# HELMUT WOLF

## The Good Engineer

 Jenean McBrearty is a graduate of San Diego State University, who taught Political Science and Sociology. Her fiction, poetry, and photographs have been published in over two-hundred print and on-line journals. She won the Eastern Kentucky English Department Award for Graduate Creative Non-fiction in 2011, and a Silver Pen Award in 2015 for her noir short story: *Red's Not Your Color*. She lives in Kentucky and writes full time —when she's not watching classic movies and eating chocolate.

# TABLE OF CONTENTS

# CHAPTER I

## The Threat

### Good Friday 2012

Helmut Wolf was the child first-responders rescued from the rubble of what once had been the Brandenburg Gate. For two days after the "Berlin Massacre" Helmut lay covered by the bodies of his dead parents, their remains protected by the toppled Quadriga that resisted the collapsed mortar and provided a small air pocket, devoid of dust, for his year-old lungs. It was their dead faces he saw before him, so loving in their final act of devotion, as he drifted in and out of consciousness while firefighters dug frantically to save him.

Gunter Wolf had been talking to the police on his cell phone, reporting the swarthy men with suitcases standing near the columns, and another two men hovering over what seemed to be a broken-down bus just under the Gate. "Something's not right. It looks suspicious. They act like they know each other," Gunter said not more than thirty seconds before one of the men, staring straight and him and Marta, and Helmut toddling between them, dropped his suitcase and ran. "Marta!" Gunter screamed, grabbing her arm as she looked at him with the words 'I love you' on her lips. She had seen them too and knew what was about to happen. They dropped to their knees, crouching around Helmut, absorbing the concussion that would have killed him. They died instantly.

Marta was killed when a sliver of stone sliced her back, rupturing her heart and snapping her spine like a twig. Gunter's limbs were blown off, but his portly torso acted as insulation.

Little Helmut was unconscious for the first eighteen hours of his ordeal. Relieved of panic and tears, he used little precious oxygen. That's what saved him, the medical experts concluded, his shallow, steady breathing declaring life to the emergency operator through Gunter's still-open cell line. GPS did the rest.

Lone Wolf Survives! *Der Stern* proclaimed, and the photograph of a blue-uniformed giant, Sergeant Emile Eisenbach, emerging from the ruins, his faced streaked with soot and sweat, with the blond baby clutched to his chest, won reporter Charles Turtletaub a Pulitzer Prize.

From that Resurrection morning on, Helmut Wolf was known as the "Miracle Baby."


2035 New Year's Eve


The premiere of the of the refurbished Berlin Opera House was an invitation-only event designed to celebrate the New Anschluss at New Years, the Vienna Philharmonic presenting a program of Beethoven and Strauss that mirrored the ambivalence of the two German-speaking nations as they hammered out a blended government for the second time in modern history.

"New this and new that. It's the same old crap if you ask me. Why can't we start over like America did?" Helmut's Aunt Patricia was fond of saying. She was her usual still-beautiful-at-forty self dressed in a grey crepe gown, a white ermine stole caressing a neck-line a twenty-year old would envy as she talked politics in the backseat of the limousine. "Tell me that, Mr. Ambassador," she said to her husband, Norman. "Why can't we scrap all this historic Teutonic bullshit and invent something really new?"

"Because Germany has never had a George Washington I expect, Dear," Norman said politely. "I have a program Helmut, want to see it?"

Helmut sat opposite them, thinking how they hadn't changed. Patricia still wanted Norman to treat her as a confidant, and he still ignored her. "No, I'll let it be a surprise," Helmut replied.

"Surprise, my ass," Patricia scoffed. "Europe hasn't had an original idea since Bismarck created the civil service. What happened with the English girl you were seeing Helmut? What was her name? Mary Magdalene or something or the other?" Helmut's love life was Patricia's second favorite subject.

"Madeline. Madeline Churchill," Helmut said.

"Oh, God spare us. Is she a drunk too?" Patricia cringed at the mention of the British name.

"No, Auntie."

"I liked her a little bit."

"She became a nun."

"Don't be stupid. British people don't become nuns. You'd have me believe you'd date a Catholic? Tripe. You hate being Catholic. You hate God. Although you might try dating a Catholic girl —they have reputations for being friendly under the right circumstances." Her wide smile showed a row of perfect white teeth. "You know your Uncle was baptized by Pope Benedict."

No, they hadn't changed a bit, Helmut thought as Patricia patted his hand. The story of Norman's conversion upon visiting the tomb of St. John Paul II was mentioned every time the press did a story about Germany's most famous Vatican ambassador.

"Even so, I'm so glad you decided to come home for the holidays. We haven't seen enough of you since graduation."

Helmut laughed. "You say that every time I come home for the holidays. I love you, Auntie, but I've never believed you – you haven't a maternal bone in your body. I've spent more time with nannies and tutors than with you."

"Don't be cruel, Helmut. A diplomat's life is not a life for a child. You'll find that out when you replace Norman in Rome," Patricia insisted, wagging a manicured finger at him.

"You haven't told her, Uncle Norman?"

"Told me what?"

Norman wiped his forehead with his handkerchief. "We're here now. Let's enjoy the concert and discuss Helmut's future another time."

Patricia dropped the subject, but her consternation lasted well into the *Blue Danube* and the entire second movement of Beethoven's *Seventh Symphony*. "Tell me now," Patricia whispered to Norman when Helmut excused himself from the box for a smoke. "He's not marrying that British cow, is he?"

Norman reconsidered. Maybe it was better to relay the information in public where Patricia wouldn't make a scene. "He's joined the army."

"NATO?" Patricia looked around nervously at the boxes next to them, hoping no one heard.

"No. Chancellor Stahl's imaginary New Wehermacht that he's temporarily calling the Fatherland Security Forces."

Patricia held her theater glasses close to her eyes, pretending to look at the stage. "I told you this New Anschluss crap would be trouble. New this. New that. It's old Nazi crap. Stahl's a social climbing opportunist just like that sniveling paperhanger was," she hissed. "He'll have the whole damn country goose-stepping again. I won't have Helmut mixed up in this, Norman."

"Just ride it out. The Christian Nationalists are going to have a hellu'va fight on their hands if Stahl tries to resurrect a field army. Pomeranz will call for new elections. The people will toss Stahl out of office —and good riddance," Norman said.

"We both know Pomeranz is no match for Stahl," Patricia said. Helmut entered the box. She didn't look at him, and he knew instantly Norman had told her about his enlistment. Her stoic jaw was set on clench till the closing strains of *Viener Blut*, and she avoided eye-contact right up to *Auld Ang Syne*.

Two bars in, a man walked onto the stage, and handed the conductor a notepad. The conductor scanned the message, turned to the audience, and began reading aloud:

"Ladies and gentlemen, Chancellor Stahl has declared martial law. Paris has been attacked by Al Qaeda. A dirty bomb has taken out the Eiffel Tower and President Matisse has left he city."

"Bastard!" someone shouted.

"Not again," Patricia whispered. "God, can't these Muslims find something better to do with their time?"

"If they could, they'd be called CEOs instead of terrorists," Norman snapped at her.

The conductor looked up, his face as white as the paper he held in his quivering hands and continued. "Death toll estimates are not available." Then, as though thinking out loud, "New Year's Eve crowds in Paris run into the hundreds of thousands...God help them." Almost as an after thought he continued, "Return to your homes. There is a sundown to sunup curfew in effect till further notice. By order of the Chancellor, looters will be shot on sight."

The audience filed out of the hall while the orchestra finished a song no one was singing. Everyone knew what "dirty bomb" meant. Moscow had lost twenty thousand in the 2015 attack, Tokyo thirty-five thousand two years later. The unfathomable had become routine. There was nothing to do except stay indoors until the full extent of the damage – and the air quality – was known. "They'll be accepting donations at the door," the usher said as the balcony crowd headed downstairs.

Patricia shrugged her shoulders. "Do they take credit cards?"

"Anything will be appreciated," the young man stammered.

"Patricia, please," Norman whispered, taking her by the arm.

"Well, who brings a check-book to a symphony?"

The usher was right and so was Patricia. At the door stood a forlorn musician, his drum up-side down, murmuring thank-you as the men took out their wallets, grabbed their Euros, and tossed them in. The women fumbled with their clutches, some tossing in loose change that hit the skin with a thud. Patricia tossed in her purse. "Who cares?" she said as Norman gave her an icy stare, "My ID's in there. They'll mail me the damn thing."

Twenty minutes later, Norman ushered his family into a stately brick townhouse on the Schillerstrasse.

"I must be losing my mind," Patricia said as they shed their snow-dusted coats in the foyer. "Helmut's decision is starting to make sense to me. I'll make cocoa."

The two men headed for the living room, and turned on the television, watching the familiar images of a city in chaos. The fires. The women screaming in agony over mutilated loved ones. People being loaded into ambulances headed for overwhelmed hospitals that could do nothing except tally the deaths. Choked-up voiceovers of aging anchormen who believed pictures weren't worth a thousand words.

"Another symbol of Western culture condemned to the flames," Norman said hitting the mute button as Patricia entered the room.

"Well, I never thought the Eiffel Tower was anything special, but the French certainly came to love it. Tourist dollars buy a lot of love in Paris." Patricia put the tray of cups and saucers on the sideboard and returned to the kitchen.

"Do you think the Americans will help Europe now, Uncle Norman?" Helmut said as they watched a crowd of dancing Arabs in Riyadh burning a French tri-color.

"I'll call Pomeranz in the morning. He'll have the Foreign Office's official assessment, but you're probably in a better position to answer that question. What was the situation when you left America?"

Helmut went to the library and brought back a map that he unrolled and spread over the coffee table in front of Norman. Pencil in hand, he made small exes in Brownsville, Texas, Las Cruces, New Mexico, and

Eureka, California near the Oregon border, then connected the exes with a red pen.

"The Mexicans are in de facto control of all the territory to the west and south of this line since the siege of Sacramento last fall. La Raza leaders have the governorships of Arizona, New Mexico, Utah and California, and there is talk of formal secession. The hell with cocoa."

Helmut went to the liquor cabinet, poured two glasses of cognac, and handed one to Norman. "La Raza wants to declare California an independent republic —they've been waiting for a signal that they won't face military intervention from the feds. The National Association of Governors gave them that signal three days ago, stating they'll refuse to release their National Guard troops to Washington even though President Franklin has declared La Raza a terrorist organization."

"Hummm. So that's what Pomeranz meant yesterday by secession fever in Frisco. How long can the American economy hold out, do you think?"

"It depends on how fast Franklin can get the oil shortage under control. The biggest refineries are in La Raza controlled territory. But, if he can divert the Alaskan pipeline to the refinery in Montana, he can delay the recession for six months. Realistically, he needs to take military action, but this is an election year. He won't."

Norman sat down and stared at the map. "He's too weak. His own party is clamoring for him to resign, according to Pomeranz. Behind closed doors, of course."

"Franklin's a Southerner, but he's no Bush," Helmut said, rolling up the map. "What's funny is that Franklin could win reelection without the La Raza territories. The Cubans and the Puerto Ricans will vote

11

Republican, of course, but Franklin could carry New York and Florida because of the Jewish Liberal vote."

"Is that where the Jews stand now, with the Democrats?"

"The Jews feel both parties sold them out with the passage of the Martinez-Jackson bill that outlawed any aid to a state considered a theocracy. The legislation cut off aid to every Mid-east country, but the Jews believe it was aimed particularly at Israel given that the UN is still funding Palestine. Still, the Republicans are just too Christian for them. Maybe someday they'll figure it out."

"You mean that Jesus is a better friend to them then Marx? I doubt it." Norman rolled his eyes, popped a Tums into his mouth and chewed it thoughtfully. "So that fellow – what's his name – the good-looking black fellow – Anatani Denga of the Independent Party. He have a chance?"

Patricia brought in tray full of cake slices, a pot of hot milk, a tin of chocolate, and a pink china vase holding three yellow daisies and put it on the coffee table. "Who wants cocoa?" She handed Norman a steaming cup. He took it and poured the rest of his cognac into it.

"We left America in an untenable position in '03." Norman said. "We wanted the United States to protect us, but not herself. Stupid, really. Now we're paying for it. If only NATO had the balls... but we can't berate Franklin for hesitating out of fear of the Mexicans when the EU is immobilized by fear of the Muslims. Why should America come to our aid when we wouldn't go to hers?"

"Because a man like Stahl is far more dangerous than barbarians like Al Qaeda or a retro Black Panther like Denga. Didn't anyone learn anything from Obama?" Patricia stirred her chocolate with a Pirouette and bit off the end. "Imagine how many dirty bombs Al Qaeda could produce if they had the factories Stahl has at his command. For my money, a dirty bomb every four or five years is better that a megaton nuke any day. Better body counts in the thousands than in the millions. America understands that."

"You've been watching too much television, Auntie." Helmut poured himself another drink, took a plate of cake, and settled into one of Patricia's blue velvet chairs. "America understands little of what is happening on her own shores – and nothing about what's happening in Germany. We must protect ourselves now."

Norman studied him closely. The Miracle Baby was now a strong six-footer, well-trained and fit, an Olympic boxer and a graduate of the Boswell Military Academy in Virginia who had just competed a master's degree in engineering at Stuttgart. And so quietly determined, it made Norman uneasy. If Helmut was just another idealistic fanatic, his infatuation with Stahlinists would pass as soon as a young woman turned his eye. But Helmut never argued his ideology with Patricia. He simply stated it as fact because he was, alarmingly, so sure of it.

To Norman, it seemed incomprehensible this grown man was once the toddler who had invaded their lives, overwhelming them with a responsibility they neither planned for nor desired. After five years in the Foreign Service, Norman was about to get his first appointment when the Brandenburg Massacre made everything he did fodder for the tabloids. How unprepared they were for celebrity. How ashamed they were of their bedroom conversations about whether to return the child to the Eisenbachs, or how soon they could farm the boy to boarding school without unleashing a backlash in the press. When Norman was offered the post at the Vatican, he grabbed at it like a drowning man. Finally, they

13

would be out of range of the paparazzi that lusted after any tidbit about the Miracle Baby. In Rome, Norman believed, miracles were so common no one would pay any attention to Helmut.

An Italian nanny had given the Wolfs the privacy and the freedom they coveted. Helmut was given all the advantages of a diplomat's child, being groomed for a life among elites as far from the Eisenbachs as possible. Had trauma and loneliness permanently scarred him, Norman wondered? If so, his gaze never revealed it. There was never any resentment in his voice. Yet, the glow that emanated from his eyes was not that of love Norman was sure.

"Be careful, Helmut," Norman warned. "Stahl promises Germany what no leader can deliver. Safety in our time."

"At least he won't deliver it like Chamberlain delivered peace in our time. Appeasement is worse than folly. It's annihilation. I've joined Fatherland Security and that's the end of it. There's nothing sinister in wanting to protect my country. This is excellent cake, Auntie."

"Thank-you. Then you support Stahl's Fortress Germany approach even though rearmament might mean breaking with the EU, NATO and the Americans?"

"There is no rearmament, Auntie. Stahl's doing what he has to do to protect German citizens. As loyal German citizens, I'd expect you'd support his efforts."

Patricia sat up straight. "I am loyal to Germany. But Stahl is not Germany. I want you to remember that, Helmut. When you swear an oath of allegiance to Fatherland Security, you swear it to your country – not to a man. Definitely, not to a radical like Stahl."

Norman was more diplomatic. "Democracy may seem wanting now, but a dictatorship is never the answer, my boy."

"Never? Uncle, no one takes a vote in a burning building. When the choice is life or death, there's no time for deliberation. The leader is either right or wrong. If he's right, everyone under his command survives. If he's wrong, all perish. Democracy can only flourish when there is an abundance of time and order, and we haven't had either for a long time."

"And you seriously believe that when Stahl has brought us an abundance of time and order, he will allow democracy to flourish?" Norman asked.

"I seriously believe we should worry about that after we're out of the burning building. Martial law is temporary."

"Norman, please see if you can have Helmut transferred into the Foreign Service. Now.  His Italian is good," Patricia said.

"No Auntie. I want to serve my country, but not like my Uncle."

"You mean you want to go to war."

"I mean if I'm going to be a good officer, I need to learn my trade. You wouldn't expect me to learn cobbling in a kitchen, would you?"

Patricia's eyes filled with tears. Helmut handed her a Kleenex. "It's time the German people returned to self-reliance, Auntie. America can't continue to fight the world's battle with terrorism alone. She needs strong allies. I know. I've lived in America. I've seen the product of German ancestry – how industrious and resolute we used to be. Now, we bellyache if we have to work forty hours a week when the average American works fifty."

"Germany hasn't had a field army for almost a hundred years, Helmut. Raising that demon – first destroy terrorists, then what? That's

15

what everyone fears most. How many holocausts lie ahead?" Norman demanded.

Helmut nodded towards the television that had gone to black-out screen. "Do you want to live in a world like that? Dark. Silent. Empty. I don't. Islamofascism is a plague that must be destroyed."

"How? By trading one fascist plague for another?" Norman's question hung like a fog. "Answer me, Helmut."

Helmut thought for a moment, then went into the library and returned with a worn photograph that he handed to Norman. "I can answer your question with one word. Eisenbach."

There was a knock at the door, and Norman motioned for Patricia and Helmut to stay put and stay quiet as he took a pistol from the sideboard drawer.

"Polizei!" a voice shouted.

Norman stuffed the pistol into his tuxedo pocket and opened the door.

"You are Ambassador Wolf?"

"Yes."

"I am here for Helmut Wolf. Is he here?"

"Yes. Helmut, come here!"

"I must speak with him privately, Sir."

Norman excused himself when Helmut appeared, and returned to the living room where Patricia sat stoic and pale. "What is it, Norman?"

Norman sat by her, offering the shelter of his arm. He hoped the summons was for a threat, not an emergency, but from his conversation with Pomeranz, he knew better. Rumors had been circulating since the New Anschluss that Stahl was preparing, not only to rearm, but to invade

16

Middle Europe under the Bush Doctrine of preemption. With the attack on Paris, the terrorists had invited Stephan Stahl to their doorstep "Stahl has his army, Patricia, and our Helmut is in on the ground floor. He'll be a Field Marshall before we know it."

Helmut overheard. "Maybe you're right, Uncle," he said. He put the cognac away. "But for now, I have to report to the police station for street patrol to make them safe for the postmen." He took off his jacket and tie, and went upstairs.

"Oh my God, stop him, Norman," Patricia pleaded.

"No. He signed up for the job, now he must do it."

"All that time in America. He's in with skinheads, I know it!"

Norman pulled her closer. "Don't make things worse with idle speculation." He looked at the blank TV screen staring back at him, and he couldn't help but feel it was an invitation into an abyss. Part of him was comforting the fragile side of Patricia. Another part was fighting the urge to jump into the void of the black screen at the side of the youth that now stood before him in a meticulously pressed uniform.

"I'll call you as soon as I can. I promise." Helmut said as Norman stood to shake his hand. Their good-byes were always awkward.

"There are no secure phone lines now. We'll hear from you when we hear from you. Until then, we'll just pray." Norman embraced him, and then turned away so the boy wouldn't see his watering eyes. Norman knew Helmut was leaving – really leaving - even if Helmut didn't know, and he felt both fear and pride. Was it possible he loved his nephew after all?

Helmut hugged his Aunt and gave her textbook instructions. "Do not drink tap water. Do not flush the toilets more than once a day. Remain

17

in the house from sundown to sunup. Keep use of all electronic devices to a minimum. Report any suspicious persons, smells, and activities."

She smiled weakly. "We know the drill, Helmut. Take care"

At the sound of the door closing Norman and Patricia went to the window and watched the two soldiers, laughing as they made their way through the snow, approach an official-looking black car. Helmut was pulling on his kidskin gloves, the red wool scarf Patricia gave him for Christmas wrapped around his neck. He could be going skiing, Norman thought. Or maybe off to see Madeline-the-Boston-veterinarian-student for coffee. Instead, he would be issued a weapon, hunting looters, and loving every minute of it.

"What do you think he meant by this?" Patricia said, picking up the famous photo and returning it to the library.

Norman was staring into the fire. In the flames, he imagined he could see the future burning along with Paris. "Like everyone else of his generation, he sees Eisenbach as a hero," Norman said. "Heroes are much more appealing than old bureaucrats like me. What Helmut doesn't understand is that yesterday's heroes so easily become today's villains."

# CHAPTER II

## *Blitzretten*

Stephan Stahl had accompanied Bundestag Member Leopold Stassner on his fact-finding junket to Moscow following the dirty bomb attack of 2015. He saw for himself the human toll – the three-foot by five-foot high pile of torsos, arms, and legs of those who had caught the initial blast, the hospital emergency rooms overflowing with people with radiation sickness, burns and hysteria, the sounds of bewilderment, rage, and sorrow as people lay bleeding on gurneys in hallways – left to die.

"The doctors are blind to them," Stahl observed to Stassner as medical personnel scurried around them. "The Russians are a barbaric people."

The eighty-nine-year-old Stassner, a survivor of the liberating Russian Army of 1945, had stopped abruptly, snatched the young Stahl by the coat-sleeve, and maneuvered him out a side door and into a small garden. "For someone who recently graduated from the university, you have learned little at the taxpayers' expense, Herr Stahl. Study the Ruskies' Great Patriotic War and you might understand what's going on in this hospital. It's filled with memories of horrendous feats of human sacrifice. If Stalin hadn't thrown three million people to the German butchers in 1941, the swastika would be flying over Moscow today. Triage works in government as well as hospitals. Learn its meaning in their war, Herr Stahl, if you want to survive your own."

And study the Russian war he did, reading long into the night in the dim light of a foul-smelling hotel room, determined to remember the lessons of history. Stalin's scorched earth policy, he learned, bought him the most precious commodity of war: time. Time to move factories, build tanks, and transfer troops from thousands of miles away; time to lure the German army farther and farther east until the Russian winter could paralyze it. What made a leader great was neither his cruelty nor his kindness, but knowing how to be each in turn, knowing how to make people accept the rightness of his decisions concerning life and death. But most of all, the great leader like the great actor, had to know the value of timing.

The drawback for the early terrorists, Stahl noted, was indeed their bad timing. Had the 9/11 attack on America lasted eighteen days instead of eighteen minutes, the world's economy would have collapsed like the towers of the World Trade Center. They sacrificed the goal in exchange for a dramatic headline. Lucky for America. Had Bin Laden been smarter, he could have finessed that trade-center attack so there would never have been a war on terror. Never underestimate the effect of the word "war" on people who are willing to fight one, Osama, he said to himself. Ah, but in America's case you had plenty of evidence that there wouldn't ever be a real war.

With Stassner's words of admonishment echoing in his brain, Stahl shut out the sights and sounds of suffering as he toured the blood-stained buildings and streets of Moscow. He paid attention to an objective, larger picture, now. The frightened faces of the people taught him the real horror of terrorism — the vulnerability that resulted from it, a vulnerability that sprang from complete demoralization, a vulnerability that could last a lifetime unless exorcised with purposeful activity. Russia is a country filled with rape victims, Stahl thought, as he saw the passivity in their eyes, a passivity he had easily mistaken for graciousness in the restaurants and hotels when he first arrived. Everywhere there was a defeat-induced humility hiding behind the smiles.

Had the Chechnyans had been able to mount an all-out military invasion, Russia would have collapsed, Stahl concluded, watching the people go about their daily lives. They seemed to be casting about for any authority that could save them from their fear. Someone, anyone, to look to for an explanation, for guidance, for strength, for ultimate justice for their suffering and loss. Failing that, they looked for vengeance.

Stahl remembered his assessment in Moscow now as he talked with his cabinet about the "French situation". Through the cacophony of voices, he heard his own whispering to his sense of historical opportunity. Now was time to exploit the chaos of civilization gone awry. And time was running out. It would be daylight in seven hours. That left only five to put his plan in motion. "Gentlemen," he said finally to his ministers, "I think it's time we get some rest. There's nothing we can do as long as we can't get a plane in the air. Humanitarian aid has to wait on Mother Nature, so we'll accept it and just make sure we're ready when she's ready to smile."

"It may be a week before anything can get through." Karl Halderman complained.

"We'll be more than ready then, won't we?" Stahl said.

Everyone stood up to go except one man – Fritz Pomeranz. "I want to make sure you realize how important it is for the world to see that we stand by our French allies in their time of need, Herr Chancellor. We

21

can't let the New Anschluss or our friendship with America interfere with the goals of the EU. We have to think unity."

"There's no need to make a speech, Fritz," Alexander Tanzer said. "We all want to go home."

"No. No, I think Pomeranz has a right to know where I stand. So I'll tell you all. The Christian Nationalist Party will do everything in its power to protect the interests of the EU. Whatever it takes, I stand ready to defend the integrity of Europe against all attacks."

"Now who's making speeches?" Pomeranz stood up and offered Stahl his hand. "Don't let the people down, Stahl, they trust you."

Pomeranz was right. In his two years as Chancellor, Stahl had been building strong support for the Christian Nationalist Party. His approval ratings were holding steady around 70%, a success, however, he never took for granted. The public was fickle even if Party membership was over thirty million and thousands lined the streets wherever he went, even if each speech was greeted by adoring crowds. Center Socialist Pomeranz, a member of the Old Guard, was wary of Stahl's popularity, his uneasiness growing along with the support of the throngs that mobbed Stahl wherever he went.

"You've given me valuable insight, Fritz. All of you, I couldn't manage without you. It's awkward, but I do wish you all a happy new year. We'll get these European attacks under control, God willing." Warm handshakes dispelled many anxieties for them all, except Pomeranz, and he had good reason for his misgivings.

Ten minutes after his official seven-member cabinet left, Stahl welcomed another set of advisors in the bunker seven floors beneath the Reichstag: Christian Nationalist Party members William Olberman,

Herman Beuhler, Gerhardt Frict, and Emil Eisenbach, Minister of Fatherland Security and creator of the Eisenbach Brigade, Stahl's elite guard.

"I know it's short notice, but there's much work to do." Stahl bid the men make themselves comfortable in the same leather chairs the elected members of the government had just left. He turned on the Elmo, and a map of Paris flashed on the wall. "What news of the City of Lights, Gentlemen?"

Frict, Stahl's intelligence officer, lit his pipe. "President Matisse is in Calais, about ready to take a plane to Quebec – not London as was first reported. He got to DeGaulle airport a little ahead of Abu Al Muhammad. It must have scared the piss out of him, seeing the runway blow up just as his plane took off. Muhammad, Mighty Mo, as we like to call him, has taken control of all communications. But Inspector Picot, the Chief of Police of Paris, has a laptop and tells us he's in charge of the asylum now, poor bastard. Matisse didn't even mobilize the army before he bailed."

"You've had contact with Picot, recently?"

"He asked for your "input" not more than a quarter hour ago. Meaning he wants to know what the hell NATO is going to do and will somebody give him a coherent order before he shoots himself."

"What's his assessment, Frict?"

"The dirty bomb was small one. It was the other three conventional IEDs that took out the Eiffel Tower. There have been several more explosions, but no report on the targets. Grand as the Eiffel explosion was, it was still a diversion."

"A diversion that sent the Parisians into a panic so Mighty Mo could get his hands on the airport, the water plant, and the government computers." Beuhler interrupted. "By now Mo knows Picot is desperate."

Frict continued. "We do know Mo's blowing up planes and runways to seal off escape, or rescue – if we could get through. The streets are already impassible between fleeing people and the damned ice. People are setting out on foot just to get out. Mo's using the Ecole Militaire as his headquarters, the audacious son-of-a-bitch."

"So, you have the usual looting and raping. Picot's forces can't control thousands of terrified people," Eisenbach said. "More people have died from exposure, heart failure, and crime than from radiation though. You know the French can't organize a picnic, let alone respond to a terrorist attack."

"This isn't a terrorist attack. It's a coup d'etat," Stahl said to the men. "They're getting smarter."

"Probably meant as a counterweight to Fortress Germany, and to you, Stephan," Emile said. "He knows the day Europe has a real leader, Al Qaeda's days in the West are numbered."

Stahl exploded. "A counterweight. Certainly, the Arab press will see it that way. It's always our fault these fuckin' Muslims go crazy. It's easier to cast terrorism as a counterweight than call a spade a fuckin' shovel. As though we're supposed to cheerfully hand over two thousand thirty-five years of Western culture to bunch of rag head freaks." He stopped himself, and said coolly, "What about Orly airport?"

"It's been abandoned for so long, I doubt Mo has given it much thought. The runways are pitted. Nothing can take off or land safely. God, the terrorists must have shit their pants when Matisse bailed. Can you hear them yuckin' it up like they did when the Towers fell?" Frict was studying the map. "If we knew it was going to be this easy, we would have done it

24

years ago." Frict said sing-song. "Paris itself isn't that big is it? What, forty-two square miles?"

"Mo's as surprised as Hitler was when the world gave him the Sudetenland," Olberman said. "Al Jazeera will tell us all about that in the morning too. Comparisons of you to Hitler are de rigor these days." As current secretary to the Minister of Intelligence, William Olberman had been chosen to lead Stahl's Ministry of Propaganda and had already prepared his family for the eventual comparisons of himself with Goebels. "We've got that black-out in force, Stephan, but people can see all the brutality they want on their computers, so does it really matter?"

"You're right. Remove the black-out. Show the public everything these animals do. What does Picot need, Herman?"

Herman Buehler, the most pensive of the group, served as Stahl's personal secretary and was making notes to review and archive later. "Manpower."

"We'll give it to him."

"How? It will take the UN weeks to mobilize a force, and NATO is depleted. It has weapons, but most Germans refuse to fight under its command. Hell, most of the enlisted are ready to pack it in now that America and the NATO are split over the energy shortage," Olberman said.

Stahl turned to Eisenbach. "Can we get Picot a Fatherland Security strike force?"

"They're ready, Stephan. Give us the word and we'll liberate Paris, then cleanse it. We can't let this crisis go to waste."

"We can't mobilize any force that looks like an army without every reporter broadcasting it to the world," Olberman cautioned. "The bloggers will have the information global before one boot hits the ground."

Stahl lit a Cigarillo. "I don't give a rat's ass what it looks like," he said quietly. Eisenbach borrowed a smoke from the pack, and Stahl tossed him the lighter.

"To hell with the reporters and the bloggers. The people will support a German field army," Eisenbach said quietly. Though now 43, Eisenbach was still an imposing figure. Standing six feet five, he forced people to look up to him. "Stephan there's no doubt this is the opportunity we've been waiting for. Everything's in place. Uniform designs, insignia, ranks, pay-grades – we've been preparing for two years." He paused. "On the other hand, you know the Liberal press will put the anti-army protestors on center stage. We do have our Muslims to contend with, and there's the weather. It's your call."

"Well, if we can't fly in supplies, we can load them on trucks, and load the trucks on railway flatbeds. Fill 'em up with food and FS troops, Emil, and paint every vehicle with a red cross to keep the protestors quiet. We can be in Paris within twenty-four hours by train, can't we?"

Olberman was incredulous. "German soldiers disguised as relief workers? It's a violation of the Geneva Convention."

"The Parisians won't mind." Frict said, as Eisenbach smashed the cigarillo into the ashtray. "If they're any still alive."

Stahl ignored their commentary. "If we can get our forces in there first, it will legitimate a German army. If we're effective — and fast – no one argues with success. Tell Picot to stop relief efforts, move what's left of his forces and supplies to Orly airport, and defend it," Stahl commanded.

"Are you ordering Picot to abandon the people?" Buehler asked.

"I'm ordering a military triage, Herman. Tell Picot it's a NATO command, if it makes you more comfortable. He's no good to anyone dead. We need a secure base of operations. I'm not sending in German boys if he's going to run like Matisse. How many FS troops do we have Emil?"

"Counting the NATO defectors? Forty thousand. Deferred enlistments make it over a hundred and eighty thousand."

"How many in Berlin?"

"Almost ten thousand. Half of them are patrolling the streets with the police tonight. The other half will relieve them in ten hours."

"They go first. Have them round up the other half. We'll need about a thousand truckloads of supplies, but five hundred will do to start. Get every man between fifteen and fifty loading the trucks immediately and send out the order for all FS troops to muster at the railway stations in Hamburg, Hanover, and Düsseldorf. Frict, you'll swear them in. Buehler, you take the southern route via Magdeburg and Frankfort. Tell the boys they get their new uniforms after they complete the mission."

"What is the mission?" Emil asked.

"The mission is to deliver humanitarian aid to the French and take the Ecole Militaire away from Al Qaeda. Call it a *Blitzretten* —Lightening Rescue."

"We've ordinance and military gear, but where do we get the supplies, Stephan?" Frict asked, expecting Stahl's predictable reply.

"The Wal-Mart warehouses, and requisition their trucks. Get receipts. We'll pay. I want every soldier to have everything he needs, razors, soap, socks, and lots of chocolate."

"You do realize, Stephan, there's no turning back once we deploy an independent military force. You'll be accused of treason and Pomeranz will probably have you arrested."

"He can try. I'm not afraid of a pretender like Pomeranz."

"He's layin' dead for you."

"Is Paris burning?"

"Yes."

"We can't sit around playing fiddles. I'll take care of Pomeranz."

"How?"

"I'll Dissolve the government and call for elections myself. That ought to keep him and his Center Socialists occupied."

It seemed so easy to say in the silent, shadowy darkness to loyal spectators. Stahl couldn't even hear the men breathing.

"Then you're taking over." Emil said as Stahl stepped in front of the bright-white screen.

"If we don't move, in twenty-four hours Muslims from all over France will head to Paris to celebrate a new Caliphate in Europe. Do any of you believe there is another man in Germany who can prevent them from marching into the Rhineland? If so, name him, and I will swear my allegiance to him because, once these animals get their hands-on Matisse's nukes, Germany is gone forever."

The words hadn't left his lips for more than a second before Eisenbach was on his knees, his right hand raised, avowing the familiar soldier's oath:

*I swear by God this sacred oath: I will render unconditional*
*obedience to Stephan Stahl, the Fuehrer of the German nation and*

*people, Supreme Commander of the armed forces, and will be*
*ready as a brave soldier to risk my life at any time for this oath.*

Olberman, Frict and Buehler did the same, repeating the words that sealed their fate with Stahl's. It was time to mobilize. It was time to protect all they held dear. They were ready, and Stahl had his army. He thanked them for their trust, offering his hand to each man as he stood. He had hoped for their support but was unprepared for their display of loyalty. Yes, he wanted to be the leader of a Fourth Reich, but the words themselves conjured up the power of the great armies of history —Caesar, Stalin, Eisenhower —and yes, now once again, Adolph Hitler. He would not make the mistakes of those great commanders, he swore to himself. He would always put the nation before his own desires. But he had little time to reflect as his men were already carrying out his orders.

On came the lights and out came the laptops, calculators, and a bottle of brandy as the men estimated timetables, tonnage, and logistics of the *Blitzretten*. Frict messaged Picot and gave the order for his withdrawal to Orly. Picot acknowledged. He would pull back and defend the airport. Eisenbach downloaded copies of commissions, filling out the names from a master list that established a formal chain of command. Fatherland Security Forces were now under Stahl's direct command, an independent German army. "Sign these," Eisenbach said, handing Stahl a pen.

Stahl affixed his name to each. "I'll draft the dissolution of the Bundestag document myself," he said. "I want to protect all of you as much as possible … in case."

"Failure is not an option, Stephan," Frict stated offhandedly. The other murmured "here, here" in agreement as they pored over their paperwork. Stahl, steadying himself from the weight of their loyalty, raised his glass in salute.

"Gentlemen," he said, "We're going to be in Paris before Berliners recover from their New Year's hangovers. And, after we've liberated the city, we're going to build the biggest goddamned concentration camp the world has ever seen, so get me some soldiers who know how to fight, and a damned good engineer."

"I have just the man," Eisenbach said, thumbing through the stack of commissions and handing one to Stahl. "The face of the future – the face of the new Wehrmacht – Helmut Wolf.

\*\*\*

Helmut and Paul Brandt tumbled into the Mercedes. "We're not going to the police station, are we?" Helmut said as Paul eased away from the curb.

"No, the armory. You need a weapon." Paul was smiling an easy-going smile. A boy known more for his good nature than good sense, he had known Helmut since their sixteen weeks of Fatherland Security training.

"Have they told you anything about Paris?"

"No. My orders are to pick up every FS member we can find and report to the armory. That's all. But there was something in Reinhardt's voice, Helmut. I could hear it. It's comin' down, I know it. We're going to get these motha' fuckers. Kill 'em dead."

The car was warm. Paul had stopped off for coffee and doughnuts, and Helmut tore open one creamer after another, adding them to his coffee until it was a pale tan. The night had been long and tiresome, but now he was awake with the electricity of danger, hungry for action.

"Who are we picking up?"

"Manfred, Johann, and Klaus." Paul took the corner too fast, and the car fishtailed. He took his foot off the gas and let the car coast to a stop just shy of the streetlamp's glow. "Sorry, did you spill?"

"No. We can do without Klaus, you know."

"Don't be hard on him just because he's married," Paul said, reaching for another doughnut.

"He shouldn't have joined," Helmut said. "Are the glazed ones for me?" Paul handed him the sugar raised. "He believes this job is like any other job and it isn't. It's …"

Paul motioned for him to be quiet. "Someone ran across the street," he whispered.

"You're seeing things. No one would be out after curfew knowing the order to shoot on sight."

"What if they don't know about the order, Helmut? What if he's a rag-head who doesn't listen to German language television or understand some guy shouting through a megaphone? I saw him, I swear."

The young men exchanged worried glances. "You're sure?" Helmut said. He looked to the right and saw a neon sign staring at them through lightly falling snow: Das Rheingold —a jewelry store. There was a "closed" sign in the window, but a light was on inside. "Would anyone be stupid enough to violate a curfew in front of a police car?" he wondered aloud.

"Our car's unmarked," Paul reminded him.

Helmut saw a figure peak out from the shadows to the side of the store.

"Maybe we stopped before he got here. Maybe he thinks the car is empty – or a driver passed out from too much New Year's cheer. It could be anything," Paul said.

They watched the figure duck in and out a few more times before he came into the light of the storefront, motioning "come here." Another figure, a scarf covering his face to his eyes, scurried across the street, shimmied up the utility pole, cut the wires, slid down, and ran into the shadows with his accomplice as the wires floated to the snow.

Helmut felt his heart pound. "They're looters."

"Maybe not. Maybe they're the owners," Paul said. He put his coffee on the dashboard, and Helmut saw his hands were shaking.

"Cutting alarm wires? Are you crazy?" Helmut said.

"What should we do? Report them?"

"And have Reinhardt climb up our asses for cowardice? What are our orders?"

"Looters will be shot on sight."

"It looks like they're looting, and they're in our sight."

"Yeah, well I never thought we'd actually see anyone out," Paul said. His breath came in short spurts. Helmut saw his hands stiffen around the steering wheel. The men were already jimmying the lock. "We could arrest them," Paul offered.

"Give me your pistol," Helmut said. Paul didn't move. "Give it to me, I said!"

"Christ, Helmut, we don't know them."

"You want an introduction?"

"Please, Helmut, let's let them go. If I beep the horn, they'll run."

Helmut put his coffee cup on the floor, and wrenched Paul's service revolver from his holster. "Touch that horn and I'll shoot you. What will we tell Reinhardt? Sorry, but we didn't know if they were terrorists or tourists, so we let them have all of Mr. Rheingold's diamonds? Cover the light till I get out and hold the door fast behind me."

Paul took off a glove and held it over the car light. Helmut eased out of the door. It had stopped snowing, but he had to get nearer for a clear shot. He walked into the darkness, skirting the glow of the streetlamp, the snow muffling his footfall. He could hear the two men talking now. They had decided to forego the lock, and one raised his wire cutters to break the window. The other man stopped him, took off his fur lined cap, and wrapped it around the cutters.

"Halt!" Helmut shouted. Panicked, the first man ran towards him. Helmut fired directly into his face, and the man dropped backwards onto the snow without making a sound. As Helmut approached him, the other man dropped the wire cutters as he raised his hands.

"Don't shoot! Don't shoot!" the man pleaded.

Helmut fired again, and the man fell to his knees, pulling off the scarf as he struggled to breathe through his blood-filled windpipe. Helmut could see his face. It was young, the eyes bulging with surprise that he was going to die.

"Allah forgive us," he choked out in garbled German before falling, face down, in the snow.

"Helmut!" he heard Paul scream. He turned and saw Paul running towards the store. "Oh, God, you killed them. You really killed them. Jesus, Jesus!"

Helmut backhanded him, and Paul reeled backwards, landing three feet from the first body, sobbing through snowflakes that melted on his hot flesh. Helmut walked over and stared down at him. "If you can't follow orders, don't wear the uniform," he said through clenched teeth. "If these men had been suicide bombers, we'd both be dead. Now get up, the police will be here soon."

Wailing sirens came closer. In what seemed like a matter of seconds, two squad cars rolled to a stop, one in front and one in back of the boys' unmarked car. Helmut called to the officers, his identification badge held high in the air. "Fatherland Security. Helmut Wolf and Paul Brandt." he yelled at three approaching officers.

"We recognize the uniforms," one of the men yelled back.

A fourth officer ran to the group. "I checked their plates. They're good." A coroner's wagon rolled up, and people could be seen peeking out of their windows from behind their curtains at the commotion.

"We were on our way to the armory when we saw these looters. I shot them," Helmut explained handing them Paul's pistol and his I.D. Brandt, on his feet now, looked at the bodies lying in blood-stained snow, and vomited.

One office laughed. "He a first-timer?" Helmut nodded yes.

"You'll need to make a report, Wolf," he said. "We'll notify the armory you'll be a little late. You'd better drive, your friend looks like he's about ready to faint." The officer turned to Paul, who fished out his I.D. and handed it to him. "Paul Brandt is it?"

"Yes." Paul coughed and spit.

"Take it easy, boy. You'll get used to it. Follow us, Wolf."

When the three-car convoy pulled away, the coroner's wagon was loading the bodies. Paul sat silent, staring out the window as Helmut drove off slowly. "What are you going to tell them, Helmut? How will you explain shooting them with my pistol?" He pulled at his blond hair, wiping the sweat from his forehead with his still-gloved left hand.

"I'll tell them the truth. We approached to arrest, and they came at you, knocking your gun from your hand. I recovered it and shot them."

"Thanks for saving my ass. Helmut, I want you to know, I'm not a coward no matter what you think."

"No. You're unseasoned, as Captain Hobart would say."

"Who's he?"

"My CO at Boswell. That's what he told me when I hesitated at the training range. They put in a pop-up of a young Muslim woman – a child in a headscarf. I froze. Theoretically, she detonated, and I was killed along with the two soldiers standing next to me. I felt like hell. My mistake cost our team the game. In real life the stakes are higher. To hesitate is to die. No second chances. I told Hobart it would never happen again, and it won't."

Paul pulled off his left glove, picked up his coffee cup and threw the lukewarm liquid out the window. "It won't happen again, Helmut, I swear."

***

Helmut filed his report, and Paul signed off on it. It was routine, they were told. A dozen looters had been shot since the curfew was imposed. The police were actually surprised the number was so low. They blamed it on the weather. As soon as the two looters were identified, their names would be added to the list. When all the families had been notified, the list would be published in the evening newspaper as a warning that, yes, looters *were* shot on sight. Paul and Helmut were congratulated by the police officers. They had done their duty.

Norman and Patricia Wolf never knew Helmut had killed two people early New Year's Day. They didn't even read the list of names of the dead looters in the newspaper. But the next time they saw Helmut, they noticed he'd changed. He was a man.

# CHAPTER III

## A Good Engineer

At Fatherland Security headquarters, Sgt. Georg Reinhardt read Major Schultz's fax about the Wolf-Brandt affair, as it was called. Schultz stated he knew Wolf was covering for Brandt; Brandt's proximity to the bodies of the two looters indicated he wasn't close enough to have had his gun knocked out of his hand. Wolf had Brandt's gun. Brandt had either given it to Wolf, or Wolf had taken it from him. In either case, Brandt was in dereliction of duty. It was now Reinhardt's decision. Did he want to punish one man or two, and if one, which one?

He would have to make a careful - read political - decision, Reinhardt thought as perused the folder containing Wolf's commission. Helmut Wolf was now Captain Wolf, chosen by Emil Eisenbach himself for special treatment as an officer in the Eisenbach Brigade Corps of Engineers. Punishing Wolf, satisfying as that might be to the aging socialist Schultz, who believed in equality in all things, was out of the question. He toyed with the idea of letting Major Schultz make the decision, but feared it might be seen as a lack of decisiveness on his part, an irreparable career mistake he could ill-afford at thirty two.

Outside, both Wolf and Brandt were waiting. The looting incident had made them too late for the swearing-in ceremony, yet neither could be briefed on the mission until, and unless, they swore the oath. They must know by now that the circumstances surrounding the shooting had been relayed to him, Reinhardt decided. Were they worried?

37

Reinhardt felt a nudge on his leg. It was Bootsie, his white Persian cat. "You're hungry, Frauline," he said as he sprinkled some kitty kibble into her silver bowl. "Lying on an official report is reprehensible, yes," he told her, "But is it the worst thing a young hero can do?" He petted her as she sniffed at the kibble. "You're right. I'll let our new Captain decide Brandt's fate." He opened the door, motioned Helmut to come in, and closed the door behind him.

"Sit down, Wolf," he said, returning the young man's salute. "I heard about the looters. Schultz told me you'd be late. I want to know what happened." He was standing above Helmut, arms crossed over his chest.

"Schultz faxed over my report?"

"Yes," Reinhardt said.

"Then you know what happened."

"Schultz thinks it could not have happened as you state."

"He wasn't there. I was."

It was clear to Reinhardt the man before him was not easily intimidated. "Is this the first time you killed someone?"

"It's the first time I have killed criminals."

Reinhardt sat down and made direct eye contact with Helmut. "You don't seem upset about it. I hear Brandt got sick."

"You'll have to speak to Brandt about that," Helmut replied.

Scanning Schultz's fax, Reinhardt decided to test the boy's resolve. "Schultz says he thinks you're covering for Brandt, that you lied in this report."

"He's entitled to his opinion."

"What is Brandt's opinion?"

"Brandt wants to serve the German people."

"I see." Reinhardt got a lint brush from his desk drawer and went after the cat hair clinging to his uniform. "Fatherland Security is asking every officer to swear a loyalty oath to Chancellor Stahl. Are you willing to take such an oath?"

"Yes, Sir."

Reinhardt handed Helmut a card. "Raise your right hand and read what's on the card, please."

Helmut stood, raised his right hand, and read the words carefully, adding "So help me God."

It unnerved Reinhardt. Wolf was so steady, so solemn. Four hundred ninety-eight men had said the same oath just an hour before and Reinhardt hadn't noticed if any of them meant a word of it. Suppose all of them have the same conviction as Wolf, he thought now. What a formidable fighting force Stahl has at his command.

Helmut put the card on his desk. "Will there be anything else, Sir?"

"Yes." Reinhardt handed him the three-star insignia. "You're a Captain now." Helmut pinned the bars to his collar. Reinhardt saluted, and handed Helmut a file folder. Inside was a certificate, signed by Stahl, and a sealed manila envelope. "Your commission and orders, Sir."

Helmut opened the envelope, and read the documents stamped "CLASSIFIED". With a stroke of a pen, he was now in charge of the men Reinhardt had sworn in, who were being loaded onto railway cars for the cold journey to Paris.

"Do you want to swear in Brandt, Sir?" Reinhardt wanted to see what Wolf would do now that he was in charge.

"Let me see your roster," Helmut said. He found the name he was looking for - Klaus Dieter. "This man, Dieter, have him replaced. Swear in Brandt and send him and Dieter to the requisition area. They need more training."

Reinhardt understood. Wolf had covered for Brandt, and thought he was salvageable. He also understood why Wolf was commissioned. He was ready to command. "Sir, you'll be choosing your staff. I'd like to be considered. You'll need an experienced aide de camp"

"Do you know anything about engineering…or security?"

"Two years at GemCorps, Sir. We specialized in oil reclamation."

"Take care of Brandt. Then meet me at the loading docks."

\*\*\*

The men had worked for three hours without a break, loading crates of food, water, and medical supplies, and the strain was taking its toll. Many were middle-aged workers too old for the army, stripped to the waist, wiping the sweat and melting ice out of their eyebrows with dirty hands. "At ease," Helmut yelled as he walked onto the dock.

The men sank to the ground where they stood, and pulled their water bottles from their back pockets. Within seconds they were scrambling for coats as their bodies recognized how cold the warehouse was.

"I don't think the French are worth my aching back," complained one lader.

"At least when all this shit gets to Paris, we're not gonna' have to unload it," said another.

"They can't wait," Helmut said, as he dragged a dolly stacked with boxes into the truck. "Every minute we delay may cost someone his life. That's why it's called *Blitzreten*."

The men watched Helmut empty the dolly, and then like a machine, return to load again.

"Are they gonna fly any of this in?" Petersen had recovered his wind and was loading his dolly next to Helmut.

"No, these trucks are going by train," Helmut said.

"It might clear." Another man joined them.

"Not for a week at least, I heard," said Petersen.

Helmut felt a hand on his arm. A wiry man in his mid forties was staring at him plaintively. "Sir, do they know how bad it is? My son is on his honeymoon … Nicholas and Lena Grothe."

Helmut stopped, and motioned the men to come near until they formed a circle around him. "We don't know how many people are dead, but we do know that we are going to save as many as we can. We have all we need, gas masks, protective gear, and plenty of bullets, but we have to learn how to do this. We're trained, but untried."

He saw the men's faces brighten with determination. "Then Stahl's army is not just a rumor?" Petersen stammered.

"We're going in because every relief agency in the world says it's impossible. We're going to prove them wrong, and we'll be shooting back. Be assured the days of terrorism are numbered." Helmut walked over to a case of beer. "Will you be able to work after a beer, mein Herren?" Helmut threw each man a can and took one himself. "I am Captain Wolf, your new commander. I'm a graduate of Boswell Military Academy, and I just killed two men for looting. I have only two policies that I borrowed from Noel Coward. Do you know the name? He wrote a movie about the British Navy in World War II called *In Which We Serve.* His policies were a happy ship and an efficient ship. I believe he got it right." Helmut lifted his can. "Will you abide by these policies?"

"Yes, Sir!" they shouted, lifting their cans in a toast to their new commander, and guzzling the cold beer.

"Now go back to work and stop your whining," Helmut ordered, and the men returned to their grueling work.

Helmut told Reinhardt to divide the men into teams of four, rotating odd and even teams – one team packing the other loading - every hour. "They'll be more efficient if they can rest some. I want no coronaries showing up at the hospitals. Be sure to get Grothe's address and make a note to look for Nicholas and Lena. We'll want to let him know."

Helmut gave the men a salute before leaving the dock, and they cheered him. They will tell their families the German Army knows what it's doing, Helmut told himself, and they can tell their families they are part of a war effort not just a rescue.

***

The images of shredded shrines and mangled monuments that were once the City of Lights were archived in Helmut's brain under "H" for hate. He had taped copies of the reconnaissance photos of the destruction on the wall next to his bed - Picot had made bedrooms for the German officers by sectioning off space with movable office partitions - along with a holy card of St. Boniface, who converted the Germans to Christianity.

Every morning he was reminded of why he made the trek to hell, as he called the trip to the Paris perimeter. Every soldier, he thought should have such reminders if only to keep his sanity in the midst of the debacle they had to deal with.

It was estimated that twenty thousand people had died from the explosions, and the toll was expected to reach half a million inside of a week, mostly from injuries and suffocation. Daily, half-tracks loaded with freshly dug up corpses, made their way to a mass grave Helmut ordered dug on the west side of the City. Thank God for the cold, he thought, it suppresses the stench of death.

Each soldier was issued a pen knife kit and plastic bags. A patch of skin was removed from everybody, or parts of bodies, and sealed in the bags for later DNA identification, if possible. The children's corpses were the most difficult for the soldiers to handle. Many had young ones at home.

"*Always Before Me*". Helmut repeated the now-familiar slogan of the Eisenbach Brigade of the Fatherland Security Forces, making the sign of the cross before forcing himself out of his blankets. Commissioned especially to lead the Corps of Engineers of the new army, Helmut now wore the controversial black retro-uniform of the historical Death's Head Division, duplicative in every way save one. Instead of a skull, his hat and buckle insignia bore the Sacred Heart of Jesus with two crossed swords in front and flames rising in the background. The Liberal press around the world decried the reinstatement of the uniforms, but the German people gave them one hundred percent approval in addition to handing Stahl a landslide victory at the special election.

*Always Before Me*. Helmut often contemplated the dual meaning of the words. He had not known four weeks ago what really lay before him, nor could he have imagined that the mission would come before everything else in his life, including sleep and food and his own "self".

In the darkness of the blizzard he eventually deployed a hundred thousand German troops in an ever-decreasing circle around Paris, searching for survivors and terrorist alike in a block by block, building by building, room by room slog-fest.

By the second week, Helmut's strategic demolition, including the underground train system, had successfully cordoned off the center of the city where the terrorists held their position at the Ecole Militaire.

By week three, the Ecole Militaire was in German hands and was being refurbished as administrative headquarters for high command, and a detention center for high ranking terrorists. Mighty Mo had attempted to commit suicide by dynamite, but had been stopped before he could detonate by a quick witted sharpshooter who shot off his right hand. The shock of going to Allah with only his left hand made him hesitate just long enough for two soldiers to tackle him. He was now in prison cell in the Ecole Militaire basement wearing a muzzle to silence his shouts of hatred and waiting for trial for treason and war crimes.

The soldiers had their orders: separate Christians from Muslims, rescue the former, and shoot the latter if they put up any resistance to being relocated in the city's center. Evacuees were taken to the train station, given first aid as necessary, hot food, water, and transportation to Calais where empty warehouses transformed into emergency shelters awaited them.

How many people had been killed by the Germans in the Paris liberation no one knew for sure. No one really cared except the foreign press and the Liberals, and no one was paying attention to them. What the world saw was a military spectacle that ended in Germany's quick and decisive victory over Muslim terrorists.

So many shocked and traumatized people, Helmut thought. Fear was a powerful sedative. He remembered their wet kisses and tearful thank-yous as German troops brought order to the crippled city, reining in looters and rapists, dispensing street corner justice at the end of their AK47s. No one was immune from retribution. When a German soldier was caught forcing a young French woman into an alley and ripping off her skirt, his Lieutenant shot him. The would-be victim was covered in blood and brains, but otherwise unhurt. The crowd had gone silent in amazement.

"There will be no violence against women tolerated here," the Lieutenant said to the onlookers, covering the woman with his coat as he led her away. When the reporter who witnessed the incident demanded an explanation as to why the soldier's rights to due process had been violated, the French crowd stoned him almost to death. Only the intervention of that same Lieutenant sent the reporter to the field hospital instead of the morgue. Now, when a German soldier told the Parisians to do something, they complied without comment.

"Captain?"

Helmut returned to the present at the sound of Reinhardt's voice. Helmut was coming to see that Reinhardt knew and did his job well, and could be trusted with the most sensitive information.

"What is it, Georg?" Helmut called him by his first name now.

45

"The Louvre is burning."

"Jesus Christ, have these animals no decency?" Helmut pulled on his uniform and strapped on his gun belt. "Let's go."

"Are you sure you want to get in the middle of this, Sir? You're too valuable to lose."

"Just drive."

The back humvee rolled towards rising flames, past squads of soldiers, and amassing tanks.

"That's it, Georg. We gave them an ultimatum, and they've called our hand." He contacted his tank commander, Sgt. Vincent Rudolph, by cell phone. "This is Captain Wolf. Seal off the area to begin the reprisals. I'll be there shortly. What? Who? Thank-you, I'll write his family. Helmut turned to Georg. "Nicholas and Lena Grothe were found, dead. Get with Rudolph for the details."

"We shouldn't get much closer, Sir." Georg came to a stop behind an armored line a mile long – Helmut's part of the perimeter —a line that secured the only passable road in, and out, of Paris.

Helmut stepped out of the vehicle and walked over to Sgt. Rudolph who stood staring at the burning building, tears involuntarily streaming down his face.

"My parents brought me to see the Mona Lisa when I was twelve. I was going to art school after that. All that beauty —gone," he choked out.

"I under….," Helmut said. Before he could finish, a shot cracked the early morning air. Helmut felt Rudolph's hand clench his arm and drag him to the ground. Rudolph was right on top of him, shielding him from another shot.

"Anyone hit?" yelled Rudolph to the three soldiers who had dived to the ground near them. No sir, no sir, and "nicked in the right shoulder" came the replies.

"Georg? You OK?" Helmut held his breath. Georg had remained in the car, a sitting target.

"OK, Sir!"

"You under cover?"

"Yes, Sir!"

"Where's it coming from, Rudolph?" Helmut demanded.

"A sniper. Up there." Rudolph pointed to a brown brick building a half a block away to their right.

"Can you get him?"

"No. The snipers go up to the roofs, take a few shots, and then hide in any convenient apartment. Most of them miss. They're weapons are first-rate, but they're not well trained. Most terrorists aren't. They're like buckshot. Once in a while, they get lucky and hit the target."

Helmut thought for a few seconds, and then asked, "Sergeant Rudolph, are those two tanks to the right of us in range?"

"You bet!"

"I have a target for them."

Rudolph called in the order. "Count ten and take out the apartment building," then yelled to his men," Put in your plugs, Gentlemen!" Everyone stuffed in ear plugs and hugged the dirt as the tanks unleashed their payloads. The ground shook, and Helmut went deaf as pain pierced his ears. He looked up as the top two stories of the brown building crashed downward. He and Rudolph stood up cautiously. A woman carrying a dead child staggered out of the doorway, followed by a man with a bleeding stub where his arm used to be, and a seven year old boy. They might have been screaming, but Helmut couldn't hear them.

"Fire again, Rudolph, level the son-of-a-bitch," Helmut commanded. He knelt down, and Rudolph motioned the men down again, as he spoke into his headset. In seconds the tanks fired another two mortars that demolished the rest of the four-story building. "From now on, any roof that has a sniper becomes a basement, understand?"

Rudolph nodded, and whispered, "Yes, Sir," his eyes looking past Helmut to the orange flames that were consuming the greatest art collection in the world. Helmut put his hand on Rudolph's shoulder, bringing his attention to Helmut's intense gaze.

"What are they telling you?" Helmut said.

"It's hopeless. No water pressure. It has to burn its self out." Rudolph was staring at the flames again. "Oh, God, will it ever stop? There'll be nothing left."

"Look around you, Rudolph. Your men are counting on you."

"Yes, Sir. I know. What are your orders?"

"Pull your squad out of the perimeter. Get them some water…"

"I'm sorry to have bothered you…for this," Rudolph managed to say.

"No. I'm glad I had a chance to say good-bye to Da Vinci and Delacroix with someone who cares about them. I visited the Louvre with my Aunt Patti the summer of my junior year. She tripped on the stairs - I'll never forget it - and I carried her back down like a child. I was shocked at just how fragile the ol' dragon really was. But she was determined not to cry even though her ankle was swelling like a balloon filling with water.

This is a disaster, Helmut, she said to me. I wish she could see Paris now. Now, Auntie, *this* is a disaster."

The two men stood silently, stealing a few minutes away from the chaos of exploding shells and screaming mothers to mourn the loss of the irreplaceable.

"About the people we've got in the city center," Rudolph said, "When will we start feeding them?"

"High command says not till we can let our soldiers in safely. They want to wait another twenty-four hours."

"The ragheads are running short of water."

"Then they'll learn to conserve. Eventually, they'll give up the terrorists, or they'll die."

"I don't think they'll learn anything, begging your pardon Sir," Rudolph said. "Death doesn't seem to matter to them."

"Then we can't let it matter to us," Helmut said, giving Rudolph a pat on the back.

There were no miracle babies in Paris. Four weeks after the attack, a hundred thousand French Muslims had been corralled in the city's center. Only twenty-five escaped, and they were caught and executed without trial. One escapee, Helmut was told, begged for more food and water for those inside before a bullet ripped through his belly. The stench of dirt, disease and death made many of the soldiers sick, but high command would not relent. Until resistance ended, no one, and nothing, moved in or out of the perimeter.

"We must do something about the women and children at least," Inspector Picot argued. "You've created another Warsaw ghetto."

"I am not at liberty to give you orders regarding civilian affairs," Helmut told Picot. "German authority extends only to military decisions. So, it's up to you, Picot. Do we give the Muslims French rations?"

Picot stared at Helmut's unmoving eyes. "Have we enough to give them?"

"No," Helmut said. "We can feed the French survivors long enough to get them to safety, or we can feed a few thousand or so Muslims. We could cut the French rations in half and feed a few thousand more Muslims for a few days, I suppose. But High Command has forbidden me to cut the rations of German soldiers. They have to be strong enough to continue rebuilding the runways for supply deliveries.. You can understand that. Another trainload of supplies is coming, but not enough to save everyone."

"Of course, Captain. Of course. What about the Red Cross? The Red Crescent? Where are they?" Picot clasped his hands to his forehead. Was he frustrated or praying, Helmut wondered?

"Their resources are exhausted. Spread too thin around the globe helping every storm victim and AIDS patient they can find," Helmut said calmly.

"America?"

Helmut laughed. "We can't rely on America anymore. All her resources are directed to Hispanics. Chancellor Stahl is mobilizing an airlift, but nothing can change the weather or make the runways usable instantly. Without runways, there is no more rescue."

"What about the English? Why doesn't the UN make them open the Chunnel?"

"London's Muslims are demonstrating in the streets and the Chunnel has been sealed off as a precautionary measure. Germany can only rescue one nation at a time."

"The trains?"

"Once in French territory they supply the countryside, and the refugees at Calais. We've slowed the French death toll there to a trickle."

Picot buried his head in his hands on the desk. "I'll be honest, Wolf, I don't want to make this decision. No matter what I do, I'll be accused of war crimes by half the world and incompetence by the other." Helmut took a seat opposite him. "There are women and children inside the city, Wolf." Picot said as tears spilled from his eyes.

"There are women and children outside the city. Which do you want to save?"

"Is there no way out? Stahl told me to hold out. I did. He told me to let you make the military decisions. I do. I obey orders, not give them. I'm not a government. Come on, Wolf, I'm desperate."

Helmut could barely hear Picot through his muffled anguish. "You want someone to do your dirty work, Inspector, someone else to shoulder the responsibility. It's the chronic French disease." Helmut pulled a document from his briefcase and slid it towards Picot. "Very well. I'll raise the German flag over Orly and communicate to Chancellor Stahl that all France is now under German military command. Is this your decision?"

"Unconditional surrender? My God, we're not at war with Germany!" Picot's hand was shaking as he reached for the pen Helmut held out to him.

"Germany is at war with terrorism, Sir. And if you are friends with the enemies of the Fatherland, you are at war with the Fatherland. This is not surrender, Picot.  It's a temporary contract giving the German government temporary authority to protect French territory and European interests."

"Another Vichy government?  Petain, Picot, what's the difference?" He signed the document and five copies. "I'll sign, but you and I both know it is meaningless. President Matisse has not resigned."

"No. He deserted and is in sunny California by now making a movie deal. Georg?"

"Yes, Sir."

"Fax Chancellor Stahl this document and send the original by courier to Berlin immediately. High command will need a copy too."

"What will you do now?" asked Picot.

"Wait for orders while high command hammers out a solution to the terrorist problem."

Georg had returned, carrying an armful of firewood, and an envelope for Helmut. He opened it, read its contents, and smiled broadly as Georg served the men coffee.

"A final solution, Captain?" Picot spat at him, his voice as brittle as the chunk of the black bread he dipped into his coffee.

"The only solution is to finally rid the world of Islamofascism, and it looks like I have been given that task in France. Paris has been designated a European repatriation center, and I've been ordered to build it."

"You're a dangerous young man, Wolf. You feel nothing for your enemy. Nothing." Picot stared into his bowl of thick red soup.

Helmut put a copy of the contract in his brief case, took out a handful of photographs, and spread them in front of Picot. He glanced through them, threw them on the table, and ran to the bathroom. "Why do you show me these obscenities?" he demanded of Helmut when he returned to the table, wiping his face with a paper towel. Helmut had straightened the pictures into a neat pile, and Picot sat down at the table, averting his eyes from the stack.

Helmut picked up the top picture, examining it as he spoke. "This is a picture of the decapitated bodies of newlyweds Nicholas and Lena Grothe, aged 21 and 19 years respectively, recovered at the Mercury Hotel." He put in on front of Picot who winced but peeked at it from the corner of one eye. Helmut picked up the next photograph.

"The terrorists put the heads on the footboard bedposts. The doctor that examined the photographs said the beheadings were done with a small handsaw rather than a sword. He could tell by the jagged tears of the skin." Helmut put the second picture alongside the first and picked up the third photograph. "This is a picture of Nicholas watching the terrorists butchering his bride. The doctors say he is in traumatic shock, given the whiteness of his skin and the dilation of his pupils. The doctor says he may have been dead from heart failure – heart explosion actually – before he was butchered."

"Stop it. Stop it," Picot pleaded. Helmut picked up a fourth photograph and examined it.

"This is Anne Carpenter, a retired third grade teacher from Valdosta, Georgia. An African-American on a vacation for which she saved for years. We know this because Private Silberman found a letter in her pocket, a letter from her daughter saying how happy she was that her mother finally got to go to Europe after twenty years of planning. There was a photograph in the letter too – a photograph of Mrs. Carpenter's third graders standing before a mural they painted of Paris."

Picot grabbed the photos and tore them into strips, flinging them into the air. Like feathers, they tumbled lightly to the floor. "Goddamn you, Wolf, I know these fanatics are fiends. I know. But children are neither fiends nor fanatics and right now they are starving to death in a cesspool they didn't make. Can't you see them? Can't you hear them?"

Helmut handed Picot a list of names and addresses. "This is a list of the families of the slaughtered identified at the Mercury Hotel. Since you are now under German command, I order you to write to notify these families of the death of their loved ones. We have to keep you busy – wouldn't want you to go crazy with boredom. Since you have such a warm and caring heart, you're the right man for the job. The families will want to know how their loved ones died. You know, did they suffer, how were they found, who found them? Things like that. Ah, but a picture is worth a thousand words, right? Well, I can get you copies." Helmut put a stack of stationery and a pen on the table. "Have a good night, Picot," he said as he stood up to leave.

"You think your enemy is different from yourself. He is not. You are the same, Wolf. Ruthless. Heartless. Insane."

"That's why I'm going to win and you're going to be safe." Helmut leaned over Picot and whispered in his ear. "Do you know where we got those pictures? They were in an office at the Ecole Militaire along with a list of names and addresses. The terrorists were going to mail the pictures to the families. The goal of the terrorist is to inflict as much pain as possible on the greatest number of people to further a political end. Remember those pictures Picot. Keep them always before you so the next

54

time you see those starving children you will see them as the future butchers they are."

* * *

The Red Cross, the Red Crescent, Al Jazeera, and hundreds of humanitarian organizations screamed that the permanent facilities in the city, termed the Paris E'tat De Guerre, were a concentration camp. The UN Security Council met in special session to condemn German intervention, and to determine if Germany was committing war crimes.

In reply, Chancellor Stahl produced the contract with the provisional French government signed by Picot. Now that Parisian terrorists had been subdued, however, he agreed to withdraw his army and leave only a reconstruction force commanded by a low-ranking officer named Captain Helmut Wolf. He would be in charge of building and maintaining permanent repatriation facilities that, Stahl promised, would meet every standard of non-combatant care.

"Let the UN fuss and fume," Stahl told his Party cabinet. "All it does it pass resolutions that everybody ignores."

But, while the UN vigorously protested Stahl's actions in France, NATO was a different story. The Baltic States, the Balkan States, and the Low Countries unanimously elected Stahl Supreme NATO Commander and requested their troops be sent to Germany for anti-terrorist training. Britain demurred. Germany had already confiscated France's nuclear arsenal and King William instructed Parliament not to allow Germany control of its nuclear arsenal. At the same time, Parliament secretly communicated to Stahl that Britain could not make a formal, unconditional commitment due to its relationship with the United States government, but that it supported Stahl's election.

And, after two successive violent demonstrations by British Muslims against deportation of terrorist suspects, Parliament passed the Protection Act which, in part, allowed Prime Minister Alastair Howe to request that a quarter of London's Muslims be ordered to Paris through the Chunnel. All Muslims already out of the country – students, business travelers, tourists - were denied readmission.

America reacted to the Protection Act with predictable outrage, vilifying its passage, and vowing to revert to isolationism if it was not repealed. Britain, offended that America would try to control its domestic politics, responded by sending rotating contingents of British troops to Germany for Fatherland Security anti-terrorist training, just falling short of full military commitment.

Emboldened by Britain's willingness to participate, the signatories of NATO responded to America's opposition by issuing President Franklin an ultimatum: if America did not approve of Stahl's election within thirty days, she would be expelled from the pact. Threatened with impeachment by a swiftly disintegrating Congress if he accepted Germany's command over a field army and command of NATO forces, Franklin withdrew America from the pact before the thirty days had passed. Turkey, who had fought so hard to join NATO in the first decade of new century, withdrew as well.

\*\*\*

*Blitzretten* was a Herculean challenge to German ingenuity. Not since the twentieth century world wars had the world witnessed such bold maneuvering. Now, with trepidation and astonishment, the leaders of free and fascist nations alike paid their respects to Stephan Stahl, the mastermind of the greatest relief effort in German history.

Cynics called it the second Burning of the Reichstag, but to those who understood Stahl, it was keen foresight. From his first week in Parliament ten years prior, Stahl had been remolding German society, especially the young men. Helmut, in fact, was one of the first recipients of Stahl's' Study Abroad program which granted paid tuition for young upper-class men to study in American military academies.

Over the objections of Social Democrats, Greens, and Liberal Coalition parties, Stahl re-militarized the general population as well as soon as he was elected Prime Minister. Everyone was expected to learn civil defense procedures and first aid. Every able-bodied man between 12 and 60 was expected to join the Homeguard where he learned how to obey orders, fire a weapon, and do regular physical exercise. Every town, village, and hamlet had its own youth group called the National Watch that mentored younger boys, steering them away from drugs and petty crime amidst accusations of being another Hitler Youth.

"I knew from an early age that my peers were lazy, and thus dangerous, because we had no guidance, no expectations of duty, competence, or self-discipline from our leaders," Stahl said in his interview with CNN. "I set as my goal the re-invigoration of masculinity through a government sponsored program to address these deficiencies. As a result, we will see the German bloodline increase tenfold."

It was a fact. Before Stahl's election, fewer than three live births out of ten were to non-Mideastern women. Two years later, the rate had climbed to five in ten.

"German blood is worthy of Darwinian success," Stahl taught German hausfraus once again. "Without your wombs, German cities will be tombs."

The "Cult of Motherhood" was as pernicious as militarization, the feminists and Leftists screamed. Stahl only countered with appeals to cultural diversity. "Diversity, yes," he shot back with propaganda campaigns in posters, print, and public airways, "And that diversity included all that is great in German culture from Blitzkrieg to Beethoven."

Always controversial, Stahl shocked the world the day he was elected as Chancellor by invoking Adolph Hitler as a role model for determination and social engineering. "Of course, we reject the barbarism of the Third Reich," Stahl asserted at a NATO conference, "But to deny Hitler's ability to mobilize the national will would be to deny the German people of the memory of that will - a will that can triumph over great adversity," he told the world. The Germans perfected organization, he argued, why not put that talent to use fighting terrorism? "Israel knows our intentions are to protect her and every Jew abroad from the rabid anti-Semitism that plagued our early history. We affirm Israel's right to exist as she affirms our right to shield the world from Islamic barbarism."

Confronted with a crumbling French society, and the all-to-near specter of a Muslim state on its border, the German people responded to Stahl's sense of mission with fervor. They must prepare, Stahl instructed, and the people welded together an intricate communication and supply system whereby the entire country could respond to any threat or disaster.

New Year's Day, as the trains in Berlin were loaded with men, arms, and supplies, citizens in every municipality roused each other by phone in the wintry night to load their trucks with supplies also, driving them to depots and onto railway flat-beds, and standing vigil till their connection with the engine of salvation chugging towards Paris.

"History holds many lessons," Stahl was fond of saying. "If the Russians could supply Leningrad by rail across a frozen Lake Ladoga, then surely the Germans can supply Paris by rail when it is half as cold and two thousand times safer."

The German people went further. In countless homes, spare rooms were readied for survivors when Calais became overwhelmed. One, two, a family of five —somehow they were kept together. Hospitals and clinics prepared to receive casualties as returning trains brought back burn and blast victims. The men donated their muscle, the women their blood, all to rescue their ravaged neighbors.

The count of survivors rose into the tens of thousands. It was, according to Fox News, an atonement of epic proportions for Germany. Stephan and Frieda Stahl were praised around the world. Stephan was portrayed as a Teutonic knight slaying the Four Dragons of Destruction: hunger, violence, war and terrorism. Frieda's resolute bearing, her white skin accentuated by auburn hair, and always shown with a rosary woven in her fingers, was imaged on postage stamps and commemorative plates as the Servant of Mercy. But by far, the most widely distributed photo was that of Stahl shaking hands with the country's young hero, Helmut Wolf, accepting the Kaiser Cross, flanked by Frieda, and Francesca and Emil Eisenbach. Behind them all a huge blow-up of Turtletaub's photo of the Miracle Baby's rescue. *Every Life Has A Purpose*, the headline read, and became the title of a poster bought around the world. The "Unholy Trinity of Destruction", the Liberal press dubbed them, but the public couldn't get enough of its inter-generational super heroes as sales receipts showed.

The Miracle Baby had grown up to be the closest thing Germany had to a crown prince. To millions of French survivors of the terrorist attack, Helmut was a miracle worker in the tradition of Saint Bernadette, and Olberman made sure they had a steady supply of photographic relics to venerate. Helmut's classic profile, his eyes gazing into an eternal vista, was printed on posters, post cards and key-chains.

In Germany, enlistment applications in the Eisenbach Brigade became so numerous, recruits were being turned away. There was even an application from a fraternity in America for an international unit, reminding Eisenbach of the Americans who joined the RAF. Eisenbach agreed to let members of NATO nations join if the individual serviceperson already had critical skills such as emergency medical or hazmat training, and could learn German within the four month basic training period.

The more vocal the denouncement by the media, the higher the enlistment numbers climbed. Said one Swiss recruit in answer to an anchorman from Fox News: "I'm tired of talking the problem to death – I want action."

# CHAPTER IV
## Death Tempts Us All

For Fritz Pomeranz, Olberman's propaganda machine brought daily frustration. News of Helmut Wolf fighting a tireless war on terror in Paris was a daily staple. In the left hand corner of Olberman's latest creation, a grocery store rag called *Der Taggekrieg*, was a weekly column, allegedly written by Helmut himself, featuring a color picture of him and a recitation of the latest feats of daring-do by local boys – Private Bliss from Marburg killed so many terrorists, Corporal Blatt from Mainz killed a Muslim sniper - followed by trite pieces of advice for young people: the body is a temple, motherhood is a sacred duty, bravery, obedience and loyalty are the hallmarks of manhood and virility. Teen-age girls kept scrapbooks of these sops to their female hormones. Young men wondered how much female attention they too could garner by putting on a well-fitting black uniform.

More demonic to Pomeranz, however, was Helmut's web site that included downloadable video clips of Muslim atrocities and German vengeance in real time. There was talk of a video game.

Yet, Pomeranz couldn't argue with success. The successful branding of a renaissance of German manhood meant awe-inspiring profits that were financing Stahl's Party entertainments. These too were displayed in *Der Taggekrieg*: pictures of Stahl with King William at a polo match, Stahl with President Franklin laying a wreath at Arlington, Stahl with President Yeshenko at the Stalingrad memorial at Volgograd.

This was the new Big Three: Germany, Britain and America, scheduled to meet at Malta to discuss the "Muslim Problem", and Pomeranz was not a part of it. "My biggest fear is that Stahl's repatriation scheme will be legitimized," he explained to Tanzer and Halderman. "Now that Russia has again adopted the Russian Orthodox Church as the state religion, it will be happy to rid itself of Muslims in its remaining spheres of influence. It's flirtation with Stahl has turned to lust. Can America be far behind given the rampant Catholicism of the Hispanics?"

"Extermination is not on the agenda, so far. Why the panic, Fritz?" Tanzer wondered aloud.

"You think they're stupid enough to broadcast another holocaust in the making to the world?" Pomeranz closed his eyes and sighed heavily. We can't let Malta become another Wannasee Conference."

Halderman felt caught in the middle. It was true Stahl had marginalized the Center Socialists by calling the Party weak on national defense. On the other hand, his Party didn't have a coherent plan to substitute for Stahl's draconian measures. "You're aware that Spain has asked Stahl to send in advisors?"

"No," Tanzer said, "When?"

"Gentlemen, please," Pomeranz pleaded, "one crisis at a time. We have to have a spy at Malta. Stahl keeps us ignorant of everything important in this war. It's an gross insult to the Party, not to mention democracy, fairness, legality —sanity. We've got to lodge a formal protest —take our case directly to the people."

Halderman handed Tanzer a memo from the Foreign Bureau then turned to Pomeranz. "If you press the issue, Stahl will dissolve the government again and ask for a confidence vote. The party won't survive another election. We barely managed to stay alive in the last one. Stahl has unlimited resources. Keeping the smaller parties around gives the appearance of proportional representation, but the truth is the German people have chosen him."

"Do we do nothing as this Unholy Trinity takes the world to hell?" Pomeranz smashed the table with his fist. "I say, no."

"What I'm saying, Fritz, is that maybe its time we considered drastic measures ourselves." Halderman stood up, and motioned Tanzer he was leaving. "Think it over. I say we bide our time until we can spot a weakness to exploit. An overt confrontation will be as disastrous as the Democrats who forced a show-down with Bush in 2004 over Iraq."

With the summit just a month away, it was time for the Center Socialists to find that weakness, concluded Pomeranz. He called Norman Wolf.

The situation would have to be handled delicately. Norman was sensitive about his nephew, announcing at the Party's convention, behind closed doors, that Helmut was not fodder for Center Socialist cannons. No matter what his private convictions, Norman had told the steering committee, publicly an ambassador must remain neutral and a-political. Or appear so, Pomeranz had countered.

"Come in, Norman," Pomeranz said. "We haven't seen each other since the last election."

"Licking our wounds in private, I guess."

"How's Patricia?" He had made sure Helmut's picture was visible as he put down his copy of *Der Taggekrieg*.

"She's well."

"How's Helmut getting along?"

"Famously. As you can see," Norman said, nodding at the newspaper.

"He does take a great picture." Pomeranz offered him a cigarette. Norman declined, but Pomeranz lit up, tossing the match into a crystal ashtray. "All this fuss about no smoking in buildings. It's my office. Though not for long if Stahl has his way. It's not like I'm killing people in death camps, right?"

"Germany's through with that nonsense, Fritz. Haven't you heard? I'll take an afternoon beer if you have it."

Pomeranz got two bottles of Corona from the refrigerator and handed one to Norman. "The Pope isn't so sure about Stahl's intentions."

"Did he tell you that?" Norman said examining the label. "Corona? What's wrong with Becks?"

"You said you wanted an afternoon beer."

"Oh my, I forgot you're the reigning expert on beer."

"Stahl has consistently refused to allow inspectors into E'tat de Guerre. Every relief and human rights group is pounding away at my door, and the reports of the deportees are alarmingly consistent."

"Did the Pope pound on your door?"

"You know John's no push-over. You've been ambassador to the Vatican for over twenty years, Norman."

"No doubt because I refuse to politicize or theocratize the post. Governments come and go, but the need for communication survives. You didn't set up this meeting to swap public administration philosophies."

"No." Pomeranz contemplated Helmut's picture. "I want to know what you think about this government loyalty oath the Christian Nationalists have introduced."

"I haven't been asked to sign it, if that's what you want to know."

"I want to know if you'll sign it if you're asked."

"I'll make my decision when it becomes necessary." Norman sighed. "I understand the position you're in, Fritz. We go back a long way. The opposition seems to be beating up the party on every issue."

Pomeranz was pacing with anxiety. "The world is looking at Germany as a reawakened monster."

"Only half the world, Fritz. Two of the Big Three see Stahl as the leader of the free western world now that America is in its twilight. He's seems one of the few leaders willing and able to protect his citizens. Everyone else has appeased their Muslims and got hammered by them. It's the sad truth."

"Jesus," Pomeranz exclaimed, "Are the only choices in the world dictators or dickless wonders? You want another beer?"

"Are you courting an afternoon drunk?" Pomeranz got two more bottles, but Norman waved him off.

"I did talk to His Holiness, Norman. He's concerned about the rumors, and about the meeting at Malta."

"I spoke with him too, and I know about his reservations."

Pomeranz's voice was deadly low. "Are the rumors about E'tat De Guerre true?"

"I don't know. I do know the deportations are problematic for John. Muslim countries see many of the expatriates as quasi-infidels. They're afraid of cultural contamination. Many deportees consider themselves citizens of the EU. His Holiness understands the implications of those opposing views. Repression, execution…"

"Stahl's violating the Geneva Convention by making stateless people out of the deportees," Pomeranz declared.

"Repatriation of people who hyphenate their citizenship is not making them stateless, and the EU agrees. You're on the losing side, Fritz. It's detain or deport. The attacks must be stopped."

Pomeranz took a letter from his desk drawer and handed it to Norman. "Read it. It's from King Saud. Arabia is not going to accept anymore deportees. Syria, Jordan, Palestine, and Iraq will follow suit. Thousands of homeless, starving refugees will overwhelm their governments."

Norman skimmed the letter and sighed as he handed it back to Pomeranz. "Stahl wants to force Muslim governments to use their OPEC-dollars for relief instead of nuclear weapons. But I'm not a politician. I communicate policy to His Holiness and relay messages to Berlin. There's nothing else I can do."

"And if the Pope excommunicated Stahl and Frieda?"

"Is the Pope testing the waters on this?"

"We discussed it."

"You mean you suggested it, Fritz."

"It gives us some leverage."

"Us who? You, the Pope, or the Center Socialists?"

"Humanity. Norman, there has to be a way to resolve the terrorist issue without killing millions of people."

"A political ploy will backfire on you and the Pope. Remember Luther? Germans will see the excommunication as Rome trying to control national policy. So far, Catholics haven't had to choose between the Church and Stahl, but if they are forced to choose, they'll choose living safety over dead virtue. After what's happened in New York, Moscow, Berlin, Tokyo, and Paris, people can't be blamed for looking at all Muslims as potential threats."

"What are our options? Off the record."

"Patience. Persuasion. Putsch." Norman took a deep breath before stating the obvious. "Arrest. Assassination."

Pomeranz walked slowly to his desk. Norman had at last spoke Halderman's drastic measure. The unspeakable had now become a viable option. Maybe now they could discuss it openly. Was there a way to spin such a radical action as a public service? The Center Socialists did not want to inherit a country in chaos. "If we could get evidence of war crimes, we could have Stahl prosecuted and executed. But the Unholy Trinity is not likely to let us get evidence —unless Helmut could be persuaded to help us get it."

"What would you do differently, Fritz? I mean, if you did get control of the government, what would you do? Dismantle Stahl's organizations? The people wouldn't stand for it."

"They would if people like Helmut and Eisenbach denounced Christian Nationalism and its organizations."

Norman couldn't help laughing. "You know nothing about Helmut or Eisenbach."

"Tell me about them. Tell me about Helmut. What motivates him? What does he love?"

"Not much, my friend. Dr. Stossel diagnosed him with attachment disorder."

"He's a sociopath?"

"No, he's fond of society. It's individuals he can't stand. Not unlike you and your Center Socialists. He'd have made a good party member if he hadn't been seduced by a shadow."

"You lost me."

"We lost him. No, let me be accurate. Patricia and I threw him away, left him floundering. Attachment disorder is usually socio-hereditary. You catch it from the relatives who were supposed to love you but ignored you. Helmut held on to the one person who held on to him, the person who wanted him to live more than any person on earth: Emil Eisenbach."

"And Eisenbach is in Stahl's pocket. That's my point. We don't have to bring Helmut down —or Eisenbach. All we have to do is redirect their loyalties," Pomeranz said.

"Get them to switch sides? I applaud your efforts even though they're doomed. They're true believers."

"True believers following a false prophet."

"Perhaps. But we all follow false prophets, and the falsest of all is ourselves." Norman paused, letting his words penetrate his own mental prison. "Have you considered, Fritz, what if the Unholy Trinity —my God it sounds like the back-up group for a demonic rock star —what if they really are the saviors of western civilization? Have you considered you might be wrong?"

"Why?" Pomeranz demanded. "They never consider they might be wrong."

"Because in a contest of wills, only the strong *do* survive. Stahl may be an opportunist, Eisenbach a puppeteer, and Helmut a golem, but they all share the same mission. Read your Bible, Fritz. The first commandment: Thou shalt have no gods before me. Did you know Helmut

68

chose the motto of the Eisenbach Brigade? *Always before Me*. Mottos have meaning."

"Maybe so, but all men have their price. I need to find out what Helmut's price is. Can you help me do that?"

"I may know someone who can."

***

The true nature of Helmut's relationship with Madeline Churchill was a mystery to Norman. He believed they were more than friends as he had seen the many scented pink envelopes she addressed to Helmut in her distinctive hand. A Left-hander, he remembered thinking as he held the envelope to his nose, who loves lilac. Like Patricia. What a coincidence.

The envelopes began to arrive shortly after Helmut entered Boswell, every holiday, every summer visit. And stopped coming after Helmut graduated from Boswell and returned to Germany. Norman wondered which was the cause, and which the effect. As much as Patricia ragged on Madeline, she would admit, in private, that Helmut seemed unhappy when he moved back to Germany permanently.

He and Patricia had met Madeline only once, at graduation. She was a big girl, at least five-foot-ten, and plump, with large breasts and a wide smile. She looked Helmut straight in the eyes when she spoke to him. He had nudged a wisp of her long brown hair out of her eyes and over her ear, and Norman recalled thinking how gentle Helmut was with her, and that he really liked her. Helmut framed the picture they took together that day, she in a calf-length maroon dress and Helmut in his white dress uniform and kept it on his dresser for months after his return.

It disappeared around Oktoberfest when Helmut entered his graduate program in Stuttgart. Norman never asked why.

He regretted that now. He should have asked, encouraged Helmut to work out their problems. Why didn't he tell Helmut to go after her? London was so close. Madeline could have done her graduate studies in Berlin; Patricia would have adjusted. They spent most of their time in Rome, anyway. Helmut and Madeline could have had the house all to themselves. She could have softened Helmut's sharp military edges.

"This call is for Madeline," Norman said to the Churchill's answering machine. "You may not remember me. I'm Helmut's Uncle Norman. Patricia and I would like you to visit for Helmut's twenty-fourth birthday. Reach us by phone. Overseas operator 7."

He sounded diplomatic, he thought. She couldn't read anything more into his message. Oh, hell, he concluded, so what if she did? So she knew that Helmut's family believed he missed her. If it turned out badly, he'd apologize to Helmut. And if all went well, Patricia would welcome her as a daughter-in-law, and have tall, plump grandchildren with round faces.

Norman congratulated himself on his recklessness. He would get Helmut out of Paris if only for a week-end.

*Dearest Nephew:*
*Your Aunt has planned a surprise for the weekend*
*of the 17th. It's my job to make sure you will be home.*
*Don't disappoint her.*
*Regards, Uncle Norman.*

It sounded like a summons. He changed regards to love and printed the note on slate-grey stationery. Helmut would do his duty quicker than a kindness. Hopefully, Madeline would change that.

When the postman picked up Norman's note, he delivered a letter to the Wolfs. It was notification that Norman was to be the first recipient of Stahl's newly created civilian Iron Cross called the Citizen's Freedom Medal, presented by the Chancellor himself in front of the world media.

Norman shuddered. Once again, celebrity came knocking at the door all because the world couldn't get enough of Berlin's Miracle Baby who was now the star of his own war show. Madeline Churchill was smart to bail out when she did.

His thoughts drifted back to his conversation with Pomeranz. Helmut could bring down Stahl. He had global adoration. Stahl was reviled by the mainstream media, Eisenbach was criticized, but Helmut was still the darling who sold newspapers. If he did reject the Christian Nationalist Party, the world would forgive him the annexation of France. Helmut had power, Norman conceded, but was in great danger too.

***

While Norman plotted the lovers' reunion, Emil Eisenbach traveled to Paris to inspect the E'tat de Guerre. Stahl had promised the press a full investigation of deportees' accusations amidst growing UN Human Rights Commission concern. The deportees, it was claimed, had no prayers rugs, or Qu'rans, and were not allowed to gather for daily prayers. Women were photographed without their veils. Children under the age of three were being baptized and sent to European homes. Their names were changed, and original birth certificates destroyed. The deportees were underfed, ill-housed, and there were few interpreters to explain regulations and orders to them. The women were raped and the men beaten if they refused to sign away their children and property. There were accusations of forced sterilization, forced labor, and forced attendance at indoctrination meetings.

Some of the accusations were strategically true. Since much of terrorist violence was preached and planned at the mosques, people were not allowed to congregate for prayer. Prayer rugs and Qu'rans were not confiscated, but none were provided by the German government because of cost.

All deportees were identified, photographed, and finger printed, and the information stored in a ID mainframe. Yes, the women were unveiled, but only women administrators did the photographing, Helmut explained to Eisenbach as they drove from Orly to Paris.

Every deportee, man, woman and child, was given a medical examination as part of the ID process that included blood typing, HIV testing, and testing for chronic illnesses such as diabetes, arthritis, and high blood pressure.  However, only women doctors examined Muslim women, and only male doctors examined the men.

Some of the children were "recultured", Helmut explained. It was entirely the parents' choice. They could take the youngsters to third world countries, or they could leave them behind to enjoy a western way of life with guaranteed educational and employment opportunities. It was either take them to the past or give them a future.

"And the forced baptisms?" Eisenbach asked as they drove past rows of whitewashed barracks where men in orange jumpsuits swept walkways, picked up trash, and scoured pots.

"The children are welcomed into the Christian community. The adults can believe as they choose. No one is forced. Some try to buy their way out of deportation by claiming conversion, but nationality is the sole determinant for the adults. If they want a priest to comfort them, we have a chaplain."

"They are expected to work, though," Eisenbach stated.

"Of course, able-bodied men are made to work. It's the first real work many of the younger men have ever done. They've lived on the dole too long. We teach them as best we can about what they can expect in their countries of origin. That, yes, they really will get their hands chopped off if they steal, so they'd better learn to work."

"That's the indoctrination process?"

"Partly. We teach them about the West – why democracies do what they do. It doesn't hurt to have some who can try to change their government of origin, impossible as that seems."

"Stop the car," Eisenbach told Reinhardt, and chose a barracks at random. "I want to visit that one."

He and Helmut went inside. The room was separated into cubicles divided by curtains. "There's a bathroom at this end of the building, and showers at the other. Cleanliness and safety is up to the occupants. We've had few acts of vandalism, but when the families saw we weren't going to clean up after them or unstop a drain or replace a window, they came around. Now anyone who decides to be dirty is policed by the other families. The word gets out. Same with the food. The rule is no contraband in the dorms —we call them dorms —because of bugs. Once they see a cockroach, they make sure everyone follows the rules."

73

"How long do they stay in these dorms, on average?"

"Processing takes about three weeks. When one contingent leaves a dorm, it's disinfected, and the water is tested. We damn sure don't want any cholera outbreaks."

"How many families to a dorm?"

"It depends on the size of the families. We had one family that was so big, they had a dorm to themselves: two sets of grandparents, four sets of parents and many, many children. It wasn't quite forty-five, but we felt it was safer to leave them alone."

Eisenbach walked down the center aisle, pulling back curtains at random, noticing that most of the beds were made and the personal effects, soap, hair brushes, and shoes, were neatly arranged. "Where are the occupants now?"

"Some of the men are on work detail building dorms, others are cleaning up the bombing site. The women are with the children in school. We hold classes on nutrition and contraception for them. You'd be surprised at how many groups decide not to tell their husbands about the contraception part. They'd be killed in some of these countries if the mullahs knew they had that information. We don't sterilize anyone, I assure you. We care nothing about their fertility now that they're not our problem anymore. Such accusations are ridiculous."

That no member of the EU sat on the Commission meant perfunctory oversight at best, but Olberman made sure Stahl got political mileage out of Eisenbach's visit, proclaiming to the world that if any truth of the accusations existed, the perpetrators would be severely punished.

"What's the daily calorie intake?"

"It isn't the Ritz, but they don't go hungry. Twelve hundred calories for the women. Two thousand for the men. Oatmeal for breakfast, soup and bread for lunch, meat and turnips for dinner. Orange juice, water, milk and tea. They get a box of sandwiches and cookies for the trip. The westernized Muslims have it the roughest. You can understand that. They really don't want to leave their SUVs and their nightclubs for camels and tents. We call them the "McDonald Contingents." They're the ones who need the most supervision. Always looking for a way out, begging and crying as they get on the planes."

"The grist of civil wars."

"Freedom is everyone's fight. If they haven't learned that in three generations, it's not our problem."

They returned to the car.

"How many dorms do you have?"

"Right now, fifty-two. Another five under construction. With more manpower, we can cut processing time in half."

"If the Muslim countries don't start refusing repatriation," Eisenbach said. "King Saud is making a formal protest to the UN, Stahl has heard rumblings that Turkey and Iraq are voting on a moratorium in the next two weeks."

"To hell with them. Let them shoot down a planeful of their own people and see what the world has to say," was Helmut's reply.

Reinhardt drove them past the dorms to the Ecole Militaire, which had been transformed into the deportation processing center. "This is the receiving hall," Helmut explained as the men strode through heavily armored doors and metal detectors. The walls bore framed blow-ups of the terrorists' photographs of the Mercury Hotel massacre. Eisenbach walked around the room, looking at each one. On each of the eight-foot by five-foot pictures was written in Arabic: This Is Why.

"It saves so much time," Helmut said. "Some of the people get sick. Especially the McDonalds. He pointed to a stack of plastic 'hurl bags'. "If they miss, they have to clean up their own vomit, but we disinfect the floors after each group comes through. That's what you smell – perfumed soap."

Eisenbach nodded his head in approval. "This is where they are I.D.ed?"

"The women and children go through this door, the men the other, for their medical examinations, finger and eye printing. They are issued an ID card too, and then assigned a dorm and a work detail. They can discard the ID, of course, but we still have their vitals in case they try to sneak back into Europe."

"What are the radiation levels like?" Eisenbach asked as they headed upstairs to Helmut's office.

"Acceptable. We covered the detonation site with a lead plate, covered that with concrete and put in a fountain of remembrance. You saw it as we drove in —the small Eiffel tower amidst the flames. At night, red lights make the flames look almost real."

"It's beautiful."

"It's was designed by Sgt. Rudolph, the man responsible for capturing Selah Chaobli, the terrorist who ransacked the Lourvre." Two soldiers snapped to attention as the men approached. "At ease," Helmut said as they passed. Helmut stopped, and turned to one of the soldiers. "Has Sgt. Rudolph been in today?"

"I haven't seen him, Sir. But a runner brought a note for you. It's in your mailbox."

Helmut unlocked the door, and pulled the note from the drop-box, gesturing Eisenbach to sit as he opened it. "It's from Norman, Emil. He wants me home on the 17th."

"We can go together. Is there an emergency?"

"Lord, no. A birthday dinner."

"Excellent." Eisenbach sat down, smiling. "Maybe you can find out why he went to see Pomeranz, who's in a snit over the upcoming Malta conference. Good ol' Fritz, he still makes daily demands for concessions from Stahl for techno-Muslims. Says the country will fold if they get deported. It's crap. American requests for immigration to Germany based on education are pouring in. Franklin's got himself in a mess over there."

"Is that why Franklin agreed to meet at Malta?"

"According to the Leftist press, Franklin's just going so he can solve the capitalist employment problem which can only be solved by Marist-Leninism. The usual bullshit. Franklin wants Stahl to tell him how to get America back from the illegals. It's hopeless, of course. Once you give people the right to vote, you're done. Imagine giving voting rights to non-citizens. How stupid can you be? You'd think the country that put a man on the moon would be smarter than that. Stahl's not going to make the American mistake."

It was true. With the amnesties of 2012 and 13, America's economy had been destroyed from the demand for social services. Globalism had allowed thousands of middle-class blacks and whites to

77

emigrate. Countries like England, Scotland, and Ireland welcomed them, and their wealth, with tax breaks and cheaper housing.

"Sir…"

"Let's drop the formalities, Helmut. My official business is through. You've done a marvelous job here. Marvelous. It's no resort, but it's hardly Auschwitz. Stahl is going to be very pleased. When can the Red Cross come? It's time we let the world see what's going on."

"Anytime with 48 hours prior notice – only because I'll have to arrange quarters and transportation for them."

"Excellent. Olberman can come with them. You were about to say?"

"I've heard rumors that the Chancellor is going to replace my Uncle as Ambassador to the Vatican. Is it true?"

"Honestly, he thought about replacing him with a man more friendly to the Christian Nationalists. But …"

"You told him not to."

"I pointed out to him that removing the uncle who raised you merely for party purposes would be bad publicity. Norman is harmless unless Pomeranz can manipulate him into doing something dumb, and it throws a crumb to bipartisanship. Norman didn't say anything about going to Vienna, did he?"

"No."

"That means he hasn't decided whether to accept the Citizen's Freedom Medal. Perhaps you can make him understand what an honor it is to have the Chancellor recognize his long career. Unless he's ready to retire."

Helmut was mulling over an idea. "Norman always wanted me to take over for him. My Italian is good."

"It's a possibility. We're not going to waste your talents in Paris indefinitely. Is there a good administrator you could recommend?"

"Vincent Rudolph," Helmut said immediately. "He's long overdue for a promotion. He and Reinhardt will make a capable team if I'm posted in Italy." Helmut noticed it was Emil who was now deep in thought.

"Did you know why Stahl chose Vienna for the award ceremony? Emil said.

"Norman and Patricia prefer it to Berlin. Too hot there."

Emil smiled. "Pomeranz complains about the heat all the time too." His face clouded then as he spoke softly. "It's prostate cancer."

"Oh, Jesus." Helmut said a quick prayer and made the sign on the cross. "How bad?"

"He's on chemo. He'll recover, the doctors say. But it's made him consider Germany's future – and the future of the war on terror. I wanted to get your take on the situation before suggesting a way to help calm his fears. You're not involved with anyone, are you? You're not in love?"

Helmut remembered Patricia's worry about him and Madeline, and shook his head no. "I'm not involved. Why?"

"No one lives forever. How do you feel about marriages of state?"

"They're Medieval."

"Teresa Jean Stahl is a pretty girl. Well educated, well mannered. Healthy. Devoted to her father. She's been with Stephan and Frieda every minute since the diagnosis. She knows that men have duties that sometimes take them far away for many months. She wouldn't be —shall we say —an impediment to other, discreet, relationships with people from England, for example."

"You mean Madeline Churchill."

"Norman has invited her to your party. We tap his phone lines, of course."

The thought of Norman playing matchmaker made Helmut grin. "You're serious, Emil! Well, I wish him all the luck in the world on that one. Tell me, has anyone asked Teresa Jean how she feels about this?" he asked half jokingly.

Emil moved closer to Helmut. "Stephan would rest better if he knew there were loyal people around to protect his family if the doctors are wrong. And knew that his work would not be sabotaged. No doubt Frieda and Teresa Jean know that too. Promise me you'll think about it."

"Yes. I promise," Helmut said, fully intending to wait five seconds before saying no.

"After the 17th," Emil said, "Call me. I can set up an accidental meeting between you and Teresa Jean when you attend your uncle's ceremony. The public needs a little romance, Helmut. It helps them bear the sadder parts of war. There'll be a movie, I'm sure."

"I'm a loyal to Stahl, you know that. But isn't it enough that I fight his war and am pedaled to children like Spiderman? I never asked to be a celebrity."

"You and I are accidents of fate, my boy. You were supposed to die in the rubble, and I was supposed to let you. We defied time and space. I don't know if celebrity is the price we pay, or the reward that makes it all bearable." Emil sat next to Helmut and put his arm around the boy's shoulder. "Remember Diana Spencer?"

"The English girl who married Prince Charles?"

"That's the one. She could have been queen, but threw it all away, endangered the monarchy itself, because she wanted romantic love. How naïve to think love had anything to do with marriage to a prince. She needed someone like me to explain it to her. I would have told her that all parties make trade-offs when they make a contract. Just because she was young and stupid doesn't mean the terms of the contract were unfair or that she could change them at will. Olberman got it right. Every life does have a purpose. Many times, it is not the purpose we would choose if we had a choice."

It wasn't his commander that was speaking now. It was his father. It was the man who cared about him, understood him, and wanted him to live. "I used to read the celebrity rags. I read books about old movie stars and their publicity marriages, Marilyn Monroe and Joe DiMaggio. The sex kitten and the baseball player. The gay ones who married for cover. And those that traded in partners like used cars because they were bored. I compared them to Norman and Patricia, two pragmatic politicos who chose not to be in love, who cheated fate by falling in love when no one was watching. Maybe Stahl will cheat fate too," Helmut said. "Arrange the meeting with Teresa Jean."

"Good man." Emil stood up, and motioned Helmut to follow. He walked to the computer and entered a series of codes that let him into a secure web site. "I think it's time you saw this." He popped a CD into the computer.

Helmut was looking at another of Olberman's video games. The images were clear, crisp, life-like and deadly. Hypnotized, he watched plane after plane spit missiles onto an urban landscape, followed by

81

thundering explosions and clouds of black smoke. People staggered out of buildings, clutching their necks; body parts flew through the air; and in the clouds, mythical warriors rode across a flaming sky brandishing sparkling swords. "What's it called?" Helmut said.

"*Damascus Demolition*. Stahl's virtual reality warning of what will happen to every city between Kabul and Gaza if there's another dirty bomb. What do you think?"

Helmut felt his pulse race as the game took him inside the Stealth cockpit. "It's me. Olberman made the pilot look like me. How fuckin' cool is that? So this is full scale war?"

"This is what happens when a player wins."

"Does the player ever lose?" Helmut's eyes riveted on the screen as reconnaissance film followed the bombardment. Every building was leveled, every pole and palm tree snapped in half, and everywhere flames and smoke climbed to heaven.

"Don't sell the bastards short. Anti-aircraft guns, shoulder missiles, heat-seeking missiles, tactical nukes. They have the best Iran and North Korea have to offer. If they get one shot on target, the player is dead. It's state of the art, Son."

"Those planes, what are they dropping now? Leaflets?"

"Salt." Emil logged off and handed Helmut the CD. "Do you know what the release date is on this? June 10th. On that day, in 1942, one thousand people suspected of being involved in SS Leader Reinhardt Heydrich's death were arrested. Three thousand Jews were deported from the ghetto at Theresienstadt for extermination. In Berlin, five hundred Jews were arrested, and one hundred fifty-two were executed. The Czech village of Lidice was liquidated. One hundred seventy-two men and boys over age sixteen in the village were shot while the women were deported to Ravensbrück concentration camp. Ninety young children were sent to the concentration camp at Gneisenau, though some *were* eventually taken to Nazi orphanages. Lidice itself was destroyed. Every building demolished, and salt was spread over the fields where grain was once planted. Even the name Lidice was removed from German maps all because of the assassination of one man. That's a true reprisal."

The CD felt hot in Helmut's hand. Was it on fire, or was he? "Can I keep this?"

Emil nodded yes. "Olberman's has had a four-week ad campaign out for *Damascus Demolition* … pre-orders are running into the millions. The U.S. Army alone has ordered fifty thousand for its recruit training. Olberman mailed a copy to General Davis," Emil continued. "At forty Euros a pop, do the math."

"Olberman's a marketing genius," Helmut said respectfully.

"Started the game engineers working on this the second Franklin delivered the Stealths to us. How Franklin got the Congress to approve that deal, I'll never know."

"America needs money and allies if she's going to survive. Even the dillweeds in Congress know that."

"Government costs money. And the wars they fight cost more money. Enjoy the game, Helmut. Play it till you get good at it and get ready for the next one. *Mecca Massacre*."

\*\*\*

Norman headed straight for the bar. Patricia didn't look up till she heard the ice tinkling in the glass, and then put down *People* magazine and watched him pour two fingers worth of scotch. "It's Helmut, isn't it? That bastard Stahl has had him killed."

Norman winced. "No. He's not dead."

"Worse then? Crippled?"

"No." Norman poured another two fingers. "I did something stupid. I decided – no Pomeranz decided – Helmut ought to have a normal life, that he should marry Madeline Churchill and that would take him out of every teeny-boppers bedroom fantasy. But Helmut wasn't lying." He grinned weakly. "Madeline really did become a nun."

"Churchill's in a convent? That's hysterically funny."

"Yes, she's Sister Clare of the rosary, or clouds or something. I didn't listen too carefully after Mother Ignatius told me Madeline wouldn't be coming to Helmut's birthday bash because she married God."

"Where is she?"

"Some Carmelite convent in Vienna."

Patricia envisioned Sister Clare draped in long brown robes standing next to Jesus in a Las Vegas wedding chapel. "That's a tough act to follow. How did it happen? I mean, when? I don't remember Helmut telling us she was a Catholic. He was desperately in love with her. Poor boy."

"So much for our surprise and half-baked intrigues."

"It isn't the end of the world, Norman. We'll have the party anyway." She went back to her magazine "According to *People* magazine, Helmut loves healthy girls, walks on the beach – when he's not torturing Muslims, of course, they left that part out - and Fig Newtons." She threw the magazine to the floor. "People call him Germany's Prince. Honestly, you'd think he was a playboy instead of a war criminal."

"We don't know that he's tortured anyone, Patti. It's all speculation. You're beginning to sound like Pomeranz."

Patricia sat back in the sofa and folded her arms over her chest. "When my Norman hits the bottle at eleven in the morning, I know there's more to the story than an ex-girlfriend taking the veil. Helmut's a fall-guy, a side-show in Stahl's freak circus. Stahl comes off like a statesman while Helmut does his dirty work." She stood up and walked to the phone.

"Who are you calling?"

"My manicurist," she sighed. "I can't possibly have a Party party sporting Revenge Red. Ambassador Pink would be more appropriate, I think. Pomeranz is coming, right?"

"Stop it Patti."

She put down the phone. "Oh, for God's sake, what can the girl be thinking? I don't understand young people today. Girls locking themselves away in convents. Helmut dedicating himself to a vendetta against Islam. They should be out partying, fucking their bucolic brains out in the Tyrolean Alps."

Norman smiled at her frustration. "No adult understands young people...except someone like Stahl."

She plopped down on the sofa again. "That rascal! Heroes. Sacrifices. It's unnatural —ridiculous Romanticism."

"The young want to be heroes, Patti. That's the point. It's their generational 'thing'."

"Do something, Norman."

"What? Kidnap Churchill so you can take her shopping? It's not like she's joined a cult. The Carmelites have been around for eight hundred years." Norman joined her on the sofa. "You can't change some one's heart, Patti." He put his arm around her.

"Is she a lesbian, do you think?"

Norman groaned.

"Talk to Umberto, Norman."

"I talk to him everyday, and everyday he tells me the same thing you and Pomeranz tell me. Do something. Do something about Paris, about Germany, about my nephew, the Anti-Christ. But what can I do about any of them?" Norman sighed now. "Sometimes I think Umberto and Pomeranz want me to assassinate the Unholy Trinity myself."

Patricia was staring at him, boring into his face with expectation. "Perhaps Rome understands Berlin better than we think," she whispered.

"I won't be a party to murder, Patti." Norman removed his arm and stared her down.

"Then you'd better stay away from Pomeranz because we both know that's the direction he's headed," Patricia said.

"Fine. Let him be the Quisling, not me."

Patricia turned away from his eyes, wondering if assassination was the only way out for countries in the grip of madmen. How much grief would the world have been spared if Stauffenberg had been successful at Rastenberg? If Umberto Cardinal Corigliano was giving Norman the imprimatur of the church to sacrifice the three for the good of the millions, then Norman shouldn't shirk his duty. "Are you going to accept the Citizen's Freedom Medal?"

"I haven't decided yet. Goddamn Stahl. I'll give him credit for one thing, he knows his politics. He's maneuvered me into a corner. If I accept the medal, the Vatican will revoke my portfolio. If I refuse it, I'll be retired. Either way, my career is over, Ol' Girl. You know that."

"I'm not ready to give up the good life just yet, my sweet. What exactly did Umberto say when you discussed the medal?"

"He said that a diplomat's success was directly related to his anonymity. I can't do Stahl's dog-and-pony show and remain anonymous, now can I? As in war, nothing is certain in diplomacy except the efficacy of secrecy."

Patricia thought for a few seconds, then asked, "It's all about the refugee problem, isn't it?"

"The world's got too many people with too many problems they look to government to solve. Rome sees its wealth and power slipping away like all the other governments. Even America can't afford to be generous anymore. Stahl's ethnic cleansing of Europe is simply too expensive for global charity, and no country can absorb so many displaced people who need emergency housing and food. What happens when the Mid-east countries stop accepting the refugees? Stahl won't be able to feed Paris indefinitely. It doesn't take a soothsayer to know it would mean a final solution. How ironic that Jew-hating Muslims now face their own holocaust."

***

There was no advance media announcement of President Franklin's meeting with Stahl. With surface to air missiles now available on the open market, the travel agendas of American leaders were seldom publicized. Al-Qaeda regularly appeared on Al-Jazeera to remind the world there was a hundred-million-dollar bounty on the head of any

American president, a bounty already paid once to two Cuban Castro retro-loyalists who shot down Air Force One on it's way to Bogotá.

Without fanfare or press corps, Franklin and Stahl exchanged small-talk in the smaller of the two Chancellery reception halls. Ten minutes into swapping compliments to their respective families, they were joined by British Prime Minister Alastair Howe who had slipped across the channel in a small, private jet. The question they were to consider was clear, if informal. Under what condition would Stahl accept American and British Muslim repatriates at E'tat de Guerre?

Stahl's position was firm. Germany would only internationalize the repatriation center if other countries shouldered the cost of expansion and basic services. What was the cost, per capita? Stahl wasn't ready to quote them a price, demurring till Amnesty International and the Red Cross/Red Crescent inspected the facility and made their recommendations. He did offer, however, the assistance of planning teams who would conduct feasibility studies for repatriation centers on their own soil at a nominal cost.

America and Britain rejected the offer, pleading domestic political resistance. "Americans want them gone, not imprisoned," Franklin explained. "Imprisonment is a lengthy, high-profile, process in America, and the Liberals, who had demanded and won full constitutional protections for non-citizens on American soil, would stage massive demonstrations against the federal government if it even looked like it was trying to expedite the process. They can't deny to Muslims what they won for Mexicans."

Stahl agreed that differing political climes and cultures militated against seemingly draconian solutions to multicultural problems. Still, he asserted, populations can be persuaded that desperate times call for desperate measures. It was matter of finesse.

"Perhaps America's strident rhetoric aimed at Germany's approach had been premature and unwise," Franklin conceded. "But anything less that vehement condemnation would have given the Republicans a we-told-you-so advantage in the elections cycle. And the actual numbers of deportees from America would be so small, it would not be cost effective to build a repatriation center," Franklin added.

Stahl suggested revamping Ellis Island. Franklin shuddered. "The political fallout from that would be catastrophic. Removing Lazarus' poem from the Statue of Liberty was traumatic enough."

"To be president in America must like being the captain of an oil tanker on a skating rink. All that power and no where to go," Stahl observed, and turned to Howe.

Britain's argument against a national repatriation center was geographic. "We don't have the room. We're a small country without empire. Where could we build such a facility that we could operate securely? It's cheaper to transport Muslims to Paris than to warehouse them in Wales," Howe concluded.

Stahl proposed a temporary repatriation insurance fund, administered by a Swiss commission that would defray costs until a fee schedule could be created. "Medical care is our single biggest costs because we can't buy it in bulk like oatmeal. If a deportee needs medication for TB or prescription glasses or dental implants, it all has to be calculated into the average and we can't do that calculation yet. We've only been up and running six months, Gentlemen."

Franklin and Howe agreed to fifty million dollars in an interest-bearing account as an initial deposit —twenty-five million each. Stahl guaranteed expansion to two hundred dorms by June 1st, and personnel to process the first wave of repatriates by July 1st. Security must necessarily be absolute, Stahl was told, because the American and British deportees would be the worst of worst, those convicted of terror-related crimes.

"Starting with convicts will make repatriation politically marketable," Franklin said. "I can sell it to the Liberals as a humane compromise. Let the countries of origin decide how prisoners are to be treated. That's politically palatable."

"You understand that it is sometimes necessary to be very firm about keeping order in the center. I can't guarantee that everyone you send to Paris will survive the discipline we maintain. Especially violent prisoners could be subject to execution."

"How common is execution?" Howe wanted to know.

"I leave that to my officers. I only insist that all punishments be neither cruel nor unusual," Stahl replied.

"Is it true Muslims are required to wear yellow crescents sewn on their clothing?"

"Prime Minister it is necessary to distinguish between custodians and deportees given sheer numbers and the fact that some Muslims have assimilated so much they no longer resemble their countrymen. The insignia is not a badge of shame, but of identification only. It's all explained in the disciplinary clause."

Franklin read the discipline clause of the agreement. The language was sterile, but included terms such as "fair", "equitable", and "recourse for deportees". Outlined was a process for filing complaints against over-

90

zealous officers, and the penalties for officers found at fault. There was even an appeals process for deportees convicted of center infractions. What was not appealable was the repatriation itself.

Howe did not hesitate to sign in the name of King William, but Franklin's hand shook as he picked up the pen, and he had to press hard to keep his signature legible. "You realize I must get approval from Congress, Chancellor Stahl. The Senate must approve the treaty and the House must appropriate the funding."

"Yes, Mr. President, but I predict even your Liberals will be thankful they can rid America of its Muslim problem with so little political effort."

Predictably, news of the Repatriation Accord with Germany was leaked to the press before Franklin and Howe made it home. A half million Muslims met Howe at Heathrow airport. Franklin's plane had to be diverted to Philadelphia when over a million people gathered at the White House and spilled over into the Capitol Mall. The UN Security Council called an emergency meeting, and listened as the leaders of Iran, Iraq, Saudi Arabia, Syria, Somalia, Afghanistan, Indonesia, Lebanon, and Egypt voiced their concerns to the permanent members. Repatriation of millions of Muslims was impossible, they insisted. It would overtax existing inadequate economies of the Mid-East nations and invite domestic unrest. Iran threatened to shoot down any German repatriation planes entering its airspace and offered aerial protection to any country who asked for it.

Bruno Muller, Stahl's UN Secretary, responded by announcing at a press conference that cultural cleansing was necessary to prevent terrorist attacks, and was precipitated by Muslim refusal to learn tolerance. "All nations have a right to confer or withdraw citizenship," Muller said directly into the camera. "Germany is committed to the safety of its people and its nationhood. The repatriation of undesirables is part of its humane approach to multiculturalism and non-assimilation of those who profess a dangerous and uncivilized belief system. Germany refuses to extend the benefits of its culture to those determined to destroy it. No responsible government would do less than Chancellor Stahl has to insure the preservation of his people and the Fatherland."

It was a short, uncompromising assertion of nationalism that the world press denounced, but non-Muslim citizens of Germany, America, and Britain applauded. Within forty-eight hours, Franklin had the approval of the House and Senate, and twenty- five million dollars in the Swiss account, only three hours after the British deposit.

## CHAPTER V

## False Starts and Heroes

The Villa San Rafael was the ancestral home of Umberto Cardinal Corigliano. It lay twenty miles from Rome, and still produced a popular local wine known as Sangria Christi. Umberto felt most at home here, walking through his mother's favorite olive grove, tending the rose garden, and sitting in the courtyard contemplating the grey granite statue of the archangel. It was here, under his patient gaze and gentle wings Umberto studied his Latin, prepared for confession on Sunday mornings, and joined his Grandmother in saying the rosary. It was here Rafael called him to service in the church.

"Or so it seemed to me, Norman," Umberto said. "Who knows where or when Madeline Churchill received her call. All I know is that, if she has been called, she cannot refuse."

Norman and Umberto often strolled through the Villa's holdings. The walk allowed them to shed their official titles and roles, and speak as friends. All Norman had to do was call and ask if the wine was ready to be tasted, and Umberto understood there was a problem that needed tending as much as his roses. Norman made such a call on Thursday. Umberto heard the concern in his voice and told Norman to meet him at the vineyard at noon.

"I saw them together," Norman said as they picked ripe grapes and put them in a basket. "They were in love. I know that."

"You're probably right. Helmut and Madeline were deeply in love. But God is a persistent suitor. He will not be denied the soul he has chosen."

"Patricia believes something must have happened. An argument maybe, or …"

"Or what?

"Patricia didn't like her. She feels guilty."

Umberto laughed. "So, Madeline Churchill locks herself in a cloister because her beau's Aunt rejected her? Norman that's the silliest thing I've heard come out of your mouth in years. Straight out of Hollywood."

"It didn't sound silly when Patti said it. You had to be there, I guess," Norman mumbled.

"Patti sounds like my father who accused me of becoming a priest because my girlfriend wouldn't sleep with me."

"Did she reject you?"

"Are you kidding? No girl ever rejected me. Rosina and I were passionate lovers from the first day we met."

"But…"

"But what? I've never aspired to sainthood. It's pointless and I'm sure it's tiresome to Christ."

"Then why didn't you marry? You know how good sex is."

They were in the olive grove now, grateful for the shade. Umberto stopped and motioned Norman to sit down. He pulled a bottle of water from his robe pocket and offered Norman a drink. The water was hot, but Norman didn't care. He gulped a few sips, and handed the bottle back to Umberto, who finished it off like it was cold beer.

"Rafael, the messenger, told me something I never really understood before. He told me it doesn't matter if we love God. We can never really love Him anyway because we are so weak and so morally infirm. No, it doesn't matter. What matters is that we accept that God loves us. Rosina Manetti, with the blackest hair and the bluest eyes I ever saw, could give me everything she had including her precious hymen, and it would never be enough. My friend, Rafael, made me understand that. My father was right, in a way. I am selfish enough to want perfection all to myself, and that perfection can only be found in God. But Manetti's good for the imperfect side of me... even now."

"Don't expect me to swoon with renewed faith, Umberto. You're a practical fornicator. Madeline may never have talked to an angel. She may just be a hysterical young woman suffering from a mental disorder. Don't you think you should find out?"

"You want me to talk with her?"

"Well, yes. More than that, I want you to —how can I put this delicately? What if she has a mission greater than her personal salvation pursued in a convent? What if God wants her to prevent a cataclysm?"

"Come on, let's get to the house." They helped each other up, bracing themselves with each other arms. Umberto set a faster pace than usual. "We have much to talk about and I talk better on a full stomach."

Once the pasta and wine were devoured, Umberto bowed his head for a short prayer before speaking. "The Holy Father is hurting, Norman. He prays for the souls at E'tat de Guerre. He's worried history may repeat itself on a bigger, more tragic scale. I have been little help to him."

Norman heard the pain in his voice and patted Umberto's arm. "I know Fritz Pomeranz has spoken to him about excommunicating the Unholy Trinity if they continue their repatriation program."

"The Holy Father's position is one of political neutrality, of course, but he cannot continue to turn a bland eye to such heinous immorality. The risk to the souls of millions of people who are supporting this insanity is too great."

"It would be unwise for his Holiness to force the Germans to choose between Berlin and Rome. It didn't work in the 1530s, or the 1930s, and it won't work now. The Germans have opened their hearts and their wallets to the victims of the Paris bombing. They look on Stahl as the only person who can protect them from Islamofascism. The Holy Father may have prayed for the Parisians, but it was Stahl who rescued them in the dead of winter. We can't deny that he alone acted when we all sat around wringing our collective hands."

Umberto clasped the crucifix he wore around his neck, and exclaimed, "God help us if it has come to this!"

"He saved millions of lives, Umberto. It's this part of the equation that has me tied in knots. I know Stahl's dangerous, but he's so damned effective."

"Only because your nephew has the gift of organization." Umberto took a drink of wine, still clutching his crucifix. "You think this girl Churchill, you think she can persuade your nephew to give up his devotion to Stahl and his Christian Nationalist Party?"

"She can at least give us some insight. If there's something else - anything else that can derail his slavish devotion to the devil he serves, it's worth exploring before there's an official break between Stahl and the

Church. Helmut is a star. Pomeranz wants him to denounce the Party and encourage political dissent. Now, anyone who speaks out is branded a traitor. He thinks Helmut can mount a public relations coup."

"I cannot jeopardize Madeline's vocation even to save the world. It would be a mortal sin to come between her and God. If God has called her to the cloister, she must stay. Norman. You understand my position?"

"I do."

"I will talk to her, though. Perhaps she *can* help."

"You know I too pray for peace, Umberto. The interests of the Vatican and the interests of Berlin are not that dissimilar when the right people sit down to talk."

"His Holiness will be most pleased that you have lit a candle for us in this time of darkness. He would certainly not object to the whole world knowing what a valuable asset you are to Berlin and to Rome."

Norman left the Villa with a hope he hadn't had in years. Umberto was a pragmatist, Archangel Rafael notwithstanding. If Umberto believed Madeline could serve humanity better without her veil, he would instruct her to do so. Marriage was a vocation too, and a sacrament. As Patricia's husband, he had a duty to her as well as to Helmut. He called Patricia on his cell phone. "Call Stahl's secretary and tell her I'll be accepting that medal he wants to give me after all. Love you."

* * *

Madeline rose from her bed every morning at four AM, showered, and put on the white blouse and brown jumper of the postulant. She brushed her hair, tied it in a bun, and covered it with a short white veil.

She prayed as she headed for the kitchen where Sister Catherine's to-do list waited for her on the refrigerator – the profane work, Sister Catherine called it - mopping, laundry, and taking care of the elderly nuns. It would be three years before she would report to the chapel before eight o'clock, five years to learn how to walk without making a sound, to keep her eyes lowered without bumping into things, and how to ignore the ache in her heart for the warmth and conversation of her family. The brides of Christ lived more like widows, she thought, as she prepared the breakfast trays for the nuns in the infirmary.

Three old sisters had to be fed, washed, and dressed and taken to the chapel in their wheelchairs. A fourth nun, Sister Agnes, was now eighty-five and had lived all but twenty-two of those years in the cloister. She no longer remembered her cloister years though. She was now somewhere in Massachusetts on her family's estate, enjoying regattas and gymkhanas with her now-deceased siblings who were more real to her than Madeline.

For Sister Agnes, every day was spent in anticipation of September 12th, the day of her debutante ball, a ritual of the rich that introduced her to Boston's polite society. Every day was spent planning for the big event, deciding on a dress and the color that would best match her eyes. How wonderful, Madeline thought, to be forever in sweet expectation, forever young and beautiful and sought after, and never disappointed by reality.

Madeline smoothed the old woman's hair and fed her the thin cereal that was all she ate. "My book, Sissy," she'd say after Madeline had washed the limp folds of skin that hung on her frail bones, put her into a clean chemise, and helped her into a green satin chair. Madeline, or

"Sissy" as Agnes called her maid of yesterday, handed Agnes her *Bride's Magazine*, then changed the urine-soaked bed linen.

"One morning you'll find her dead, "Mother Ignatius told her when Madeline confessed that taking care of Sister Agnes was the hardest part of serving Christ. "Her soul is already with God. It's her body that's hanging on. That's what we tend to, keeping the temple as clean as any other where God dwells"

"Think of it as caring for a puppy that you can never paper train," Sister Catherine whispered to her when they passed in the hallway.

The advice helped a little, but it was not the physical work that was difficult. It was the temptation of Sister Agnes' book. For two years Madeline had no contact with the outside world. No television, radio, visitors, or newspapers, least of all something as worldly and vain as photographs of young men and women dressed in splendid clothes, surrounded by cherub-faced children, and airbrushed to remove any flaw. Yet, every month a new volume arrived in a plain brown wrapper like pornography, Madeline thought. She tried to keep her eyes away, but Sister Agnes demanded girlish company.

"Look at this one, Sissy. I wouldn't wear a pink sash with that white. Too much contrast. I'd keep it all pearl colored. Except for the bouquet. That's the time for pink roses. What do you think?"

How is it, Madeline wondered, that Sister Cecilia, who was seventy-eight, was still sane and practically blind while Sister Agnes was batty but had the eyes of a hawk?

"You look pale, Sissy. You should get some sun, but not too much. Not enough to freckle, but enough to bring a blush to your cheek. Men like that. They like women who are pink and dress in lace. Why do you wear that same old rag every day?"

It was difficult to treat Sister Agnes like a puppy when she spoke like a budding teen-ager.

"When I marry, I will wear a white peignoir on my wedding night and have lots of sex," Agnes vowed. Too late, Madeline wanted to tell her. Your bridegroom is an asexual being that will never look upon you as the woman you believe yourself to be. Or remember yourself to be once.

Was she pale as Agnes said, Madeline wondered? No doubt she was, but there were no mirrors in the long, cool, dark hallways of the St. Elizabethkirche. Madeline knew she'd lost weight. The extra-large blouses hanging in her closet looked huge to her. When she put on her jumper, the folds of material hid the shapely curves of her arms and legs. An austere diet, hard work, and deep sleep made Madeline look more like an athlete than a nun. But the race to heaven was not won by the well-toned body, but a well-disciplined soul.

Her daily prayer had become a plea to relieve her from the job taking care of Sister Agnes, who was doing what Helmut and her parents could not do: make her doubt her vocation.

When Cardinal Corigliano asked Mother Ignatius for a private visit with Madeline, her first instinct was to refuse. "Without a grill, Your Eminence? The Rule forbids any man from speaking to a sister in private. What ever you have to say to her, must be said to me also."

"Yes, Mother. Except that His Holiness insists I examine her claim to a vocation with absolute freedom to question her, and he insists she be able to answer under no duress whatsoever. I'm not here to sell her into slavery, Mother."

"It's good to know the Inquisition is alive and well in Austria. As is Nazism. I know she was involved with that Wolf boy. That *is* what you want to talk with her about, isn't it?"

"We have a report from someone who knows her that she may not be suitable for the religious life."

Mother Ignatius opened her desk drawer and handed Corigliano a green ledger. "This is my personal accounting record. I too had a life before coming to the Carmelites. I was a CPA in Britain and worked with the finest legal agency in the world. Fisher and Greenberg LLC. You don't recognize the name, but Madeline Churchill would. Her mother is a solicitor who represents many prominent couples in overseas adoptions."

Corigliano open the ledger and perused the pages, noting the last entry. "You're operating at a loss, Mother, but so are many cloister convents."

"Ah yes, but notice the date on that last entry. It was six months ago. You see, Your Eminence, Madeline comes to the Church with a very generous dowry. Mrs. Churchill, nee Greenberg, who happens to be a Jewish convert, is determined to give Madeline whatever makes her happy. If she wants to play nun for a few years, mama is willing to foot the bill. And in a few years, Madeline will know if the religious life is for her. Hopefully, with some wise investment, Madeline's contribution can keep us solvent till the crones die. I have nuns here who simply cannot survive in a place we could afford without Madeline's money. Is it wrong of me to want them to be taken care of, Your Eminence?"

Corigliano turned the page, and a saw a deposit of 1.5 million dollars. "I've put the money in a trust," Mother Ignatius continued. "I swear, I won't touch the principal —the interest more than pays the bills."

"Of course, I understand, Mother. I hope we can come to a mutual understanding. It may be that Ms. Churchill has a larger cross to bear than living behind a wall for the rest of her life. Did you know that Wolf asked her to marry him?"

"Most young women have relationships before coming here."

"Does she know about the Paris bombing and the deportations?"

"No, she does not." Mother Ignatius paused for a brief prayer. "I can't tell you how many prayer requests I get to end this madness."

"His Holiness is looking for information, any clue about how to end this madness. If an interview with Madeline would help the Holy Father …"

"I see. You can use my office to speak with her."

\*\*\*

Madeline weighed Corigliano's words carefully. He had asked her to do something she was forbidden to do - remember the love of another human being. She had almost succeeded in suppressing her emotions. When thoughts of Helmut intruded on her meditations, she dutifully distracted herself with the work at hand. Do that enough, Mother Ignatius told her, and the memories become fleeting echoes. The old self must die, and it never gives up without a struggle. Eventually, the new self emerges, the God-centered self. But it was her entire self that Madeline doubted. Why did she ever have to meet Helmut, anyway? He was such a heavy cross to bear. How long would it be before she confessed to her nightly self-love for want of him?

Now she was being freed from the struggle to forget him in the name of a higher good. Was this evil or God's sign that she was not meant to be a nun?

"Sissy, when is the hairdresser coming?"

"Soon, Sister Agnes. But you have to choose your dress first. A gown with a high neckline demands an upswept hair-do. A plunging one, ringlets."

"You're so right. Pull my hair up. Let me see."

Madeline brushed Agnes' long white hair until she held all of it in her hand, then pinned it in a bun. "You look beautiful," Madeline told her. It wasn't a lie. Freed of worry and knowledge of deprivation, Agnes had assumed an angelic countenance.

"I can't wait for tonight." Madeline saw a look come over Agnes' face she never seen before, a happiness that made her skin glow and her eyes intensify with a secret passion. "Gerry's coming. Did I tell you I've chosen him to escort me? I suddenly realize I love him, Sissy. And he loves me. When he proposes, I'm going to accept. What have you done with my silver mirror?"

"I put it in the bathroom. I'll get it for you in a minute," Madeline said. She returned to the bed to put on a fresh pillowcase, knowing that Sister Agnes would forget her request in a few seconds. There was no silver mirror. She heard a deep sigh, and when she turned around, Agnes was staring at her with a peaceful smile on her face, a smiling stone.

"Sister Agnes?" Madeline sat down on the bed. This was death. When did he enter? She didn't hear him. He just stole the breath from Agnes and left before Madeline could catch a glimpse of him. She took the *Bride's Magazine* from Agnes' hands and thumbed through the pages.

Agnes would never see the happy people again. This one, she said to herself as she ran her fingers over a picture of a woman in a white satin and lace gown, this was the one Agnes would have chosen.

She thought about the dress again as she sat in the garden, paper and pen in hand. Mother Ignatius had told her to make some notes for the Cardinal, and get it over with, but it wasn't that simple now.

Sister Agnes hadn't died with thoughts of God on her mind. She died with the name of Gerry, whoever he was, on her lips. Would Gerry care? Did he remember Agnes? Perhaps he was in an old folk's home somewhere thinking about her, missing her, and the years they could have shared. And Agnes? She had passed from the world without a hand to hold, or a child to kiss goodbye. I was all she had, Madeline thought, and even I was an imaginary person. None of her real "sisters" paid her any mind. To them she was a puppy. She might as well have been a talking plant. Agnes had only the convent, its hallways and corridors the only arms that embraced her, its smell of incense and fresh scrubbed floors her only sensual stimuli. Madeline drew the word "Agnes' in the dirt and placed pebbles in the lines. Underneath Agnes, she scrawled the word "Gerry" and put pebbles in his lines too, a silly homage to wasted years.

Corigliano had told her things about Helmut she couldn't believe. What did she know of deportations and refugees? Even if the things the Cardinal told her were true, what he asked of her sounded like betrayal. Yes, she would tell what she knew of Helmut, but she would not tell anyone about the shoebox she had hidden in her closet at home, full of letters that shared with her his personal, inner thoughts and feelings of love and affection for her. Someday, she had promised God, she would burn them. Never had she promised God to give them to another to read.

104

*Dear Cardinal Corigliano:*

*I have searched my memory for any information that might assist His Holiness in persuading Helmut Wolf to renounce his political affiliation. I have remembered nothing of importance about him, unless you want to know he likes peanut butter cookies and the American holiday of Thanksgiving. I cooked a turkey for us in our Junior year, and a pumpkin pie that never quite set. He told me it was the best dinner he had ever eaten. He even ate two slices of gooey pie. I believe he loved me. That is all.*

*Yours in Christ Jesus,*
*Sister Clare*

"You're disappointed, Your Eminence?" Mother Ignatius watched him read Madeline's note, and put it in his brief case.

"No. It's what I expected. She's a young girl, and reticent to tattle on her boyfriend. You have to know young people, Mother. They're more loyal to their peers than we ever were. No, I'm encouraged. She's remembering him fondly and that's what I want to tap into."

"Sister Agnes died while Madeline was attending her. It's natural she should be upset about it. Distracted, Eminence."

"She may need to talk. Let her know she can call me." Corigliano handed Mother Ignatius his card. "Anytime. Oh, and I think you should know that I've spoken with Mrs. Churchill. She liked Herr Wolf very much. She hoped for a good marriage. I told her about Sister Agnes, and the other old nuns too. She said if Madeline should discover that she does not have a vocation, say within the next few weeks, Mrs. Churchill will withdraw Madeline's dowry and replace it with a two million dollar endowment for the convent. Just thought you might want to know, either way, God will provide."

"That's certainly good news. Do you think it's possible that Mrs. Churchill knows her daughter's heart better than Madeline does herself?" Mother Ignatius said cautiously.

"Maybe."

"Did Mrs. Churchill say whether she has had recent communication from Helmut regarding Madeline? Perhaps there is a letter from him that Madeline ought to see to help her examine her true feelings about him."

"Would you let her read such a letter. Mother?"

"I believe any contact with Wolf would hasten Madeline's decision-making process. That would be a positive development."

"I will convey that information to Mrs. Churchill. She misses Madeline terribly. Won't you miss her, Mother?"

"She's an enthusiast. I have no use for enthusiasts."

"So much for Maria von Trapp."

"Who?"

"The Austrian nun who married Baron von Trapp. You remember. I run to the hills instead of doing dishes. The nuns in that convent loved their Maria," Corigliano explained.

"Maria Von Trapp was no offspring of neo-hippie culture. Madeline's a child. If I wanted one, I would have married and had one of my own. Mother, indeed! I'm too busy running a convent to worry about Madeline's relationship with the Devine or the Devil."

"So it would appear."

"Just as you're too busy protecting the Vatican from the Germans to worry about it."

"Touché. We are of like mind. Let's hope Helmut isn't too busy as well."

# CHAPTER VI
## The Show Goes On

The first shipment of 1,150 repatriates from America arrived in Paris on June 28th. With the UN Human Rights Inspectors looking over his shoulder, Helmut personally monitored their disembarkation and transport to E'tat de Guerre. His soldiers proved their mettle, ignoring the taunts and threats of the Muslim men as they were herded into the newly-constructed holding facility. According to UN Resolution 20015, each repatriate had to be accounted for, and each stage of the repatriation process documented in his file. Copies of those files were to be turned over to the Human Rights Commission, as well as the receiving nation's authorities.

In theory, according to the UN, this documentation requirement would effectively slow down the repatriation process and buy time. Since Muller's speech, negotiations were at an impasse over definitions used in the wording of proposed sanctions for Germany. Specifically, was E'tat de Guerre a repatriation center or a deportation center? What was the exact status of those being returned to their "countries of heritage" as opposed to "countries of origin"? And of what crime were these repatriates guilty that they should be expelled?

The new terminology used by the Big Three to explain the massive relocation of millions of people had no accepted legal definitions and were therefore nebulous as best. The repatriates were not criminals in that most of them, particularly women and children, had never been convicted of anything in a court of law. The Big Three simply called them "cultural threats", that is, any persons who swore allegiance to another political authority other than the constitutional government of the county. Muslims who avow that a foreign text, in this case the Qu'ran, supersede national constitutions fit the definition and were subject to immediate repatriation.

As predicted, the International Court was inundated with appeals from human right organizations that intervened on behalf of the repatriates. In an advisory brief to the UN, the IC argued that the Repatriation Accord was used as a method of stifling political dissent and cultural diversity. The IC also argued that Christians had their Bible and the Jews their Torah that preceded the Constitution of governments and were thought to be above the laws of men, and that singling out the Qu'ran was evidence of cultural animus.

The Big Three refused to respond to the brief itself but issued a press release through their respective UN Ambassadors that maintained that neither of these Judeo-Christian texts challenged the separation of Church and state, while Islam demanded unity of church and state. There was documentary evidence to support their assessment. In a 1989 PBS interview, Hassan Nasir, the distinguished professor, described this unitary ideology as the main ingredient of Islam.

The IC objected, stating that the distinction was a matter of degree, not substance. King William, for example, was the head of the Church of England as well as its monarch, and therefore there was no separation of church and state in the Western nation. Britain countered that England's constitution bound the monarch as well as the citizens, and therefore trumped the power of the "secular pope" of the Church of England.

In America, the US Supreme Court, citing the necessary and proper clause, maintained that the Repatriation Accord President Franklin signed with Britain and Germany was within the prerogatives of the Executive branch, and that the vocabulary, while unfamiliar, was clear enough to pass constitutional muster. The Senate was within its rights to ratify the Accord. Britain's House of Lords accepted the request of the Court of Appeals to decide the case and reached the same conclusion as the American Supreme Court.

The United States dismissed the IC's entire advisory brief as irrelevant, however, as the US did not recognize the authority of the International Court precisely because it knew, eventually, the court's ruling would assert authority over the Constitution. That argument was so persuasive, that both Germany and Britain resigned their membership in the IC. Fearing the resignation of the Big Three from the UN Charter and the withdrawal of economic support for the organization, the Secretary General of the UN also rejected the IC brief outright.

It was short battle, but for some, decisive.

The UN could slow down the repatriation but could not stop it without precipitating "Western Flight". This was a truth even the Arab Council, as the Mid-east opposition to repatriation called their UN voting bloc, could not deny, and alternately condemned the repatriation policy and pleaded for financial assistance for the refugees it created.

Of the 1,150 American repatriates, all males between the ages of eighteen and sixty, 200 went to Pakistan, 100 went to Saudi Arabia, 300 to Iraq, 400 to Iran, 200 to Indonesia, and 50 each to Syria, Jordon, and Lebanon. If they returned to America for any reason, they would be subject to immediate arrest and imprisonment for a minimum of 20 years without trial. "America", according to United States UN ambassador McNulty, "Has had enough."

Germany's policy was harsher for its "cultural threat" repatriates. If they returned to Germany for any reason without prior approval, they would be executed without trial. The pictures of the nine Pakistanis who tested Germany's policy were hung in the foyer of the E'tat de Guerre processing center as a warning that Germany too had "had enough".

It was interesting to Helmut that Al Jazeera reported that four of the Iranian repatriates were wanted by the Iranian government for drug smuggling and had been executed without a trial a week after they landed in Tehran. The next morning, he contacted Eisenbach, and requested permission to cross-check the names of the repatriates with Interpol and the International Criminal Registry before processing. "There's no need to give a person medical treatment if he's going to be killed when he returns to his country of heritage. We can save time and money by separating repatriates from criminals," Helmut explained.

Eisenbach agreed, and passed the information to Muller, who informed the Arab Council that every file would contain the criminal status of each repatriate. The receiving country could thus deal more quickly with their own internal law enforcement problems. Germany, Muller said, was sensitive to the difficulties of the Mid-east nations.

The Arab Council responded by inquiring whether Germany could spare them burial expense by executing certain criminals at E'tat de Guerre. Muller declined. There would be no systematic executions at the repatriation center. Germany was also sensitive to the sensibilities of relatives of Holocaust survivors. However, should these nations wish to expedite punishment of these criminals, it would be glad to send technical advisors to assist them.

The Republic of Kurdistan requested assistance immediately, catching Muller off guard. He hastily assembled an advisory team consisting of a Fatherland Security Lieutenant, a construction engineer, a physician's assistant, and, at Helmut's insistence, a newly created Human Rights Coordinator who would serve as a legal expert and repatriate advocate.

"Make sure the co-coordinator a woman," Muller's orders from Olberman read. "She should be middle-aged, plump, and have a record of humanitarian concern. A Barbara Bush-Mother Teresa clone would be nice, but any retired kindergarten teacher who recycles will do as long as she's a chemical engineer."

The picture of Helmut introducing Frau Schiller to the male members of the assistance team and the Kurdistan delegation went global. But it was the picture of Helmut kneeling down to retrieve Frau Schiller's dropped car keys that ignited a new wave of Wolf-mania: Helmut was the dutiful son every mother yearned for. He protected German culture by day and ate apple strudel by night.

By day Frau Schiller advised construction crews building "dorms", and by night, helped the Kurdistan government build environmentally friendly oil refineries.

Egypt, desiring to reassure European tourists that it was once again safe to visit the pyramids, was the next country to jump on board. "We live on the fringes of the Oil Hole that is the Mid-east and, like Israel, must market the only asset we have —history," Abnel Sadr Ibrihimi confided to Muller. "Someday, some Arab Nietzsche will quite rightly declare that Allah is dead, and the sooner the better."

"It it's more likely that some California university laboratory will proclaim oil is dead," Muller responded.

"Then I thank God and Allah that every Western generation has a romance with Egyptology. What would my country be without Cleopatra and Caesar? Just another starving African country."

Ibrihimi's passing comments were forwarded to Olberman with a notation that Egypt had much to offer Germany. While the UN continued to grapple with the de facto acquiescence of one Mid-east country after another to Stahl's repatriation program, and human rights organizations were staging protest marches and broadcasting their opposition over Radio Free Earth, Helmut made a trip to Cairo with another repatriation assistance team. He returned with a Memorandum of Understanding between the Egyptian government and the German Worker's Pension Fund representative for a vacation hotel and casino to be built along the banks of the Nile.

# CHAPTER VII

## The Rocky Road to Marriage

"They make a beautiful couple, Stephan, like they belong together." Emil was perusing the newspaper spread of the unofficial visit of Helmut and Teresa Jean to King William. Stephan was looking over his shoulder, beaming at the color photos of the couple getting off the plane at Heathrow, waving at the adoring crowd, and shaking hands with King William's brother, Prince Harry. Helmut was in his uniform, Teresa in a white suit, her auburn hair pulled back under a wide-brimmed black hat adorned with a single white rose. A fourth photo was of Helmut offering his hand to help her out of the limousine, her eyes turned up to him, gentle, and innocent.

"They're the darlings of the paparazzi too," Stephan said, picking up the latest edition of *La Finestro*. "Look at these headlines. Germany's New Royalty, Call him Kaiser! A Dynasty Begins? They're waiting for an announcement, Emil." He rested a friendly hand on Emil's shoulder. "Who can resist the charms of Rome, right?"

"It's a good match, Stephan. Helmut's a good man, and they get along well. That's all that matters."

Stephan sighed happily as he straightened the papers. "She's very happy. I heard her and her mother giggling this morning when they saw the papers. I haven't heard such laughter in months. You know what? I caught her smiling to herself. That's a good sign, isn't it?"

"A very good sign."

"Look at us. Hovering like mother hens when we ought to be drinking a toast like men." Stephan rummaged around the liquor cabinet and could only come up with a half empty bottle of Chivas. Emil reached for it, and Stephan let him take the bottle. "And we're looking at gossip magazines. Do you think he'll propose? Does he love her?"

"You know you aren't allowed bourbon." Emil handed Stephan another picture of Helmut and Teresa, this one showing them talking with an angel-faced Italian girl of seven offering them wild flowers. Helmut's hand rested on Teresa's as they took the bouquet. "This is Olberman's favorite. He says we should use it for the engagement photo. This is the one. It shows their best side."

"Has Helmut said something to you? He has, hasn't he?"

"He told me… he's concerned that she'll tire of the celebrity," Emil said. "You've done a great job of protecting her from the media. He's constantly in the limelight. I told him, after all she's Frieda's daughter, so she has a great role model. I asked him flat out what his intentions were, and he asked me if he'd have your blessing if he asked for it. He feels unworthy of her. You'd think Teresa can walk on water."

"But does he love her?"

"Yes, I believe he does. Do you know they met a bookstore?

"I've heard the story, how he literally ran into her. Asked her to coffee." Stephan settled on orange juice.

Emil watched Stephan pour the juice with both hands clasped around the bottle. "Imagine my surprise when I saw them together. She winked at me when Helmut introduced us. I think she liked playing a joke on him," Emil said.

Frieda had come in with a tray of pill bottles and steaming soup. Stephen grimaced, but began the afternoon ritual without a word from her. "There's no better cure for illness than happiness," she said to Emil. "Stephan's a new man since his daughter is almost married."

"What do you think about Helmut as a son-in-law?" Emil said.

Frieda tried to sound objective. "He's a thoughtful boy." Helmut had called her the night before the trip to Rome to ask which Teresa Jean preferred, white or yellow gold. He swore her to secrecy, saying he wanted to surprise Teresa. When Frieda pressed him, all he would say is that he would be talking to both her and Stephan when they returned. "I think Helmut wants to make sure Teresa will accept him before he clears anything with Stephan. He's a proud boy too."

"All men are proud that way," Stephan added. "Will she accept him?"

"Are you kidding? I found this in her room this morning." Frieda reached in her pocket and took out a folded piece of paper. She unfolded it, and smoothed it before handing Stephan a picture of a silk organza wedding dress with the words "Frau Wolf" scrawled on it. "It's a page from *Bride's Magazine*."

"It's beautiful, "Stephan said, holding the picture at arms length. "What did you tell Helmut? White or yellow?"

"Yellow. She's so pale. Yellow gives her skin warmth."

Emil congratulated the happy parents, and silently, himself. There were four very happy people now. In time, Helmut would be happy too. Emil was convinced of that. Teresa was a sensible young woman who understood her role in her father's master plan for Germany and was radiantly happy that role meant marriage to the most desired young man in the world.

Over his morning coffee, Fritz Pomeranz was inspecting the same photographs that Stephan and Emil had pored over. He was not elated, reading the headlines as the harbinger of the demise of the Center Socialist Party. A marriage between Helmut and Teresa meant the Christian Nationalists would hold power for the next fifty years. Longer if they socialized their offspring carefully. Norman's call interrupted his speculation.

***

"Corigliano has talked to Churchill. I know you've seen the papers, but give him a few days to work his magic," Norman said.

"We don't have a few days," Fritz shot back through clenched teeth. "Once the engagement's announced, it's a done deal."

"I didn't know Helmut even knew Teresa Jean," Norman told him.

"For Christ's sake, he's Stephan's protégé, of course he'd know her."

"Stephan kept Teresa in private schools. I mean, Helmut knew Stephan had a daughter, but this romance thing is sudden, I assure you, its a PR instrument," Norman insisted.

"The little opportunistic bastard! Olberman's going to have to build a bigger barn."

"What?"

"A bigger barn for all the political hay he's making over this orchestrated romance. Norman, you have to talk to Helmut. I mean it."

"And tell him what? That's he can't get married? All I can do is make sure he knows Madeline is having second thoughts. It may make him delay."

"Delay becoming heir apparent to Stahl's regime? No, he's going through with this and Eisenbach is behind it all, I know it. Tell Corigliano to keep Churchill in her cloister."

Norman hung up, wondering if Patricia had been right about what had to be done. Still, he called Corigliano and asked if he'd seen the morning paper. "What do you think, Umberto?"

"She's a very striking young woman," Umberto said.

"They dress her well."

"Stop it, Norman. They look happy in their picture, but affability could be mistaken for love in the glow of camera flashes and attention."

"They're cut from the same cloth is all."

"The best marriages are based on likeness not differences, Norman. You better than anyone knows that."

"What did Churchill say?" Norman demanded.

"She's a true daughter of the church. Obedient and naïve. Perhaps if she could see Helmut in person. Where are Helmut and Teresa staying in Rome?"

"The Excelsior, I imagine. Helmut's been there a hundred times. I have a suite there."

"Why not invite them to San Rafael? It's so private. And you could talk to Helmut, tell him Madeline wants to see him at the Excelsior suite. "

This was real progress to Norman. He called Fritz, telling him to make arrangements for Churchill's stay. "I don't want Corigliano's fingerprints on this, or mine" he warned. "Have her use another name.

She'll contact Helmut because we'll tell her he wants to talk to her, and the paparazzi will do the rest."

"Ahhh, I get it. Shoot them together, and Teresa will go back to daddy with a broken heart," Fritz said.

"Nothing destroys political careers like sexual indiscretion," Norman said. "Helmut won't have to leave the Party, the Party will leave him."

Fritz congratulated Norman on his quick action, then dialed Tanzer. Helmut was the most vulnerable of the Unholy Trinity. Derail the engine of Olberman's marketing juggernaut, and all the revue that financed the repatriation program, and the program would collapse.

"Norman said shoot them together," Fritz told Tanzer. "Let's do it."

\*\*\*

"Helmut, you look like you've seen a doppelganger." Teresa was arranging fresh-cut roses is a vase. She smiled at him, an adoring smile she'd seen on the faces of so many women he barely noticed. "Are you going out?"

"Just coming in. The Cardinal's villa is beautiful." He unzipped his sweat-shirt, threw it on the sofa, and put his arms around her, burying his head in her warm hair. "I have been walking in this Eden and I have to tell you, the world might as well be a galaxy away."

She turned to him and fell into his embrace briefly, then turned away. "Do you think his generosity means anything political?" She was going over the dinner menu. Frieda had told her that her father's health should be taken as a warning that good wives see to their husband's diet.

119

"You mean a rapproachmont between Berlin and Rome via family ties? Hardly. More like lobbying for Stephan's ear." He pointed to roast pork, but Teresa shook her head no, and pointed to eggplant parmesan. "Umberto and Norman go way back, started their diplomatic careers at the same time. I think they had a friendly rivalry going to see who could rise the fastest in their respective governments."

"Daddy doesn't dislike Norman, you know. He thinks he's very capable," Teresa said.

"Ummmm. But if he thinks a medal is going to woo my uncle away from the Center Socialists, he's wrong."

"He wants Norman on his side, Helmut. Germany's side."

"He feels he *is* on Germany's side. But it's a Germany that would not be worth living in. My uncle has been in Rome so long he's become devout without realizing it. Now Patricia, on the other hand, she despises Stephan because she despises anything she perceives as crass, and nationalism is crass to her."

"The Pope despises E'tat de Guerre," Teresa said. "It puts him in a terrible position. You know how hard Benedict tried to subdue hatred for Muslims when he was alive."

"That's my point. The Pope, Norman, Pomeranz – none of them understand that repatriation is better than the alternative."

"Which is?"

"Extermination. How else can we defend ourselves against people who want to destroy Christianity? They see Christianity as global pacifism, and it's neither of those things."

"What is it, then?"

"They've lost sight of the central teaching of the faith. That nothing is worth losing your soul over. Nothing should stand between you and God. Not your parents, your children, your spouse, or your church. Going to war is not the worst thing a Christian can do. Aiding and abetting evil is. Making Muslims unhappy because they must return to their countries of culture is infinitely more humane than killing them. Don't you think?"

"You and Emil, and Daddy - like Herr Goring said, one German is a fine man, two a bund, and three a war. You all think alike."

"That's what makes up strong. Unity of mind and spirit. And a willingness to sacrifice personal desires for the good of the country. We're not unique – just rare. Cincinnatus, George Washington …"

"Hitler?"

"Now there was one selfish bastard," Helmut said. Teresa had finished the menu and rang the chef who came so quickly Helmut wondered if he'd been eavesdropping. Georg had checked the rooms for bugs as part of his security duties and pronounced them clean. Still, Helmut new there was more to Corigliano's generosity than hospitality. "Got my cholesterol care done for day?" He smiled and pulled Teresa next to him on the sofa.

"OK, Herr Wolf, what is it?"

"What makes you think something is *it*?" He gave her kiss on the cheek and rested his head on her shoulder.

"No complaint about the food. It's a sign," Teresa said.

"A sign?"

"You have something on your mind other than creature comfort."

"Ummm. I think you're beginning to read me. Uncle Norman says Patricia can read him. That is a sign, I think."

"Oh? A sign of what?"

"I'm becoming a slave to your charms."

"Herr Wolf, national hero, big strong man afraid to tell his girlfriend what's on his mind. What if I call Georg and tell him to tell all your soldiers?" She nibbled his ear and whispered playfully. "I bet they'd laugh at you."

"OK, I'll spill it. Madeline Churchill called me. She wants to talk to me." He waited for her body to give him an indication of her reaction, but she didn't even tense.

"Do you want to talk to her?" She paused, waiting for an answer. His silence was the answer. "Of course, you do. Why don't we invite her to an eggplant dinner?"

Helmut sat up straight. "You're not jealous?" He scrutinized her face for some evidence of displeasure. She stood up and went to the piano where she put the roses, and moved the vase over an inch, then stood back as though weighing a question of state instead of the location of a decoration.

"You were in love with her. She must be a wonderful person," Teresa said.

Emil was right, Helmut thought, she was Frieda's daughter and would make a perfect political wife.

"I could set another place tonight. There's enough food in this place to feed an army. It's scandalous." Teresa continued.

The word echoed in his head. Helmut remembered what Madeline had said to him about her decision to enter the convent. He had laughed until the reality of her resolve sunk in. "I've found something worthy of a sacrifice, something more important than myself," she said. He had ridiculed her, called her immature and sexually frustrated, and made crude jokes about her wanting to fuck Jesus, as though if he made her angry enough, she would abandon her hysteria.

But, slowly, he came to accept her sincerity. Her commitment became his, and her strength became a model for his own. Did he still want her? Yes. Passionately. He wanted her to choose a real man over a perfect spirit and now she might be ready. Just the sound of her voice still made him hot and hard. He hadn't walked the villa grounds, he had run them, anything to get rid of the breathlessness he'd felt when heard those melodious words spilling from the phone as though from heaven: I need to see you. I need you. His Madeline could be his at last if not for the scandal it would bring to everything he had come to love more than himself.

Teresa was still at the piano, now sitting in front of the keys, and slowly reading sheet music as she plucked out the notes. Scandal. Yes, his opponents would like nothing better than to catch him with an apostate nun in a hotel room while the great Stephan Stahl's daughter waited for her engagement ring playing Chopin on a Steinway. He had them foiled.

"Can I help you with anything, Teri? Dinner, I mean."

"No, Dear," she said, not taking her eyes off the music. "I'm good."

He walked over to her and gave her another kiss on the cheek. "No, you're great."

She looked up at him now. "You could get the wine and pour us a glass. Is that Sangria Christi any good?"

"Norman likes it."

"Oh, then he's been here before?"

"Yes. Many times." Helmut put her wine glass on a coaster and buried his face in the flowers. "My God, they're fragrant. Why don't roses in Germany smell this strong?"

"It's the heat. It takes all the strength out of the men and puts it in the flowers. Which is why Rome fell," Teresa explained.

"You don't think the barbarians had anything to do with it?"

"Well, by the time they got here, Rome had too many flowers and not enough strong men to fight."

"I don't believe Gibbons mentioned flowers in his *Decline of the Roman Empire*."

"Then Gibbons was a twit."

Helmut wagged his finger at the flowers. "You aren't going to get my strength, you beautiful devils." When Teresa looked up Helmut was punching numbers on his cell phone. "Madeline? Teresa and I want you to come to dinner. Tonight, yes. Alright, tomorrow then. I'll send a car. Tell me where you're staying."

\*\*\*

Helmut woke up to Georg standing over him. "You're alive," Georg stammered and sat down on the bed beside him.

"What the hell? Of course, I'm alive."

Georg patted his leg. "I thought … Ambassador Wolf said …"

"What's happened? Teresa?"

"She's fine, Helmut. There was an explosion at the Excelsior Hotel and your uncle called to see if you were …"

Helmut stumbled to the bathroom and splashed his face with icy water. "Madeline," he whispered in gratitude, and made the sign of the cross.

"Sir?"

"Nothing. Wake up Teresa and bring her here." Helmut put on his battle fatigues, a pair of hunting boots, and a thermal t-shirt, then headed for the bathroom to brush his teeth.

"Do you want me to call your uncle and tell him you're OK"

"Not yet." Helmut spit into the sink. "Get me Eisenbach. We need to know who the players are … and make arrangements to get back to Austria. Teresa can't be part of this."

"You think it was terrorists?" Georg hit the direct dial to Eisenbach.

"More like traitors," Helmut said taking the phone from him. "Emil? I'm safe. Teresa's safe. What have you heard?"

"I'm with Stephan and Frieda now. I'll put you on speaker phone."

"We're alright, I swear," Helmut said.

"We weren't sure if you were at the hotel," Stephan said.

"We've been at the Villa since noon. Had dinner ... a movie …"

Teresa, wrapped in a disobedient robe that exposed half her nightgown, took the phone from Helmut and rubbed her eyes with her free hand. "Hello? Mama? Yes, I'm fine, just not awake. No, we didn't hear anything about it. Georg said there was a bombing, but we're so far from the city we didn't hear anything … we were watching *Sunset Boulevard*, haven't had the television on at all. I love you too."

"We're on our way home. No. No commercial flights. Georg's in charge of security now." Helmut hung up the phone.

125

"Miss Stahl, I'll get your clothes. Stay here," Georg ordered. He brought her a pair of camouflage pants and a green t-shirt, socks, her tennis shoes and a black hooded sweat-shirt. "You're not to be alone," he told Teresa. "You're a security problem now."

Helmut knew what that meant. In seconds a squad of bodyguards had taken up their positions in the Villa, all non-military personnel were sequestered in the kitchen, every vehicle was being searched for explosives, and snipers were in position on the roof. Only Georg knew the escape plan, and that was locked in his head

The vehicle Georg chose was the dark blue Ford pick-up used to haul stock feed. Three other people, dressed in dark clothing, got into a white Camry and followed Georg as he sped out to an open field where a small twin-engine plane and a helicopter, engines running, waited to take off. Georg and the fleeing couple boarded the plane, the decoys boarded the copter. The copter took off first, then the plane, each heading in opposite directions.

"What do you think, Capt'n Wolf? A diversion? An Assassination attempt?" Georg handed them each a thermos of hot coffee.

"Thank-you Georg." Teresa took Helmut's hand. It was cold and heavy. Like his heart, she thought.

"Let's not hang crepe just yet. We don't even know when it happened," Helmut said.

"Ambassador Wolf didn't tell me anything. We can't break radio silence, Capt'n."

"Of course not, but until we have details, I'm not jumping to conclusions."

Georg headed for the bathroom, leaving them alone, and Teresa knew they had to talk before they landed. "It's alright, you know. I know what you're thinking. Your life is too dangerous for us to be together. All you have to do is tell me, Helmut. I'll square things with my parents. There'll be no repercussions or unpleasantness. I promise."

Helmut squeezed her hand gently and brought it to his lips. "I do love you, Terri. You're bright and funny and faithful. But, when Georg told me there had been a bombing, I kept thinking that if we hadn't been at the Villa, you would have shared my fate. Do you want a life of seclusion? Always afraid I may not come back? This is so screwed up. And I wanted this to be the most wonderful, romantic time of our lives." He wiped a tear from his cheek with her hand as Georg sat down. He stayed but a minute, telling them he was going to sit with the pilot. Helmut waited till the cockpit door closed. "I'm a lucky man. I have a good team," he said.

"My father says the same thing about his cabinet. They're good, loyal men. I think he underestimates his power to bring that out in people. He gives them something to be loyal to, you know?"

"Yes, certainly."

"You're like that too, Helmut. I think you're the son he wishes I'd been."

"Oh, no. A son touches your heart, but a daughter enslaves it forever. Stephan Stahl is willing to die for his country, but he's living for you, Terri."

"He's been so sick, Helmut. I'd do anything for him."

"Even marry a man you don't love? Even marry a condemned man, and now a hunted one?"

127

"If it came to that, yes. But I've met a man I do love. In time people will see that you and Daddy are right – that the repatriation program is the only fair way to solve the terrorist problem. I know it. I'm not afraid."

Helmut took a black velvet box from his pocket that held a small gold ring with a heart-shaped diamond, and offered it to her. "If you take this, you know we're engaged. You'll share my fate." He took her hand and sipped the ring on her finger. "I hope you like it."

"It's perfect, Dear. It's beautiful," she said caressing the ring with her hand.

"I don't know the protocols of engagements. How long they last. Who sets the wedding date. I'll leave all of that up to you and Frau Stahl. I know everything will be beautiful because you're beautiful. Am I babbling, Terri?" Helmut said.

Theirs would be a polite relationship. When he lay in bed with Teri he would think about Madeline the way he did whenever he wanted to be happy. In the dark it would be Madeline he was kissing, the memory of her full, cushy body fueling his passion. Eisenbach had promised him both position and passion in the two women in his life, and for while at least, it seemed possible.

\*\*\*

"I wanted us to meet before Helmut arrives." Stephan ushered members of his party cabinet into a corner office at the country estate, referring to it as his country war bunker. Olberman and Eisenbach walked in and sat at the green-felted game table Stephan had brought in from the den. They all knew whoever was responsible for the bombing had to be found and dealt with immediately, but would that mean public trials or a midnight purge?

"What is the media saying, Olberman?" Stephan asked as the men helped themselves to coffee.

"They aren't screaming burning Reichstag yet, but you know that's what Pomeranz will say if the trail leads to his Center Socialists."

Eisenbach cut a large wedge of cheese and a slice of apple and shoved the plate towards him. "Try and eat, Stephan, You've got to put on weight."

"Where's Frict?"

"Vienna."

"Get him back here, pronto."

"Buehler's in Berlin making funeral arrangements for his mother, God rest her soul," Emil explained.

"Damn it. He's my secretary and can certainly do more for me than he can for a corpse," Stephen said. "That's selfish. I know how close he was to his mother."

"He has no sisters, Stephan. Bad planning on his part."

Olberman read from a legal pad. "According to the Roman police, the bomb exploded at about eleven o'clock. It took out the entire second floor suite reserved by the German government for Ambassador Wolf. The first and third floor rooms were empty. Whoever planned this was able to make sure no others were hurt. Unfortunately, a maid had forgotten to put a mint on one of the pillows in the third-floor suite and was in the bedroom at the time of the blast. She's in bad shape —concussion and a broken back —thrown upwards by the blast. The mattress probably kept her from exploding as well, but the other woman who was in the Ambassador's suite has yet to be identified."

"Other woman?" Stahl said.

"There are servants and maids and chauffeurs, and the paparazzi. She could be anybody. Does Norman Wolf have a mistress?"

"From what I know of Patricia Wolf, I would hope so." Stephan finished off his fruit and cheese. "Let's hope this stays down. The medicine is as bad as the symptoms of the disease, Emil."

"Yes, I know. But try."

"So, from what we know, this was either an assassination attempt on Helmut's life, or an assault on Germany itself by persons unknown."

"That's it, Stephan," Olberman said.

"Alright, gentlemen. I need the police report, and everything you can get on our Frauline Doe. Maybe, she blew herself up. It wouldn't be the first time a suicide bomber was a woman. Oh, and get a timeline going. I want to know where everyone important was for the last three days – make them account for every minute of their time. Including the generous Cardinal Corigliano. If we can get the Vatican on board…."

"Impossible, Stephan," Olberman said. "The Holy Father isn't going to want the Church involved in this."

"I'll talk to Helmut, maybe he can get Norman to put some pressure on the Pope. Our official position is that it was Muslim extremists that planted the bomb. Until we know differently, I will assume that position is correct. I want both of you here every night at seven for an update."

"The press will want a statement," Olberman said. "Should I mention Teresa?"

"No details for now except to say that Helmut and Teresa were registered but visiting the Cardinal's villa. Play down the danger."

***

"You ass!" were the first words out of Norman's mouth when Pomeranz's secretary closed his door behind her. "You stupid ass."

"You think I sabotaged your plan? Even if I'd wanted to, I wouldn't do it with a fucking bomb!" Pomeranz was on his feet now, pacing like a tiger. "Scheize. Do you think Stahl blames us?"

"Helmut and Teresa are alive, thank God, they went to the Villa early."

Pomeranz stopped pacing and fell onto the sofa in relief. "Jesus, we're saved."

"Momentarily at least," Norman said. "There'll be an investigation. Stahl can't let this pass. And there is the body of the other victim to consider."

"Madeline Churchill?"

"I'm not sure. The police haven't identified the remains. I'm not even sure Churchill made it to Rome."

"Not sure?" The blood was rushing to Pomeranz's head again, making him dizzy.

"Fritz, you did make the reservation under the name Emily Thompson, right?"

"Yes, did you tell Helmut the name she was supposed to use?"

"Yes, but he never heard from her as far as I know."

"He never saw her in Rome before the blast?"

"No. I don't think so….. I haven't talked to him."

"Any information from the hotel?"

"Only that an upstairs maid was badly hurt."

"So Madeline could be in bits and pieces….Corigliano, what does he say about all this?"

"He's as bewildered as I am."

"Then he isn't sure she ever got there. Maybe she changed her mind. Has he contacted the convent?"

"He can't, you fool. If she's not there, it'll raise a red flag. The convent believes she's taking a leave of absence under Corigliano's recommendation and is going home for a visit."

"Well, it must be her, then. Who else could it be?"

"Corigliano is having the police check the hotel register, make sure every face has a name, every name a face."

It was quiet as the men sank into their own thoughts. Pomeranz was the first to pose the question. "Would Corigliano hide her identity from the press if she did die in the explosion? How's he going to explain her disappearance in Rome if the convent thinks she's home, and home thinks she's in Vienna? You know him well, Norman. Is he pragmatic?"

"Definitely."

"So, as far as we know, no one knows Madeline was supposed to be in Rome except you, me, Helmut, and Corigliano, and …"

"And who else?" Norman asked suspiciously.

"Tanzer."

"Oh, Jesus Christ, Fritz, you are such an ass. What part of secret don't you understand in the concept of conspiracy?"

"If none of us says anything … pretend we have no idea why she was at the hotel … Corigliano can say he talked to her and she was simply a hysterical young woman stalking her ex-boyfriend when she left the convent. It's plausible, right? She knew what room the Wolf's would stay in. She could have been lying in wait for him."

"You're forgetting Helmut. You're assuming they only spoke once, but he might know whether she made it to Rome."

"Why haven't you talked to him?"

"He's under a security watch. And I probably won't talk to him until we're in prison. You know Stahl is just waiting for a chance to purge us from the government."

"If Helmut doesn't know Madeline was there, Norman, we're home free. If we dummy up, not trouble trouble … You get my drift? Sometimes the better part of survival is knowing what to ignore."

Norman thought of calling Patricia to see if Helmut had contacted her, but then thought it better not to in front of Fritz. "Exactly," he said.

***

A full security detail met the young couple when they landed at Stahl's private airport. Frieda waited in the Mercedes as Helmut and Teresa deplaned and ducked under umbrellas to avoid a summer shower. Teresa slid into the back seat to the arms of her frantic mother. "Good job, Georg," Helmut said. He patted Georg on the back before climbing into the front seat. "Get some rest. I'll call you tomorrow morning."

"Your Uncle Norman called you, Helmut," Frieda said.

133

"How is Daddy?" Teresa said, ignoring the information. "I hope he's not terribly worried." She held her mothers hand in hers and covered it with her left hand, casting her eyes towards the gold engagement ring on her finger.

"Of course, he's worried." Frieda glanced down, patted Teresa's hand, and touched the ring with her fingertips.

"He doesn't blame Helmut for any of this, I hope," Teresa said.

"No, no… We're relieved you're both safe."

"Please don't spoil this for me, Mama. Please. I'm so happy. And this is just a freak thing, the work of some crazy people who want to get their names in the papers. I'm sure of it."

Frieda reached over the seat and gave Helmut's shoulder a tender squeeze. "You're alright, Helmut?"

"We're both fine. Just a little dazed from the rush. It looks like a plot, but I'm inclined to agree with Terri. It may even be just a weird coincidence. I'm making no judgments till we have more information." He turned in the seat and smiled at them, huddled together like Eskimos, Frieda bracing herself as though protecting her daughter. He saw her face soften as she stroked her daughter's hand.

"It looks like we have a wedding to plan," she said, smiling in approval at Helmut.

"I'm leaving all the ribbons and bows and flowers and jam to you and Terri. I know nothing about planning ceremonies, but please, let my Aunt Patricia do something that will make her feel important or it will break her heart."

"She will choose my bouquet," Teresa said. "And the table centerpieces."

"Agreed," Frieda said. She took a small black book from her purse and made a notation. Teresa couldn't see that Frieda had already made consultation appointments with the dressmaker, the caterers, and the florists. "I'll call her first thing in the morning."

Helmut sat back in his seat. He'd successfully distracted them from contemplating the night's happenstance even as he calculated how he could save Norman from a drop of suspicion he'd been involved in the explosion.

*** 

"Have your spoke to your Uncle, Helmut?" Stephan was at the window gazing down at his wife and daughter as they pored over swatches and color palettes in the garden gazebo.

"No. I love my Uncle. I know there has to be an investigation and I want no special consideration, given that Norman's a member of the opposition."

"What does your gut tell you?"

Helmut joined him at the window. "My uncle is a diplomat, not an assassin. As for Corigliano, it was his idea that Terri and I use his villa. If he'd wanted me dead, he'd have poisoned the wine like any other descendant of the Medici."

Stephan directed his attention to the women who were having a good laugh at something unknown to the men. "I feel like a thief, stealing a bit of their joy while they're not looking."

"Terri's so lovely. I can't believe she said yes."

"I have it on good authority that she's been planning this wedding

135

since the day you met. Many hearts will break when you two take your vows. You realize that." Stephan lit a cigarillo, and Helmut handed him an ashtray, lowering his eyes in silent rebuke. Stephan shrugged and crushed the ember end into the glass. "It's verboten, I know." He paced the floor for a few seconds before throwing a box of the forbidden tobacco into the trash. "What about Pomeranz? Do you see his fingerprints on this?"

"Killing me isn't going to stop the Repatriation Program. I'd think he'd know that by now."

"Then it was … what … terrorists?"

"I believe it was. I'm just very thankful that Terri and I were at the villa. Very thankful."

"You know the police found the remains of a young woman in Norman's suite. Do you know who she was?"

"I'm hoping I'm wrong, but it may be an old friend of mine named Madeline Churchill. She called me from the airport and said she was going to be staying at the Excelsior."

"Is that strange?"

"Oh, no. My Aunt and Uncle met her in America. Norman said she might be visiting after canceling on them for my birthday party. Terri and I invited her to dinner tonight. She begged off till tomorrow. I've tried calling, but …. Terri and I are praying that she's OK."

"Was she a troubled woman? Emil tells me she was in a convent for a while. That's where the daughters of wealthy people go when they don't want to go to rehab centers, isn't it?"

"She's been there over two years, and ready to begin her novitiate. You know, second step. It's standard operating procedures for postulants to visit home and friends, to see if it's really what they want. As for being troubled, faith troubles us all at some point, if we have real faith. She's the most devout Catholic I've ever met."

"I pray she's safe too," Stephan said.

"I think it would be best not to mention anything about this until we know what happened to her. I wouldn't want to alarm her parents. They're nice people."

"We'll let the Italians deal with it for now," Stephan said. "I'll call your Aunt and Uncle tonight and tell them we expect them here this week-end. I'll low-key the awarding of the Citizen's Freedom Medal, if that will make it easier for him. I know Pomeranz and his friend, the Cardinal, are giving him grief about it."

"That will soothe a lot of feathers. Thank-you."

"But Emil stays on the dais. We can't let the public see any rift in the government. Olberman's orders. You understand."

"Yes, absolutely, I wouldn't have it any other way."

"Now, tell me what you want for wedding present. A Rolls Royce? A chateau in Bavaria?"

Helmut laughed at the suggestions. "The first thing I want …

"The first? You have a list?"

"What I mean is, the first thing I want to *do* is get Georg a commendation for the security he provided for Teri and me. Flawless."

"Commendation, hell. Think he'd like a Rolls?"

"Yeah, if it's armored plated and the horn plays *Deutschland Uber Alles*."

"Done! We'll get him a commendation and a Rolls. I'm not so sure about the horn."

"You're very generous."

Stephan stared past Helmut wistfully. "No, I'm hungry. Hungry for life. For success. For saving the world. I want to accomplish so much, and after I'm gone, I want you to accomplish even more, Helmut. I want the German people to taste greatness – no I want them to be gluttons. I want the whole world to stand back and say, if it weren't for the Germans, we'd have nothing. I want to erase Hitler and resurrect the Holy Roman Empire. The Americans, the Brits, every civilized country in Europe is getting on board, understanding that what we're doing is nothing less than offering salvation to Western culture. If only people like your Uncle Norman and Pomeranz and Cardinal Corigliano— all of them —if only they could share our vision."

Helmut saw the glow of happiness and fervor in Stephan's eyes, heard the energy growing in his voice. Emil was right. His marriage to Teresa Jean was an elixir that invigorated the ailing man, doing for him what chemotherapy and drug cocktails could not – restoring his sense of purpose. And Teresa was right. He was the son Stephan had longed for.

"I am allowed to have a brandy. It's supposed to warm my insides," Stephan said. Helmut headed for the liquor cabinet, but Stephan was on his feet and back at the window before he reached it. He was getting stronger, there was no doubt, Helmut thought as he handed the elder man a small snifter. "You'd better see the priest tomorrow. Father Hahn at St. Mary's. Unless, you have a preference."

"No, Sir."

He and Stephan shook hands, but Stephan couldn't resist giving Helmut a brief embrace. "Call me Stephan. Or Dad. Whatever makes you comfortable."

"I've never called anyone Dad in my life. That'll definitely take some getting used to. Stephan, for a while."

"Good. Good. This is a joyous occasion." He opened the door to the hallway where Eisenbach, Olberman and Frict were waiting, and waved them in. "Gentlemen, we are to have the most splendid wedding."

"I've already worked up the press releases, Helmut," Olberman said handing him a folder brimming with photographs and headlines. "Feel free to can the ones you don't like, but I think you'll approve."

Helmut accepted the folder eagerly and thumbed through the pictures. "I'm no match for our Minister of Propaganda." It was an admission not flattery. He felt Emil's hand on his shoulder and was about to excuse himself when Stephan motioned them all to sit.

"You too, Helmut. It's time you knew the political landscape we'll be dealing with at Malta."

"Have any of the NATO partners —Poland, Hungary, Czech Republic —given us any flack about not having a representative at Malta?" Frict asked. His eyes were barely open, his clothes rumpled from the plane trip. There were no and nays around the table as Frict handed out the proposed agenda of the Malta Meeting. "Good, then I think we have a NATO consensus that whatever you decide, Stephan, is in the best interests of Europe."

"The goal is to get Russia publicly on board with the Repatriation Program," Stephan said. "They've been stalling. This delay for the wedding will give the Russians time to visit Paris. Who's coming, Frict?"

"Vasily and Natalia Provenko. They're close to President Yeshenko. Natya's his niece."

"Who's in charge there, Helmut?"

139

"The man you promoted to Lieutenant —Vincent Rudolph. I guarantee the Russians will come away on our side. He runs the place by the book. Still, I can make the church arrangements tomorrow morning and fly in for the Russian visit. Teresa doesn't need me. I've left the pageantry in her hands."

"Wise man," Olberman said. "I think it'd be a great idea to have Helmut there to meet the Russian delegation."

"Even with the security considerations so soon after the bombing?" Stephan gave Emil a quick glance.

"All the more reason for Helmut to go. We don't want our enemies thinking we're using a family event to protect him," Olberman explained.

"I'm going anyway, Stephan," Emil said. "And with Reinhardt there too, we'll all be safe."

"Well, Olberman, how will you spin it?"

"I'll get pictures of Teresa and Helmut saying good-bye. All soldiers have to leave loved ones, why not Helmut? I'll need some live footage of the Paris meeting. Lots of film about the Provenkos, maybe some character stuff, like hero relatives in the Great War. Stuff like that."

"Excellent. Now, about the conference itself. Beuler will be there, of course. When is he due from Berlin? I hate it when he's not here."

"He's tying up the loose ends. I believe they read his mother's will tomorrow."

"Thank God," Stephan said, making the sign of the cross.

\*\*\*

Across from Helmut sat Father Hahn, a Dominican of the old school, whose office was dominated by a life-sized crucifix. He had blue-veined hands and a tonsured head, and a long neck that protruded from the traditional black cowl. His eyes were violet glass surrounded by dark rings and sallow skin. He looks dead, Helmut thought, as Father Hahn thumbed through Helmut's three-page application for a church service – evidence of the German penchant for bureaucracy. Father Hahn made the sign of the cross and glared at Helmut. "Your future father-in-law is charismatic, Herr Wolf. I've seen his tricks. He walks on to a stage and millions listen to him as though he were a prophet."

"What's that got to do with Teresa and me getting married?"

"You are his protégé. He teaches you the tricks of Satan, and you want me to bless a union that violates every law of the Church?"

"There are no impediments to our marriage, Father. We are unrelated by blood, both of age, have our parents consent, are fertile and neither of us is married, and we love each other."

"You mean you each love Stephan Stahl and his Neo-Nazi Party."

"And Germany and cute bunnies. What's your point?"

"A marriage is between two people, not three or a country."

"We're just two young people who want to get married."

"A war criminal and the daughter of a despot. How sweet are the flowers that pave the road to hell."

"I thought it was good intentions that paved the road to hell. In any case, we 're not the devil's spawn, Father," Helmut said impatiently.

"You're the beginning of Stephan Stahl's dynasty."

"Most families want their gene pool to survive the evolutionary struggle. Why shouldn't Stephan Stahl be a grandfather?"

Father Hahn shook his head in disgust. "Even Hitler had the

decency to die without progeny. I can't grant your request, Herr Wolf. Marriage is a sacrament and would require you to be in a state on grace. It would mean you renouncing your sins and doing penance for the blood of thousands on your hands."

"Only one hand, Father. The other hand has saved the blood of millions. Will you praise the virtue of one hand as quickly as you condemn the vice of the other?"

"You are bold, Herr Wolf, but I am not taken in by the silver tongue of the Evil One."

"I'm truthful, Father. And what about Teresa? She's not guilty of anything but being born into a controversial family. Are you going to punish her for what I've done?"

"She can't be allowed to marry you. She risks her soul and those of her children. The Church cannot let people think Rome supports the immorality of the German regime. That is final."

Helmut put on his cap and excused himself. Not far from St. Mary's was Holy Word Lutheran Church, and he wasted no time arranging for Rev. Kohl to officiate. "I consider this an incredible honor, Herr Wolf," Kohl said, ushering Helmut into the vestibule, and holding the door open for him. The two men walked into the sun-lit church, its barren walls and hewn wood beams posing a striking contrast to St. Mary's Baroque excesses. What drew Helmut's eye was the pulpit atop a winding staircase that bore the hand-carved relief of the four evangelists. He approached it and felt the hardness of the polished wood banister as Kohl restored a fallen hymnal to its proper place in the pew. "The altar is less dramatic compared to St. Mary's, but flowers and candles change that."

Helmut's eyes graduated to the stained-glass windows, all scenes from the Bible, and focused on one in particular —The Apotheosis of Luther —done in blues and gold. In Luther's right hand was a bible, in the left, an American standard. Kohl noticed his interest.

"It's odd, I know. But the window it replaced was shattered by a misplaced partisan bomb during World War II. See the date? Nineteen forty-seven. Dedicated to the Liberating Armies of the United States. It was boarded up till then." Kohl stamped his foot on the gleaming boards. "Under the floor is a wine cellar. Our little chapel hid three United States Army flyers down there, and a few Jews. Luther was a warrior of sorts too, you know."

Helmut couldn't suppress his pleasure. "Something tells me we're fighting the same enemy." Reverend Kohl returned his smile. "I do have a favor to ask, though. I'll want statues, Reverend. I hope that won't be a problem. It's just that Teresa is named for the Little Flower, and the Fatherland Security Forces who liberated Paris have a special devotion to the Sacred Heart. This ceremony is dedicated to them, and all those who died in the Paris liberation."

"Not a problem. We welcome our Catholic brothers and sisters. We'll consider the statues ornaments not idols for purposes of your wedding, and your Little Flower will be adorned with roses. We're a small church…"

"We will make it a center of devotion, Reverend. I assure you, thousands of people will bring you their thanks for hosting our ceremony. Holy Word Church will be the Mecca of Vienna." Helmut handed Kohl a check for fifty thousand Euros. "And, maybe you could get new carpet?"

"What color would you like, Herr Wolf?"

Helmut looked up at the window. "Blood red."

The deal was sealed with a warm handshake, and Helmut's acceptance of Reverend Kohl's hospitality on behalf of the German people. A photographer immortalized the moment.

When the press release hit the newspapers announcing a Catholic wedding at a Lutheran church, Corigliano was appalled. "Father Hahn, what have you done? Have you lost your reason? How are we to exert any influence on the German government if we alienate these two devout children of the Church?" He tried to keep the anger out of his voice.

Hahn was just as outraged. "Forgive me Your Eminence, but you're making this a political decision. It isn't. Would you have had me officiate at the wedding of Goebels or Goring? These are Neo-Nazis we're talking about. Shall we collaborate again?"

"Can't you see what's happening in Europe? We're losing parishioners in every church that denounces the Christian Nationalists. Three churches have closed completely in Berlin. We have to stop the hemorrhage."

"Are you asking me to violate my conscience?"

"No, I'm ordering you to find me a priest with a different conscience who will marry Helmut and Teresa and do it quick."

"It's too late."

"Nonsense. It can be a dual ceremony. Call it interfaith reciprocity, but put it right, Willem. The Holy Father doesn't want another Reformation. Rome can't afford it."

Willem Hahn heard a dial tone and called Reverend Kohl. As an obedient son of the Church, he knew what he had to do.

Helmut left the decision of a dual ceremony up to Teresa. It was to be her day, Helmut explained to Father Hahn, and she thought Holy Word Church was a beautiful venue. It was rustic, humble, and its simple altar would not detract from the color scheme. She and Frieda had already contacted the florist and the choirmaster. The organist had already begun practicing the musical selections, and two podiums were ready to receive the life-like replicas of the Carmelite nun and Jesus with His flaming heart pierced by swords.

Corigliano called Norman. "That damn fool Hahn…. Can you sell Helmut on a dual ceremony even if it's at Holy Word?"

"I can ask, but I can't promise."

"Please, Norman, it's high profile. We can't have it look like Rome is abandoning the German people."

"You do realize there will be a sea of black uniforms in those pews, not tuxedos. It will be a military wedding. Are you sure you want the Church to be seen as supporting Helmut's Fatherland Security Force on television?"

"It's the 1930s all over again – the same predicament Pius XI faced, isn't it?" Umberto said.

"History repeats itself." Norman said. He could hear the frustration in Umberto's voice.

"Are these young people aware of that history? Really aware? All the marching and training and that damnable E'tat de Guerre … God help us, maybe they are saving the world from barbarism. Sometimes I wonder. If anyone was to save the West, how else would it be done if not through discipline and media and …. murder?"

"I don't have the answer, Umberto. I don't know if it's right for us to condemn people who believe they do know. I don't have any solutions to replace the repatriation program other than prayer and surrender. But you seem to have softened your position a little. Why?"

"Because Helmut didn't go to meet Madeline Churchill. We tempted him and he never bit the apple. Was it his moral sensibility, Devine Providence or sheer dumb luck?"

"I'll treat that as a rhetorical question, my friend. It doesn't matter if Madeline's really dead. What matters is what we're going to tell the Churchills. Eventually they'll want to know where their daughter is. Like when they see Helmut's married Teresa Stahl."

"Well, until I see a DNA report, I'm going to assume Madeline Churchill is alive. And if she's dead, she will have died of food poisoning instead of a hotel bombing that looks an awful lot like an assassination attempt. I've got a doctor's death certificate saying that's exactly what she died of. It's the only way to extricate us from the politics of this debacle. But first, we have to find out what Helmut knows."

"I'll try to talk to him. He's going to want to know who's involved in her leaving the convent —maybe he already does. He'll blame us, and you know he's merciless."

"But he also knows Stahl needs the support of the Church, Norman, and I'm willing to make a good faith effort to show him that support before Madeline turns up dead."

"Alright, I'll tell Tanzer and Pomeranz to behave themselves – no press conferences criticizing the Church's participation at the wedding. No bitching about the Citizen's Freedom Medal."

"And tell your friends that the matter of Madeline Churchill must be resolved for the benefit of all involved," Umberto pronounced, "Unfortunately if that means for Stephan Stahl's benefit as well, so be it."

# CHAPTER VIII

## The Bear Comes Aboard

The new staff headquarters at E'tat de Guerre were luxurious. Helmut had a corner apartment with his own bath, kitchen, a balcony that looked out over the Paris Memorial, and a king-sized bed. "We had a Muslim who worked in Bonn help us," Lt. Rudolph said as he smoothed the corner of the gold and white chenille bedspread. "We figured it would do until Madame Wolf arrives."

"He did a fine job. Is he the one who did the meeting room too? It's beautiful." Helmut stepped out onto the balcony. "She'll love this view. The memorial gardens …"

"He's quite good. He's hoping you'll appreciate his artistry enough to see him. He's begged me for an interview. Will you see him?"

"Yes, as soon as the Russian delegation has left."

"Of course."

"You've done an excellent job in my absence, Rudolph. I appreciate it." Helmut walked around the room, looking at the art prints so carefully chosen, the figurines angled precisely in the built-in shelves, and the silk drapes that floated in the breeze over the French doors.

"Thank-you, Sir. The entire center is ready for inspection. You won't find a speck of dust on a weapon or a fingerprint on a buckle."

"This fellow you want me to see, is he a true artist? Does he paint or sculpt?"

"He was the curator of the Stadtmuseum. His specialty is preservation. The Mid-eastern art collection there is considered one of the best in the world."

"That explains the attention to detail."

"The chef wants to know what you want for dinner."

"Roast pork *and* eggplant. Sauerkraut and cheese."

"For the Russians too?"

Helmut grinned at Rudolph. "What do Russians like to eat?"

"I have no idea, Sir. But if we serve them enough vodka, they won't care what we give them. From what I hear, Russian cuisine is pretty basic. May I make a suggestion?"

"Sure."

"Call your future mother-in-law and ask her. When I was getting married, I was given that advice. I've never regretted getting on her good side straightaway."

"How long have you been married?"

"I was married eighteen months when my wife was killed in a terrorist attack. There's no pain like a train in Spain. So they say. Her mother takes care of my little boy when I'm deployed."

"I'm sorry. I didn't mean to pry. But I'll take that advice, and any more, if you have it."

\*\*\*

Vasily Provenko was a short, dark man who sported a trim moustache, wore all thirteen of his medals, and insisted on touring the Repatriation Center in a convertible. Helmut obliged, apologizing to

Georg who had to change the security plan he'd been working on for the last forty-eight hours, and wore his Kaiser Cross which greatly impressed Vasily.

"Don't be fooled, Helmut," Stephan had told him. "The Russians are a tough people. There's a reason Stalin chose the name – it means steel just like Stahl. They'll be surprised at our humanitarian approach. When St. Basil's Cathedral was destroyed by a dirty bomb, President Borokovski purged the entire city of Moscow of anyone he suspected of being Muslim – including tourists. The slogan Bullets and Bayonets was embroidered on his funeral shroud. Just because President Yeshenko is new doesn't mean he isn't cut from the same pattern."

Helmut could see that toughness in Vasily - the way he gripped his shot glass with his whole hand, the way he devoured his food without chewing, and the way his thick-soled heavy boots drummed down the hallways. Yet, in his meetings with him and Emil, Helmut could also see a keen intelligence and admirable stamina.

"It's time we took a break, Da?" Vasily was out of chocolate, a treat which he never seemed to tire, and it was near noon. That meant consuming more vodka and a game of backgammon with Emil, who genuinely seemed to like their competitions.

"Go ahead, Gentlemen, I have a Center to run," Helmut said by way of excusing himself. Both Emil and Vasily smoked too, and Helmut wanted to get away from the sour air.

So far, things had been going well. Vasily wanted to know how much it cost to run the facility, and asked Helmut how he felt about being a famous war criminal. Prepared for the question, Helmut answered that he didn't mind, that one man's war criminal was another man's hero and he would leave it to history to judge him.

"You're so right, Captain Wolf. History has a way of changing all things. Maybe its time for the Russian government to let bygones be bygones. Our countries have mutual interests. You need oil. We have oil. You want to be rid of the Muslims. We want to rid of the Muslims. We need capital investment. You have capital to invest."

It was clear Vasily wanted to talk politics. The backgammon game was a cover for the political game that was being played between old timers, and Helmut knew his cue.

Outside the meeting room, Helmut stretched and flexed his back. Thank God, he thought, Emil was here to field the tough questions about a German-Russian entente. He had no idea this would turn into a full-scale testing of the political waters. He came out into the sunshine and took a healthy breath of fresh air. Georg approached him hurriedly, just as a vehicle entered the compound.

"What is that?" Helmut demanded as a white trailer pulled by an official-looking half-ton pick-up truck rolled through the Center gates and stopped in front of his new quarters.

Georg rolled his eyes. "Vasily's horse."

"His horse? What the hell …?"

"According to the Foreign Ministry, Vasily never goes anywhere without his horse. It's a cultural matter to which we are to be very sensitive." Georg handed him a telegram from the Foreign Ministry.

"Where are we supposed to keep him? And his groom, I assume."

A tall, blonde woman got out of the cab and strode towards Helmut with an extended hand. "Natya. Natalia Provenskaya. I am Vasily's wife."

She had child-like skin, soft and pink, and a nose speckled with delicate freckles. Helmut could imagine her naked in bed, but not with Vasily. He envied him without hatred.

"He tells me, Natya, I will be there to meet you so these German dogs don't eat you up. And where is he?" Her smile covered her face.

Helmut shook her hand, noticing the brown suede gloves she wore fit well but were obviously well worn. He returned her smile. "I promise, I won't even nip you."

"He's such an ethnocentric, that Vasily. If something isn't Russian, it 's no good and can't be trusted."

"We'll take good care of you and ..."

"Oh, the horse. Comrade. That's his name."

"You and Comrade Provenko."

His words were lost in the air as Natya was already half-way back to the trailer. She backed Comrade out of the trailer and Helmut saw at once why Vasily couldn't bear to be apart from the beast. It was about the size of a Great Dane with a smooth roan coat and a shaggy white mane and tail. Helmut heard an "awwww" escape Georg's lips, and admitted to himself that the little horse was adorable.

Natya brought Comrade to where the men stood, and knelt beside him, looking up at Helmut with her smoky eyes. "This is Vasily's heart. He won't be a bother. Comrade I mean He has all his food in the trailer and I'll clean up after him. He's a dear, isn't he? Come on, pet him yourself."

She took Helmut's hand and pulled it towards Comrade's muzzle. Helmut felt a jolt of electricity run up his arm. He couldn't have resisted her grasp if he'd wanted to. She was an angel who smelled of fresh hay and saddle soap. He knelt down and stroked the horse's velvety nose. "I think he likes you, Sir. Who are you?"

"I'm Captain Wolf. I like him. He's cute," Helmut said. "Georg, come on, I know you want to pet him too."

"He needs a walk after so long a trip. Can you take him for a walk, Georg? Your captain won't mind, will he?" Natya was speaking to Georg but looking at Helmut.

"Take him through the garden, Georg. Little fertilizer maker."

Georg took the reins and led Comrade away, softly telling the horse their itinerary.

"Oh, I forgot to give him the sugar," Natya said reaching in the pocket of her riding jacket and pulling out two sugar cubes. "He only gets it when he's a good boy, you know? Are you a good boy?"

"The best," Helmut said.

"Then here, you can have the sugar."

Helmut took the sugar and popped a cube into his mouth, puckering his lips as he sucked out its sweetness. Natya took the other cube and put it on the tip of her tongue, then slowly drew it into her mouth as she stared into his eyes. "I am a good girl. Yes?"

"Of course. Let me take you to your husband." Helmut led her into the building where Vasily was talking with Eisenbach. Matching him stride for stride with her long legs, Natya quickened the pace until they were almost running up the stairs, and when they got to the top, she stopped and laughed.

"You see? You can't help but beat me. It doesn't take much to make you run the race even when you know you're going to win!"

153

Vasily and Emil came out of the meeting room and hurried towards them. "What's going on, Helmut?" Emil said as Vasily picked up Natya and swung her around, covering her with kisses. She returned his embrace with gusto.

"Vasily, you have been such a bad boy! I bring Comrade here to see you, and where are you?"

"He's here, my little Comrade?" Vasily turned to Emil. "We have plenty of time for talk. I have to see my baby." He followed Natya down the stairs, leaving Helmut and a bewildered Emil alone.

"They brought a baby? Here?"

Helmut, patted Emil's arm. "It's a miniature horse. Cute little guy. Georg's in love. I think he misses Bootsie."

"Natya's gorgeous. Quite the odd couple, aren't they? What do you think of them?" said Emil.

"I think if every terrorist had a beautiful Natya and a cute little Comrade, there would be no bloodshed," Helmut answered.

It was an honest answer straight from his heart. As he lay in bed, Natya's innocent sensuality filled his thoughts. What was there not to love? She was beautiful, friendly, generous, and sexy. Yet, he knew as soon as he saw her in Vasily arms, she was passionately in love with him. Everything else was just play. Tell Stephan, he reminded himself, that the Russians are seductive thieves. Natya had stolen his heart, then tossed it away without repentance. His spirit had not felt so free since he and Madeline drove to Yosemite with visions of scaling El Capitan, until they saw it. Struck dumb as it came into view, they realized neither of them had the skills to attempt the challenge.

They sat in the car awestruck, listening to buzz bugs and smelling summer's dried leaves. They were week-end hikers, not face-of-God climbers.

Madeline had turned to him and asked, "Are there steps?" They started laughing, simultaneously acknowledging their human incompetence in the face of monstrous natural reality. What fools they were. They turned around and drove home instead of heading to Las Vegas to get married like they'd planned. By the time they got back to Virginia, the unconquerable mountain that had been in front of them was now between them.

He missed Madeline, ached for her, hated her for being the "good" in his life. He made love to dozens of women trying to forget her, had the adulation of millions of women around the world, but always before him was the image of her. In his nostrils, the memory of the pungent smell of patchouli and roses haunted him. He cursed her, praised her, prayed to her, and finally satisfied himself by pretending she was undulating under him. How many hours would he have to sleep alone before he'd done enough penance for wanting her to love him more than she loved God?

A roll of gunfire brought him out of his thoughts and onto the floor holding his pistol ready to fire at whatever entered his bedroom unidentified. Whatever the commotion, it was now on his balcony. He heard glass breaking and muffled voices. Someone shouted his name.

"Who goes there?" he called out.

"A silver wolf," came the coded reply, and Helmut knew it was Georg. He turned on the light, stood up and dressed in seconds as Georg came into the room, panting and blood-spattered.

"Vasily and Natya?"

"Safe. Eisenbach too."

"There is a God. What happened?" Helmut pulled on his boots.

"Damn ragheads! Damn them to hell."

"Where else? Chicago?" Helmut said. "Assassination attempts come with the territory. We are in a dangerous business, my friend."

"Two deportees went berserk. Overpowered a soldier."

"Is that their blood on your clothes?"

"No. Corporal Metzner's. But we got 'em, Helmut."

"How bad is Metzner?"

"Throat cut. Bled out in eight seconds."

"God be merciful. Where are the bastards?"

"Restrained in the brig."

"Let's go."

Helmut followed Georg to the Center's military jail. Three German soldiers, sentenced to a weekend in the brig without pay for public drunkenness but now thoroughly sober, were in the first cell. Inside the second cell, two men stood chained to iron rings on the back wall.

"Allah be praised," the men chanted as the men entered. Helmut walked over to the man with bloodstained clothes, and the man spit in his face. "Allah be praised," the man said again. Helmut stepped back, drew his pistol shoved the barrel into the man's balls and fired. The man screamed in pain, his body going limp as blood poured from his groin.

"Corporal Metzner sends his regards," Helmut whispered.

The other chained man began screaming too as Helmut approached him, looking him square in the face.

"No, don't," Helmut heard a voice say. When he turned around, Emil, Vasily, and four Russian security guards were outside the cell. "Don't kill him." It was Vasily.

Georg leaned into Helmut and whispered, "Natya was taking Comrade for a walk. She's alright, but Comrade … they cut his throat too."

Helmut put away his pistol and backed away. "Send our drunks back to their barracks, Georg, Herr Provenko is taking jurisdiction over the prisoner."

Georg unlocked the soldiers' cell. "Double-time it back to barracks, Boys" he ordered, and the men took off running. Wild-eyed with fear, the chained man struggled to get free, shouting, "It wasn't me. I didn't kill anybody. I swear, I didn't kill anybody."

Emil placed a hand on Vasily's shoulder and said, "I'm so sorry," before leaving with Helmut and Georg at his side. The shrieks of the terror-filled terrorist lasted only a few seconds. Vasily gagged him before his soldiers sodomized him, broke his bones one by one, and then decapitated him with a bayonet.

The Russian execution was neither swift nor clean, Helmut wrote in his report to Stahl, but it was just. The Provenkos were inconsolable over the death of Comrade and drank gallons of vodka to ease their pain. It's my understanding that they are unable to have children because of the radiation they received in the second Al Qaeda Moscow attack. Though nothing can replace Comrade in their hearts, I have nevertheless delivered another toy horse to them, and expressed our hope that Kachina will comfort them.

Emil wrote to Stahl: Provenko has assured me that, after seeing the barbarity of our enemies first hand, Russia is committed to erasing the scourge of Islamofascism from the face of the earth. He was impressed with Helmut's understanding of the cultural differences between our two countries, an understanding demonstrated by the way he ceded jurisdiction over the prisoner to the Russian government without hesitation. Provenko reaffirmed that the Russian government is allied with the German government in our shared war on terror.

Natya wrote to Helmut: We were so happy to meet the famous Captain Wolf. The picture of all of us together has made us famous too. People stop Vasily and me in the street and ask us if you are as brave as you are handsome, and we say yes, he is. Such a good time we had in Paris. We love our little Kachina. Your faithful friends.

The note was accompanied by a small silver tin with two sugar cubes inside. Imagining a terrorist getting his hands on Natya must have driven Vasily to madness, Helmut thought. She was as sweet as the sugar she sent.

* * *

Three months after Provenko's visit, over two and a half billion people watched Stephan Stahl walk Teresa down the aisle and give her hand in marriage to Captain Wolf. Looking on, in the front row pew was Patricia and Norman Wolf, who wore his Citizen's Freedom Medal on the lapel of his black pin-striped morning coat. Next to Frieda were Emil and Francesca Eisenbach. Behind them sat dignitaries from around the world and of both parties, including Olberman, and Pomeranz, and behind them rows of Helmut's staff flown in from Paris, including Lieutenant Rudolph, who escorted the maid of honor to the reception.

At the end of the ceremony, Teresa, accompanied by her four bridesmaids, laid her bouquet at the feet of her patron saint while Helmut, with best-man Georg at his side, placed a ceremonial dagger at the feet of Jesus. The bride and groom knelt for a moment in silent prayer, then returned to each other, and faced the congregation as husband and wife.

Father Hahn and Reverend Kohl gave the assembly the blessings of the cross, exchanged a kiss of peace in an ecumenical embrace, and then followed the happy couple as they exited the church under the crossed swords of the Fatherland Security Force honor guard.

"Blasphemy," Pomeranz whispered under his breath as the family wedding pictures were taken on the Holy Word steps. No one heard him. The bells were pealing and the crowd of two hundred and fifty thousand people who had witnessed the ceremony on two huge screens erected outside the church were cheering and waving German flags.

\*\*\*

Founded by John Calvin, and dubbed the Protestant Rome, Geneva had all the beauty of the French scenery but none of the fun identified with its neighbor. Small, compared to other travel destinations in Europe, clean and efficient, Geneva catered to business people and white tourists who soon tired of its lack of sensual pleasure. But to Helmut and Terri it was perfect.

The town was easily secured and strategically located between Vienna and Paris. It is also the home of the Musée d'Art et d'Histoire which houses a Western art collection that includes Rodin's *The Thinker* and *The Tragic Muse*, Canova's exquisite *Venus and Adonis*, and Witz's altarpiece of Jesus and the fishermen on Lake Geneva itself. Teresa wanted to see the Impressionist collection that includes Renoir and Cezanne, but she was most interested in Hodler's *Lac de Thoune*. This painting, loaned to the Louvre for a special exhibit of water pictures, was saved from the Paris bombing because a usually efficient shipment clerk was sick with the flu the day it was to leave. All Geneva regarded the delay as an act of God.

"Do you know, Terri, that before the terrorists beheaded the Louvre staff and set the building ablaze, they ripped up the world's art treasures in front of the people who had cared for them for thirty years? We know because they filmed it all and sent us a copy. I've seen those films. People pleading for their lives —and one man, a custodian, pleading with the terrorists to spare a small oil of the *Angus Dei*."

"The picture of the lamb lying on a table with its feet tied ... and a halo around its head. I know it," Teresa said.

"I saw it in San Diego. Madeline bought a small print of it and carried it her wallet like a holy card. As they cut off the man's head, he screamed Angus Dei! Angus Dei! Of all the great masters in the museum, he asked only that they spare a representation of Christ."

Teresa nestled her head in his arm as they sat in bed and watched the sailboats on the lake. They had the bed moved closer to the window just so they could see it as they made love and drank champagne. She thought she should say something to him, but she didn't know if they should be words of comfort or anger. She began to realize that she had not married a young hero, but an old soldier. Helmut was physically strong, but psychically he was made of stone. By necessity, she thought. Frieda had warned her many times not to expect an ordinary life married to an extraordinary man. You can go with him, or you can withdraw to your home and let him live his extraordinary life, she had said. You'll know what is best for both of you when the honeymoon is over, and he will respect whatever you decide. As for him, he cannot decide otherwise than to be what he is.

It was good advice, Teresa learned. After three days of museum and restaurant hopping and buying all the thank-you presents for the wedding party at the colorful shops in the center of the city, she decided to return to Vienna.

She made the decision in the train station. Helmut was buying her a Toblerone candy bar for the trip to Paris when he stopped in front a young woman seated on a green bench across from the station waiting room. Teresa judged her to be only sixteen. When she saw Helmut's boots, she looked up at him with red-rimmed eyes. She had brown hair that was tied back in a pony tail at the nape of her neck and held a small statue in her hand. Teresa could see it was a replica of the Pieta.

"Why are you crying, Frauline?" Helmut asked her. "I have a tissue, here take it and dry your eyes."

"I was in Rome just yesterday." She showed the statue to Helmut. "He blessed this for me. Mia Papa. Such a kind man. Eyes that told you not to be troubled."

"You saw the Holy Father?"

"Yes, and now he's dead."

"Dead? How do you know that?"

161

"My friend, Carol, texed me." The young woman gave him her cell phone. Helmut took it and read the message.

"Frauline, is Carol a truthful girl?"

"Yes, sir."

Teresa saw Helmut sit down next to the girl, remove the insignia from his hat, and give it to her in exchange for her Pieta. "You keep this. This is Helmut Wolf's pledge to you: the people who did this will be punished."

"You are the real Wolf?"

"Yes." Helmut gave her a hug and marched towards Terri. It seemed Helmut was returning to her, but he wasn't. He stood beside her, on the phone with Georg. "Have you seen the news?"

Within seconds Georg was at their side along with throngs of security personnel. "Get that young woman on a plane home, secure the train station, and get Stephan on the phone," Helmut ordered, then sat beside her. "The Vatican's been bombed."

"Oh, Jesus! Then the Excelsior *was* just a prelude. Helmut you have to go."

"I'm on my way to Paris to organize the rescue. Do you want to go with me?"

"No. I'll be safer in Vienna. Promise me you'll come home soon."

"I'll try, Darling. I swear. I hate to leave you." He kissed her again and again and held her so close she thought she'd faint. "I love you, Terri."

He disappeared into a sea of back uniforms, and with that, Teresa Jean Wolf became a widow to duty.

# CHAPTER IX

## The Unthinkable

Eight weeks to the day after the Excelsior explosion, four long-range missiles hit the Vatican. The first hit St. Peter's Square, the second St Peter's Basilica, the third and fourth the Vatican museums, setting off nineteen successive conventional bomb explosions, one demolishing the radio station. The worst hit was the colonnades that arced St. Peter's square where over three hundred thousand people had gathered to see Pope John XXIV say his twenty-fifth anniversary mass at an outdoor altar. As he was walking to the Square, John was knocked to the ground. He struggled to his feet and was running to the art gallery in a futile attempt to salvage some of its treasures when a second blast knocked him down again. The West Wall collapsed, pinning half his body under tons of debris. His upper body was so badly ravaged by flying debris, he could only be identified by the papal ring.

Now, the man whose election the Papacy was tainted by controversy, lay in a closed casket before the altar of what was left of St. Stephen's church. Many high-ranking prelates deemed him too worldly to be pontiff, but Edward Cardinal Hugh, the man who nominated him, had laughed at the suggestion. "You will see," he predicted, "John will be loved for his graces."

Hugh's prediction was accurate. John's piety and deep understanding of the yearnings of the modern heart endeared him to Catholics around the globe. Able to speak the language of the Anglican,

163

the Lutheran and the Episcopalian, John seemed poised to unite Christianity more profoundly than any of his predecessors.

He did not require acceptance of papal infallibility. A true ecumenist in the tradition of John XXIII, he required only acceptance of the divinity of Christ. "We are not Catholic or Protestant at the foot of the cross," he said in an address to the world's bishops. "Neither is there Suni or Shia in the mosque."

Asked to clarify his remarks by El Arabia TV, Pope John compared the Catholic-Protestant split over papal infallibility to the divide within Islam over the legitimate successor to Mohammed, and it was this comparison that sparked demonstration and deaths threats that few took any more seriously than those made against other Popes. Popes John-Paul, though an actual recipient of an assassin's bullet, and Benedict had refused to be intimidated by those that sought to silence them.

One newspaper columnist once wrote:

*Pope John XXIV constantly astounds the world with a philosophic balancing act reminiscent of Kant. He is not tortured by the existence of two realities – one spiritual and one temporal – and if you ignore his accent, he could pass for a Harvard scholar. We must be careful not to canonize him before he is dead just for the sake of time and tourism.*

As church bells around the globe tolled in mourning, the Italian government, fearing successive attacks, sealed off all transportation routes into Vatican City in an attempt to control the crowds rushing to ground zero. Thousand were searching for information about relatives and friends who had filled the Square, but despite pleas for people to keep the streets clear for emergency personnel, the crowd doubled in an hour. Mourners,

164

media, looters and hawkers pressed in on each other, congealing into a human bomb that exploded in rioting throughout Rome.

Three circus-sized tents were erected outside the Vatican perimeter to serve as morgues, but it was obvious they would be at capacity in a few hours as truckload after truckload of the dead and dying were retrieved from the Vatican complex.

The surviving College of Cardinals gathered in St. Stephen's. Amid howling sirens and screaming victims, the fifteen men had retired to contemplate the realities of their situation, and to submit themselves to the will of God rather than go mad with grief

"My brothers in Christ," Cardinal Corigliano said as he rose from his knees and faced the terrified men. "I've been in contact with President Buscolioni. He's sending a helicopter in to take us to Villa San Rafael. We'll be safe there."

One by one the men took their chairs, wiping away soot and tears. All but Edward Hugh who was lying on the stone floor, arms outstretched in a cross.

Umberto gently encouraged him. "We must have faith, Edward. I know John was your friend, but we haven't time to bury him. We have to get out of the city."

Edward got up and walked close to Umberto. "You know what will happen if we leave. How long before Stephan Stahl rescues the Vatican and makes it another Paris?"

Umberto paled. He'd been ping-ponging phone calls with Norman since the first explosion. "You speak of ghastly things, Edward."

"Yes, as ghastly as your sanctioning the marriage of a war criminal. You made a devil's bargain, Umberto. You've led the world to believe the Germans are our friends, and like any good friend, they will be at our doorstep in this crisis. It's help we'll regret."

"You fool," Umberto said lowly. "You know these old men can't stay here. The air is so bad, they can hardly breathe now, and there's no water. Do you want to kill them all?"

"If Stahl comes to Italy, he's never going home without a war. The Church needs a leader."

"Yes, we must do what we can to insure the Church survives in tact, Edward, but we can elect a new Pope at San Rafael just as well as we can here."

"No! We will elect a new Pope now, and he will stay here to make sure there is a Church to come back to. Do you remember the scandal the Church endured because of its desire to survive Hitler? To abandon this holy ground gives it to blasphemers and war criminals."

"We must turn the other cheek. Forgive our enemies..."

"Which ones, Umberto? The Muslims or the Germans?"

"All of them. As Christ did in Gethsemane."

"I am not comforted by platitudes. John could have walked the tightrope, but only because he was a sovereign. If we leave like Matisse left Paris, we're done."

Umberto nodded in agreement. He grasped the crucifix her wore around his neck, and stared at the floor, exhausted. As John's secretary he was the de facto chair of the College of Cardinals and bore the weight of their souls on his shoulders. The mourners were waiting for a reply to Edward's concerns, concerns they shared, but were reluctant to voice. "What would you have us do?" Umberto said.

"What we are duty bound to do, except do it more expeditiously," Edward said. "We must ride out to meet Henry as Pope Gregory did at Conossa. I do not believe we can prevent a reprisal for this attack. I do believe we can prevent Stahl's annexation of Vatican City as a protectorate. I also believe it is our duty to convince the Chancellor he is morally bound to protect innocent Muslims who abhor the evils of terrorism as much as we do." Edward put his handkerchief in a pocket hidden in the folds of his crimson cassock as a deep sigh escaped his barrel chest.

"Edward is right, Umberto. Muslim innocents are as deserving of protection as Christian children." It was Philipe Cardinal Nabu from Sudan who spoke. The seven-foot black man came to John's closed casket, turned and addressed the College. "Yet, we have seen generation after generation of Arab criminals slaughter innocent tribes people in Africa, poison wells, steal water and food from the mouths of children, bankrupt struggling economies, and behead captives. These radicals are a cancer, a pestilence on the earth that eats away confidence and the psychological strength to bear adversity. We cannot assume that those who do nothing to stop these outrages hate them. The UN, the relief organizations, all condone them with their silence." Nabu grabbed the Bible resting on the casket. "Do you believe this is the word of God, Edward?"

"Yes, of course."

"Then herein lies the sign we seek. Let me read to you from John's own Bible, a family heirloom published in 1945. The Second Epistle of St. Paul to the Thessalonians:

*Let no man deceive you by any means for unless there come a revolt first, and the man of sin be revealed, the son of perdition who opposeth Christ and is lifted up and sitteth in the temple, and worshiped as though he were God.*

And to whom does the passage refer? In a footnote it is spelled out. The reference is to the Anti-Christ. The footnote also explains that it is Mohamet who sitteth in the temple and is worshiped as a god, "as Mohamet has done by the churches of the East." Even then, my brothers," Nabu continued, "The Church knew Mohammed was the anti-Christ. If you need further proof, read John: Chapter 1, Verse 22, wherein he describes the anti-Christ as he who denieth that Jesus is the Christ, who denies the Father and the Son. Islam denies that Jesus was the Son of God, and sets Mohammed above Him.

The Bible tells us in the Apocalypse that the Four Horsemen are Jesus astride a white horse, and the other three —war, famine, and pestilence —are the punishments meted out to those who deny Him. The Bible does not forbid war."

Edward was not prepared for a Biblical debate but felt compelled to quiet Nabu's zeal with reason. "You make the Bible sound like the Qu'ran. To condemn a religion is one thing. To kill its followers, no matter how misguided they are, is another. Christians are also exhorted to love above all things. Wouldn't God prefer we persuade rather than persecute?"

"How do we persuade if we're all dead?" Nabu placed the Bible back on the casket and returned to his seat.

"Do you want to be pope, Nabu?" Umberto asked. "Tell us honestly if you believe God is calling you, for the Church needs a leader who is assured of the rightness of his decisions. Only this will calm the fears that haunt the faithful."

Nabu made the sign of the cross before answering. "No, Brother, I have not been called. This I know."

Umberto faced the College. "Is there anyone here who has heard God's call?"

"What has God said to you, Umberto?" Edward said.

"I confess, I am so filled with grief and loathing and fear, that I cannot hear His voice. Perhaps tomorrow he will dissolve my emotions and replace them with good counsel. This is all I can hope for."

Umberto withdrew from the sparring. Norman had asked him the same question just hours before, and he had given him the unvarnished answer. "God has told me I am lucky to have dodged the bullet with the Churchill mess, and to steer clear of German entanglements. Only a fool or a crazy man would take the job now that the wolf is at the door."

"So you've heard about the Provenko report?" Norman said.

"My God, who hasn't? Eisenbach playing the part of von Ribbentrop to Provenko's Molotov. You'd think Provenko's bragging on barbaric Russian justice would have embarrassed the German government," Umberto said. "Instead he's a hero. It's shameful."

"You've obviously never met Olberman," Norman mused. "He makes Goebels look like a lightweight. When you get electricity, boot up your computer and see the clips of Helmut and Teresa setting off on their honeymoon and look at the signs in the crowd. Helmut the invincible. Helmut the hero."

"Helmut, the blood lusting Bastard of Berlin whose policy is to execute first and execute later," Umberto said.

"Metzner's family appreciated Helmut's swift meting out of German justice," Norman reminded him.

"I should have listened to Father Hahn. Rome can't very well bless the son-of-a-bitch one day and excommunicate him the next without looking like a political player."

"I won't go there, Umberto. But you need to bury John as soon as possible and elect someone who *is* a political player but doesn't look like one. That's my best ambassador's advice."

Umberto was mulling over that advice when he heard a voice call from outside St. Stephen's. "Sirs, we're here to evacuate you." It was the Roman police.

The Cardinals filed out into the daylight where a chopper waited, and the television cameras filmed. "We'll have to make two trips, Gentlemen. Ten at a time."

"Take the eldest first," Umberto told the officer, and the remaining five headed back into the chapel.

Once inside Edward announced his decision. "I'm staying."

"Are you mad?" Nabu asked quietly.

"No, I'm following my conscience and my conscience says someone has to stay here to meet Herr Wolf."

Nabu followed Edward to the altar. "Then, God has called you?" he asked hopefully.

"We traveled a long way together, John and I, Nabu. I knew from the first day I met him, he would be Pope. I never dreamed he'd be a martyr. Who could have known?" Nabu drew closer, drawing comfort

170

from Edward's friendly voice. He needed to hear something, anything that would take away a rage that was more then he could bear. "I learned so much from my friend," Edward continued. "How to forgive myself for being human. But, no, I can never fill his shoes. All I can do is wait and hold on to whatever is left of Christendom."

Nabu slid quietly to his knees. He knew that he and Edward were not alone in the Church. John was there and so was God, telling him that Edward was the man for the job. "I'll wait with you," he said. God isn't always dramatic, Nabu thought. It is not always about raising the dead and making the sun stand still. Sometimes the signs we demand from Him are right in front of us.

"This is insane. We can't elect a Pope with five votes," Umberto said.

"As long as it's a majority vote, we can." It was Xioa Cardinal Chu from China, a seventy-year old who had listened carefully to the three men. "We have only three candidates. I and Anthony Cardinal O'Malley are too old to meet the Hun. So, it's a choice among three – one who wants to surrender. Umberto. One who wants a war. Nabu. And one who wants to temper righteous justice against the terrorists with Christ's mercy for innocents. The first two options are not credible. Umberto is a bureaucratic diplomat who will compromise. Compromise is necessary sometimes. Nabu is a firebrand who will never compromise. This too is good. Sometimes there is a need for stone walls. So, there is only Edward. The third option that is the only option. He is willing to stay and deal with the death and destruction. He has my vote."

"Mine also," said O'Malley.

"Mine also," echoed Nabu.

Tony O'Malley opened the casket and took the ring from John's finger and held it out to Edward. "I know it is supposed to be smashed, but we have no way of getting another. Take it. You were elected on the first ballot."

"Do any of you know anything about Edward?" Umberto protested. "Do you know he was married before he became a priest?"

"The information is irrelevant, Umberto. With all due respect, St. Augustine was no virgin when he entered the priesthood. Neither was Thomas a'Becket. That Edward loved another human being as well as God speaks well for the capacity of his heart. His joy will be doubled in heaven when he is reunited with both God and his wife." No longer anxious, Nabu spoke with calm authority. "We need someone to lead us through this crisis."

Umberto held his gold cross, lightly stroking its smooth yellow surface. Perhaps Nebu was right. An English Pope would throw Stephan Stahl an unexpected curve ball. Edward would be a lightening rod that would draw all the energy to himself and leave the rest of them a dark place to hide in case things went badly. "Alright. We have a new Pope. And the three of us will stay. Tony, don't let the Cardinals drink my brandy, and tell Il Presidente we need food and water."

When the chopper took off with Chu and O'Malley, Umberto called Norman from the vestibule. "We have a new boss, Norman," he said.

"You're joking."

"It's Edward Hugh. No one else wanted the gig."

"Did he want it?"

"No, but he listened to reason. Cardinal Chu's reason anyway. Three of us are staying."

"With San Rafael calling you to the Villa?"

"You think I'm going to let a new Pope deal with the Unholy Trinity alone? What do you hear from Malta?" Umberto whispered.

"Not much. Since the Excelsior, the Center Socialists have been out of the loop. But I don't think Stahl wants to move unilaterally into Italy – he'll want President Buscolioni to invite him in. That could be soon from what I hear. How are things there?"

"Hell. Sanitation is the big problem. There isn't enough lime to cover the corpses. They've taken to bulldozing everything into deep pits —bodies to bidets —its all waste."

"Stahl won't allow a cholera outbreak, Umberto. Cholera, Typhus - he'll come in when the first case is reported whether President Buscolioni agrees or not."

"I'll pass that along. Where's Helmut?"

"Still in Paris."

"That's reassuring."

"How much damage was done? Really."

Umberto told him to hang on while he blew his nose, but it was a way to stifle the sob in his voice. "Norman, St. Peter's Square is a field hospital surrounded by mountains of jumbled stone. Everything's gone. There's no doubt Catholicism was the target. The only blessing is the Vatican library holdings below ground were spared."

"Take care of yourself, Umberto. We're praying for you."

At six o'clock, two days and nine hours after the first blast, white smoke wafted from a hastily constructed furnace on top of St. Stephen's.

Nabu made the perilous trip up the ladder to the roof, deposited the ballots, and scrambled down. Edward Hugh became only the second English Pope in history, after Adrian IV, taking the name Edward I, and accepted the papal ring, staff, and miter as symbols of his authority. He also accepted the viciousness of world terrorism as his cross.

***

Pope Edward made St. Stephen's right vestibule his office as well as his residence. The situation in Vatican City was deteriorating rapidly. The Vatican still had no electricity or running water. Health advisors from Rome were telling Buscolioni to bulldoze what was left of the historic buildings to facilitate corpse recovery, and suppress the threat of fire and disease, but Edward feared that historically important artifacts would be lost forever in the name of expediency. Italy's heat became an enemy too. By noon the next day the stench of decay was unbearable, driving away survivors from Rome by droves. The relationship between the Vatican and Rome reached an impasse when Rome quarantined Vatican City.

It waxed clear to Edward that he had to make some quick decisions. It seemed he was caught between ceding authority to Rome or to the Germans, and neither of those alternatives served the interests of the Church. He called Nabu and told him he needed every scrap of information on every urban terrorist attack in Europe going back to the Madrid bombing of the early 2000s. Nabu rushed to the office and handed Edward his cell phone. "I've compiled the information in chronological order, but I can't print you hard copies. I'm sorry, Edward."

"Wait, don't go. I want to talk to you about Stahl. Umberto tells me you know him."

Nabu looked around for a chair and settled for the floor. Edward joined him, pouring them each a glass of the wine that was also spared in the safety of the underground chambers. "I met him a few times when I was secretary to Bishop Meyer in Berlin. I was there during the Brandenburg Massacre. Stahl was there too. He was born in 1984. I remember because I was born in 1984, and we talked about how wrong Orwell got it – governments had gotten weaker not stronger. Anyway, Stahl was the protégé of Leopold Stassner, the man who inaugurated the Marshall Plan for Russia after Moscow was hit. Stassner wanted Bishop Meyer to conduct the Easter service at ground zero, and Stahl and I coordinated the arrangements. He delivered a list of prayer points, you might say, for Meyer to use in the sermon, but Meyer was late. I offered Stahl some coffee and we talked."

"Did Meyer conduct the service?"

"Of course, but no one remembers his sermon."

"Oh, I remember. That's the day Helmut was rescued."

Nabu gave him a wry smile. "Like W.C. fields said, no animals, no children, and he might have added no heroes. Stahl didn't do his homework because the search efforts were still underway when Bishop Meyer arrived. There was a lot of noise and commotion and reporters. I chased them away, but the photographer, Turtletaub, was a personal friend of Stahl's. We were standing at the edge of the crowd, facing the podium, listening to Meyer ribbing Turtletaub about it being a slow news day if he was paid to cover a church service. Everything got quiet, and we heard a shout. We looked up at the hill of ruins and Eisenbach appeared at the top of the mound of rubble behind Meyer."

"Talk about being at the right place at the right time!"

"I'll never forget it, Holiness. Eisenbach had been digging for that child non-stop since the explosion. He'd dig till he was exhausted, rest for a few hours, and start again. Nothing could convince him to give up. All of a sudden, Eisenbach was standing on top of the ruins with the child in his arms. We all thought he was dead, and then a little hand reached up and touched Eisenbach's cheek – everything they say about witnessing a miracle is true. The German people have owned them both from that moment on."

"What happened after the miracle?"

"Eisenbach and his wife wanted to adopt the boy – they'd never had children of their own. They adored Helmut - visited him in the hospital, took him home and cared for him until he was positively identified as the Wolf's nephew. Losing him devastated them."

"And Stahl?"

"I was impressed with his range of knowledge, his devotion to Stassner, and there's one more thing. His patriotism."

"Is he as ruthless as Umberto says?"

"Without casting any negativity on my colleague, I disagree with Umberto's assessment. Stahl's a politician. He prefers persuasion to force. Eisenbach is unscrupulous. Helmut is the ruthless one. But, make no mistake, Holiness, they are loyal to each other. Their enemies fear them and their citizens adore them."

"I must be very careful, then. Thank-you, Nabu."

Nabu got to his feet. "You need a hand up?"

"No, I'll be fine. I've got some praying to do …"

"Let's hope God is listening," Umberto said, interrupting their conversation. He handed Edward an envelope. "It's a communiqué from Norman Wolf. Stahl is flying in emergency supplies and trained personnel."

"How did he ..."

"By invitation of the Italian government. Listen!"

"Choppers, Edward," Nabu said running for the door. Edward and Umberto followed, holding their cassocks above their knees as they bounded down the steps. "There must be twenty of them," Nabu said. "There's no room for them to all land in the square."

From out of the hovering copters, soldiers rappelled into St. Peter's Square. Once on the ground, they maneuvered boxes and crates lowered to the ground on wire cables and stacked them in neat piles.

"Got any water in those boxes, son?" Nabu asked an approaching soldier.

The soldier took a bottle out of his pack and handed it to Nabu, who gave it to Edward. "Edward, please, drink."

"Are you the Pope, Sir?" the soldier asked.

"Yes, I am," Edward said.

The young man knelt and kissed Edward's ring. "Father, whatever you need us to do, we're ready."

"What is your name, son?"

"Corporal Bob Jones from Omaha."

"But your uniform …"

"I'm part of an American training contingent of the Eisenbach Brigade. I volunteered for Operation Vatican."

"Jesus, we have a name already. Olberman will be here shortly," Umberto said.

A black Apache helicopter bearing the insignia of the Fatherland Security Forces was the only one to land. A young man deplaned, and Umberto instantly recognized Helmut. He walked over to the four men, and Jones saluted. "Sir!"

"Corporal, get that generator unloaded and the air conditioner. Father," Helmut said kneeling and kissing Edward's ring," If you'll direct the Corporal to your quarters, we'll get you out of the heat."

"I'll see to it, Holiness," Nabu said.

"The hospitals first, please," Edward implored.

"It's alright, Father, we've brought six and there are more on the way," Helmut said, as Nabu and Jones headed off. "I'm Captain Wolf."

"I know who you are," Edward said.

"We have much to deliver, so the noise will go on for some time, I'm afraid. Sorry. We're making the dispensaries a priority."

Georg came to his side. "Where do you want the porta-potties, Captain?"

"Holiness, we need to assess the situation here. Do we have your permission to do a little snooping?"

"Reconnoitering. I believe they call it."

Helmut laughed. "OK. Georg, make sure you reconnoiter those toilets down wind. We already have enough perfume le disaster."

"Captain Wolf, this is Cardinal Corigliano," Edward said, taken aback by Helmut's aplomb. "My legate."

Helmut offered Umberto his hand, and Umberto shook it for the sake of good manners. It was difficult for him to imagine that the friendly

178

man in front of him was a war criminal.

"It's nice to finally meet you. Teresa and I loved the Villa. We owe our lives to your hospitality."

"The Lord works in mysterious ways," Umberto said. Edward shot him a be-nice, but quizzical, glance.

"May I congratulate you on your marriage, Herr Wolf," Edward said to break the silence.

"Thank-you, Holiness. The Chancellor and the German government send you warmest regards and want you to know we are here to serve in any capacity you request."

"How long will you be staying?" Umberto asked sharply.

"Till the job is done, Eminence."

"We know you have other commitments," Edward said.

"May I be candid, Holiness? Speaking as an engineer, I can tell you reconstruction is going to take a very long time. Construction is my field of expertise. I beg for your prayers and your patience because that is your field of expertise. I hope you will let me do my job with as little interference as I give you in doing your job. Having said that, the job will be done better and faster if I have your cooperation." Helmut stopped for a moment and scanned the area. "I want to rebuild using all the original materials I can salvage from the ruin. And I want you to help me by providing original plans, specs, maps … And also photographs and memories. Chancellor Stahl has made the Vatican a high priority and has committed all the resources needed to accomplish the goal of giving you your holy city back."

"Well … well, thank-you Captain Wolf."

"Job one, Your Holiness, is security, protecting the Church's wealth in all its many forms. The artwork must be crated and stored in temperature-controlled warehouses —that sort of thing. Looting must be prevented along with violence directed at the artisans who are here to care for vestments and statues —that sort of thing. Violence against your person must be prevented, too. Thus, curfews and armed patrols are absolutely necessary. Do you understand what I'm saying?"

"That we're prisoners," Umberto said.

"No. I am saying rules are for everyone, including me." Helmut took a deep breath. "I know that Pope John did not approve of the Repatriation Program. Reasonable men can disagree on the wisdom of any political approach to a problem. But the people I have with me have nothing to do with political decisions. They put themselves in a threatening and unhealthy situation because they love their church, its traditions, and its Holy Father. This is the greatest job they will ever do. They will tell their grandchildren how they rebuilt Rome. And, Cardinal Corigliano, Rome was not built in a day. Excuse me, your Holiness, I have work to do." Helmut gave the men a respectful bow, and joined the men helping to unload supplies. A Cat bulldozer was already clearing space for pre-fabricated buildings, and squads of black uniformed men, like ants, spread themselves out in a ring parallel to the line of Roman police.

Edward and Umberto returned to St. Stephen's, that was now filled with stacks of bottled water, cool air, and the hum of a solar-powered generator. Inside the public restroom was a porta-potty, rolls of unwrapped toilet paper, paper towels and disinfectant hand gel. On Edward's desk sat a basket of citrus fruit and a sack of supplies that included coffee, sugar, and scones, cups, saucers, and spoons. For Umberto, a bottle of brandy, with thank-you note attached, sat in a basket of violets. In the corner was a microwave oven and an apartment sized refrigerator.

Umberto opened the door and pulled out fresh milk. "For the coffee, no doubt," he said, waving it gently. "Want a latte, Edward?"

"Wolf makes it hard to dislike him," Edward said, waving a package of tea-bags back at Umberto.

Umberto nodded towards three fold-away cots leaning against the wall. "The bastard thinks of everything."

Nabu entered, his nose and mouth covered by a filtration mask. He carried a box filled with them and put it on the table, and threw the soot covered one he was wearing in the trashcan beside the desk. "These guys are unbelievable. They've already cleared a road into the complex." He got a bottle of water and went into the bathroom to gargle the soot from his throat. "We have to wear the masks when we're outside," he called out from the bathroom. "That's the rule. Someone tested the air quality and said it was noxious." He returned to the vestibule where Umberto was boiling water for tea. "Helmut said he'd put in a call for more medical personnel, but that he couldn't let them in until the temporary housing facilities are ready. He says they should be here by tomorrow morning."

"You seem impressed with him," Umberto said.

Nabu directed his words to Edward. "He's met with Milan about NATO forces enforcing the curfew in Rome. I don't think Milan's going to want his police officers under foreign control, but oh well …too bad."

Edward opened his desk drawer and placed a purple stole around his neck. "What are you doing," Umberto asked.

"We're fed and watered and safe. It's time we did our job. The injured and the dying need us." Edward put on a filtration mask and headed for the door. Nabu stepped in front of him.

"No, Edward."

Edward motioned him aside and opened the door where he was greeted by three soldiers carrying machine guns. "Are you going to shoot me?" he asked as they barred his way.

"No, Father. But we have orders to restrain you. Curfew began at 1800 hundred, and it's 1803." Edward closed the door.

"Like I said, we're prisoners, Edward," Umberto said. He was pouring water over the tea bags.

"No. We're the living treasures of the Church," Nabu hissed. "That's what Helmut told me when I asked him if the curfew applied to us. He also said that until the streets were safe again, we could watch what was happening on the TV. And if you weren't so blinded by your hatred, Umberto, you might just realize he's protecting us. I overheard his argument with Milan, who wants to evacuate us, forcibly if necessary. You know what he told Milan? Were Pope Edward to beg me to take him to San Rafael, I would remind him of his duty to stay." Nabu threw his water bottle in the trashcan. "What do you think all the niceties are for?"

Edward removed the stole from his neck, folded it, and put it back in the drawer. "Help me, Nabu," he said. The two men set up the cots to provide seating. Nabu figured out how to plug the 13-inch TV into the generator while Umberto scrounged around in the supply sacks for something to eat. "When does curfew end? Can we go out and help in the morning?" Edward asked Nabu.

"We'd just be in the way. He said to give it a few days."

182

"I guess so from the looks of the news footage," Umberto said, turning up the sound on the TV. A dark-haired woman was standing in front of a C-131 airplane transport at Italy's Leonardo Da Vinci airport. Behind her, a never-ending stream of men in the now-familiar black uniforms of the Homeland Security Forces marched out of the plane and boarded shuttle trucks.

*This is the second contingent of Germany's combined NATO and Fatherland Security Forces to land today. Like the fifteen hundred men before them, these men are on there way into Rome to help Chief of Police Federico Milan quell the rioting that has rolled over the city in waves following Sunday's terrorist attack on the Vatican.*

The screen switched to a montage of film clips of the aftermath of the explosions in St. Peter's Square as the reporter continued.

*You're looking at Sunday's ten o'clock horror when thousand of Pope John twenty-fourth's well wishers ran in panic to get out of the Square. Chief Milan and his Roman police were soon overwhelmed.*

It was the first time the Catholic Prelates had actually seen the extent of the damage and the rioting. They sat riveted as the film footage switched to clips of Helmut's chopper landing, the unloading, and the many small units responsible for each segment of rescue: nurses and doctors treating the injured, soldiers handing our water, and donning riot gear.

*The death toll so far is estimated at one hundred thousand, but search and rescue efforts have changed to search and recovery on the orders of this man, Helmut Wolf, who arrived today in a*

*dramatic exhibition of his terror-attack response called blitzretten.*
*Developed in response to the Paris attack, the blitzretten force has*
*perfected its methods and increased it resources to insure that*
*every country in Europe receives swift and efficient assistance*
*whenever its people are attacked. All NATO countries have gotten*
*involved, but this is the first real test of multinational cooperation*
*in the war on terror rescue forces.*

The screen now showed Stahl welcoming Franklin, Howe and Yeshenko
at Malta.

*Just days before the attack the Big Four sat down at Malta to*
*discuss the world's terror problem. Russia, last to come on board,*
*greeted his fellow national leaders and told Stahl Russia would be*
*sending ten thousand soldiers for training at the German anti-*
*terrorist school in Marburg.*

The big shock came when Cardinal Chu's face appeared on screen,
announcing the elections of the new Pope, followed by archival film
footage of Edward at the investiture of John XXIV, and an enlarged
London Times newspaper picture of him as a new Cardinal.

*Though the world mourned the death of beloved John twenty-*
*fourth, the Church gave the world hope just two days after the*
*attack with the election of only the second British pope in history.*
*Edward Cardinal Hugh, was elected on the first ballot by a super*
*majority vote that took place inside St. Stephen's Chapel. The*
*building, though ravaged by bombs, still stands as does the*
*continuity of Church leadership, said Cardinal Chu, who made the*
*announcement from the garden of Villa San Rafael, a place of*

*refuge for the older churchmen. The white smoke told the tale and was greeted with Viva Papa! around the world.*

Edward fought back tears as he watched Catholics from Rio to Reykjavik, from Detroit to Dresden cheer the announcement that the new Pope was still in the Eternal City. The news story continued with pictures of Helmut and Teresa saying good-bye at the train station, and then of Helmut's giving the young woman his insignia.

*The new Pope and his closest advisors, Umberto Corigliano and Philipe Nabu remain in the Vatican complex under the protection of Helmut Wolf who left new wife, Teresa, in the care of her mother in Vienna.*

"The love affair of the century," Umberto said.

"Yes, between the media and this boy," Edward said. "But while we're busy condemning him, he's out rationalizing tragedy and bringing boys like Jones from Omaha to Rome to do good deeds. If I didn't know better, I'd believe I was a hero just for staying put."

Nabu turned down the sound but couldn't take his eyes away from the screen. The news channel was running a special on the History of the Repatriation Program and he wanted information.

# CHAPTER X

## The Game's Afoot on Day Two

Helmut's "Wolf Pack" borrowed its name from WWII German submariners but was modeled on the US Army Cops of Engineers. Recruited from European and American universities, these men formed an elite cadre of field science officers within the Eisenbach Brigade whose job it was, as Helmut described it, to "move heaven and earth to solve problems".

No man can be a good engineer, Helmut believed, who is not also a student of history and art. Saving Western Civilization required a fundamental understanding of the characteristics that defined it, and the most important facet of those characteristics was the marriage of the ideal with the real. It's the difference between a sand castle and a Gothic cathedral, he thought. They are both beautiful and man-made, they are both symbols of man-made institutions of church and state, but only one endures.

These Islamofascists wrongly believe that destroying the edifices of Western culture can destroy the spirit and the will of that culture. But if they studied ancient history, they would see that the pyramids still stand in spite of the culture that produced them, not because of it. Whereas every stone creation in Europe could be knocked down, and their passing would only inspire the children of Da Vinci to rebuild them.

This is true, according to Helmut, because of what he referred to as the "technological tipping point". That was the day the marriage of the ideal and the real was consummated: July 20, 1969 when Neil Armstrong stepped onto the moon.

From then on, all other cultures became mere entertainment, interesting diversions like the animals in the zoo, rather than Darwinian competitors. Whatever innate talent individuals in those cultures had, they would only be viable within the context of the Western methodology. Only to the extent that individuals, communities and countries employed that methodology, would they prosper.

If Western culture had a psychological failing, it was guilt for its success in providing the greatest good for the greatest number. Even China, once it adopted Western methodology, was able to feed its billion and half people three times a day and still have a surplus. If Western culture had a philosophic failing, it was insisting that science and religion are not compatible. Religion was not an alternative, compartmentalized aberration of the weak. It was the goal — the apprehension of the absolute —that science served. God, the eternal spirit makes man, and man reaches out to spirit while in the confines of time and space. Wasn't this understood by the ancient Greeks? Considering he started with nothing, he has done much in a short time relative to the time of space.

"Herr Wolf," Helmut's philosophy teacher told him, "You are indeed a product of your culture. If ever there was a modern Hegelian, you are he."

The comment pleased Helmut though, admittedly, Hegel did misstep. He believed that the Prussian state was flower of Western culture rather than the seed. But I know, Helmut thought, there is no one flower, but untold billions of blossoms. Every breath is a beginning of a process, every day a rebirth, a chance to learn, worship and admire.

"When I can look at a picture painted five hundred years before I was born, knowing that image will be seen by eyes five hundred years from now, I know the culture that created that possibility is onto something," he told Madeline the day they visited the Sistine Chapel. That was the day Madeline really began to change, before El Capitan.

"Stay here, I think I dropped my address book in the Chapel," she said as they walked out into the sun. "I have to go back." When she retuned, she was different. Subdued. Drinking lattes at the Café Excelsior, she barely looked at him.

"Maddie, where are you?" he said. "I was talking about the paintings. Which postcard do you want?"

"Yes, of course," she said, "I was just thinking about them too." She took her wallet out of her purse.

"Is this one on you?"

"Yeah, I'll get this one." She walked to the register and he knew she wanted to be alone. She had that far-away glaze in her eyes, the glaze he had seen in the eyes of the dying at the hospice his sociology class visited.

"Are you OK?" he asked when she came back to the table.

"I love you," she replied.

"I love you too, Maddie. What brought this on?"

"*Casablanca.*"

That's when he knew she was leaving him. Though they had two more vacations and three more years of college ahead of them, she was going to leave. Eventually, all he would have would be memories. Paintings last five hundred years, but each person's life is so short he has to fill it up with what is most important to him and him alone. Other people are just fellow travelers.

Helmut remembered their visit as he surveyed the ruins of the Sistine Chapel. Hunks of colored stone, like puzzle pieces, lay in a heap at his feet along with broken wood and torn cloth. "What do you think, Georg. Can we put Humpty-Dumpty back together again?"

"If it can be done, the Wolf Pack will do it."

"Let's walk around this bad boy and see what we have." The men headed off to the right to circle the ruins. "How we doin' on crowd control?"

"It's a hell of a lot easier without people shooting at us," Georg said.

"Amen."

"The first night is always the toughest. People don't really believe we'll shoot looters on sight. But, after a few are named on the TV news, people get the message," Georg said. "You remember how that goes."

"How many did you have to shoot?"

"Twenty. Milan's not happy, but he's cooperating."

"I wouldn't want my forces under foreign command. How'd the meeting go?"

"He agrees the people who did the Excelsior bombing are responsible for the Vatican blasts."

Helmut stopped. A blood-stained handkerchief was wedged between two pieces of stone. "Bag that, Georg. It may have belonged to someone's loved one." Georg put on a pair of latex gloves, carefully pulled out the handkerchief, and put it in a plastic bag. "Milan's wrong," Helmut continued. "These guys don't do overtures. They go straight to the finale. St. Basil's, St. Peter's – these guys are attacking Christian shrines not hotels."

"What about Paris?"

"The Eiffel Tower is the closest the French have to a modern church. Notre Dame be damned, they venerate themselves."

"I get it. Like the World Trade Center was a cathedral of St. Capitalism."

"That's what I'm thinking," Helmut said. "Did Milan say anything worth repeating about the Excelsior bombing? Have they identified the DNA of that Jane Doe?"

"Let's get some water, Helmut. I gotta get some of this soot out of my eyes."

They went to a water station - a tent with a few tables and chairs, and stacks of bottled water. Georg peeled of the gloves after putting the bagged handkerchief in the freezer, and put them in a hazardous waste bin with his dust mask. Helmut removed his mask, and both men washed their hands, and sponged their faces with warm water. Georg got water and juice from the refrigerator for them and joined Helmut who was now seated by the door, his legs propped up on small stool.

"I went to my appointment to talk to Milan about security like you ordered," Georg said. "He immediately started in again on how the highest prelates of the church belonged at the villa. I said it was a dead issue and that's when things turned odd. He said the Holy Father should stay, but that Corigliano should be allowed to go to his villa, that the Pope still had Nabu there to wait on him. I just told him to take it up with you, I was only there to tell him we're going to extend our perimeter around the Vatican complex to include the tent morgues. He threw a fit." Helmut nodded. "I knew he'd give us grief over that, Capt'n, but it's kinder in the long run. You don't need a whole body for ID, just a tissue sample and they take up a helluva less freezer space. Lord, don't these people realize the danger of disease - I'm sorry. It's the frustration talking. I suppose it's hard for people to have their loved ones buried in a pit without a service."

"It would be harder to see them exploding like grenades," Helmut said. "We'll build them a memorial like we did in Paris. Send some specs to Rudolph and tell him to get started on the design. His Arab friend can help. So, go on."

"Milan got called out of the office by some irate citizen who was pissed because the curfew made him miss his mistress' birthday and he had to stay the night with his wife. I glanced at his calendar. He had Corigliano's name written down for a nine AM meeting."

"Meaning he met with our friend Umberto before he met with you. Interesting." Helmut scratched his chin "He could just want to get out of this hell-hole. I got the feeling he doesn't like Edward much, either. I'll ask my Uncle if Umberto had expectations of wearing the miter."

"When I asked him for an update on the Excelsior, he said the entire investigation was on hold because of the Vatican bombing, including the DNA testing. He wants the labs to concentrate their efforts on identifying the loved ones of Roman citizens."

"He's right, damn it. You know, if we clear out morgue one, we could widen the road into the complex, and let that big dozer in, Georg."

"The problem is what to do with the bodies. We can't dig pits anywhere around here. We'll fuck up the catacombs or electricity cables – and I'm real iffy about loading bodies up in plain sight to take them out of town."

"We'll have to do it at night, then. Get a few platoons some safety suits and gas masks. Tell 'em to pretend their loading fertilizer. I want that first morgue cleared by morning. When do we get the cadaver dogs?"

"Rudolph said they're on their way." Georg looked at his watch. "Should be at the airport anytime. Are you letting Umberto go to his villa?"

"Yeah, if he asks me, the ungrateful son-of-a-bitch."

"Don't be so hard on him. He may not be as healthy as he looks."

I know why he wants out, Helmut thought, we've confiscated every cell phone and tapped every phone line. He can't contact Norman, and he's got big news. I'll force him to come to me. He will, too, when he's scared enough. "I'll think about it," he said.

*** 

Umberto was not ungrateful. When he got the pathologist's report from Milan, identifying the second body at the excelsior, he knew Madeline was alive, somewhere. He also figured Helmut knew too, and that meant Helmut suspected he and Norman were involved in the Excelsior bombing. There could be only one reason why Helmut wasn't confronting them. He wanted to get enough information to hang them all, including Fritz Pomeranz.

And yet … what had he done wrong? Questioned Madeline's vocation? That was his job as a responsible prelate of the church. Arranged for Madeline to have a chance to see Helmut? Of course, he had to respect her wishes and her privacy. It wasn't his responsibility to talk with her parents. She was a grown woman, and if she didn't want to

192

contact anyone it was her business. He had valid reasons for helping her evaluate her vocation before entering her novitiate.

But Norman was a different story. He had no cover. There was no way to hide his role in a plot to derail the Christian Nationalists. What if he and Pomeranz had masterminded an assassination attempt? Just because Pomeranz denied it didn't make it so. Assassins are likely to be liars too.

He eyed Edward entering the Chapel and debated about telling him the story. The worst that could happen is that Edward would require him to tell Helmut about his part in Madeline's sudden appearance… and disappearance. He could probably convince Edward to attend his confession. Helmut wouldn't scandalize the Church. With the Holy Father on his side, Helmut would protect him. Edward might even give cover to Norman if he knew his good intentions.

"I know it was wrongheaded, Edward, but you know we did it for the Church. You know how John hated E'tat de Guerre and everything the Christian Nationalists stand for. We thought it was a way to bring down the Party without violence. We never thought the plan would blow up." Umberto searched Edward's eyes for a sign of understanding if not appreciation for his torment. "You can see that, can't you?"

"How do you know Madeline's alive? What DNA did the lab have to compare the sample with?"

"It wasn't DNA that proved the woman in the room wasn't Madeline. It was the blood. It was type O. Madeline was A+. The convent has her medical records. I reviewed her file when I went to speak with her."

"Looking for evidence she wasn't a virgin, I suspect." Edward knelt down and said a short prayer, and rested his head in his hands, deep in thought. When he resumed his seat, he spoke to Umberto without looking at him. "For your penance, you have to contact Madeline's parents at once. Perhaps she has contacted them, though I doubt it, if neither you nor Mother Ignatius have heard from them. And, of course, you'll have to talk to Wolf. Tell him you've talked to me, and that I told you to wait for the lab report. Tell him you wanted to give her time to work things out, but now you're alarmed now that you know for certain she didn't die at the Excelsior. Whether Wolf talked to Madeline or not, he's going to find out about your involvement eventually."

"And Norman? The Center Socialists?"

"You tell me this when the Germans have been on Vatican soil for two weeks? What were you waiting for, for Wolf to tell me right before he leads you away in handcuffs?" Edwards's voice was low and calm, but his hands shook with anger. "I'm relieving you of all your legate duties. Stay away from Norman, the Center Socialists and politics in general. Do you understand, Umberto? The Church is not about assassinations of reputations, of young novitiates or political opponents."

"Yes, Your Holiness." Each of Edward's words was a stone added to a necklace of regret for having taken the Holy Father into his confidence. He had not asked for forgiveness, only advice. He was of no use to the Church outside his diplomatic role, he thought. How long would it take for Edward to see that?

"Send one of our protectors outside for Wolf. We'll meet with him as soon as we can. And tell Nabu I want to talk with him. God willing, he doesn't have any nasty secrets for me."

Umberto stood up, surprised that his knees showed no sign of weakness after such bad news. "He wants to see you," he said to Nabu.

"Are we leaving for San Rafael?"

"No. I don't think that's on the agenda." Umberto opened the front door, and Mabu heard him say, "Get Wolf. We need to speak with him."

The name Wolf made Nabu put down his pen, close the ledger he was working on, and hurry into the Chapel. "Edward, what's going on?"

"Sit down, Nabu. I need you to be honest with me. Do you know anything about this Madeline Churchill business?"

"No, Sir. I don't. I've never even heard the name before."

"I need to know if John knew of any measures that were being taken against the German government, any initiatives to curb the rise of the Christian Nationalists ... anything at all. Because I want you to meet with Umberto, and me, and Wolf and assure him unequivocally that there were no plans in the Vatican to in any way influence the government or anyone who worked in the government. Do you understand what I'm telling you?"

"Holiness, I know John hated the Repatriation Program. He hated it more than you can imagine because he felt it was killing any chance of bringing Muslim people into the Christian fold. He thought, in time, they would come to know Christ through the good-will of their Christian neighbors. He prayed for that. But he would never have involved himself in the political activities of the German people to hasten that end. As his best friend, you should know that."

Umberto opened the Chapel door and whispered, "Wolf is here, Your Holiness." Edward and Nabu joined them in the vestibule. When Helmut knelt to kiss the papal ring, Edward embraced him and pulled him

195

up. "No, this is business, Captain Wolf. Please sit down. I'm addressing you as the representative of a sovereign state, not as your spiritual father."

"Alright," Helmut said. The two men sat opposite each other, the black and white of their respective costumes matching the intensity of their impending negotiations. Umberto's confession was short, punctuated by his giving Helmut the doctor's report that Milan had given him. "It wasn't as sinister as you might think," Umberto said. "Your Uncle Norman was sure that you were in love with Madeline. So sure. I did him a favor, that's all. When the hotel was bombed, we didn't know what to do. We wanted to ascertain if she was alive or dead before we mistepped again."

Helmut said nothing.

"Captain Wolf, you've done great things here. I'll be the first to admit that the Italian government needed your assistance, and I needed your assistance. Every time I look outside and see how quickly your men have been able to render aid and comfort to thousands of people, I am overwhelmed. You have youth and training on your side. We have tradition and, hopefully, wisdom, on ours." Edward gave Umberto a searing glare. "I want to assure the German government, that despite the nonsense perpetrated on you and your wife, we are grateful to Chancellor Stahl for making it possible for the Vatican to retain its sovereignty in the midst of so great a catastrophe. We ask your forbearance. We will do everything we can to find Ms. Churchill, and to restore her to her family or to her convent —whatever is her choice."

Helmut looked at Nabu. "And you, what do you have to say about this?"

"The Holy Father asked me if Pope John had any part in this. I can assure you he did not, Captain Wolf. Interference with governments of other countries was not something he practiced, or approved of, by any of his staff."

"I'll convey your regards to Chancellor Stahl, Your Holiness. Your candor has cleared up some questions he has – that his child and future son-in-law could have been the targets of an assassination attempt caused him much worry, as I'm sure you can understand. I'm sure we can put this behind us as soon as we discover who was behind the plot. If it was neither my Uncle nor the Cardinal, then it might be some Muslim faction that may have Madeline captive.'

"Oh, my God, I never considered that!" Umberto blurted.

"There has to be some reason she hasn't answered our phone calls if she's alive. Either she can't or doesn't want to, though from what I know about her, she wouldn't hurt her parents this way."

Nabu raised his hand tentatively. "May I offer another explanation for the can't?'

"Yes, please," Helmut said eagerly.

"It could be she was in the hotel, and the blast didn't kill her, but injured her, affected her memory maybe. Say, from a concussion."

Helmut contemplated the idea. "It could be she's lost. It's a dangerous position to be in, but less dangerous than being kidnapped by terrorists. Cardinal Corigliano, why don't you contact her parents and tell them we think she's gone missing and ask them for a photograph that we can add to the wall."

"The wall?"

"That's right, you don't know, Holiness. Relatives of the missing have posted their photographs and contact numbers on the fence separating the Vatican complex from Rome. Such a tragic testimony to evil deeds. I expect you will want to continue your duties as part of the search for her, Cardinal Corigliano."

"Absolutely. We must find her, poor girl," Umberto said.

"I know my Uncle has come to depend upon your dedication and expertise. My suggestion is that you go directly to the Villa and contact Ambassador Wolf about the developments in the Churchill case. That is, if His Holiness can spare you. Holiness, I beg your permission to tell my Uncle of Corigliano's continued efforts to nurture the relationship between the Vatican and the German government."

Umberto's eyes pleaded with Edward. "What shall Captain Wolf tell his Uncle, Your Holiness?" he said.

Edward, shook his head in disbelief. "Such ardent desire to work for the common good cannot be thwarted by someone so insignificant as I," he said. "Call your Uncle, Captain Wolf, and tell him Cardinal Corigliano is still Papal Legate to Germany, though why it should be so, I do not know."

*\*\**

Stephan Stahl proved himself up to the task of bringing the Russian government on board with the Repatriation Program. The biggest hurdles were replacement labor for President Yeshenko's Muslim workforce, and Russia's insistence that Germany pledge not to interfere with recovery of Russia's lost province of Chechnya.

Once the repatriation plan was in place, Stahl assured Yeshenko, Chechnya would by purged of Muslim resistance, making a vote to rejoin the Motherland a certainty. And as for labor shortages, China had expressed strong desires for a guest worker program that would relieve some of its unemployment woes. Moreover, China had already agreed that all guest workers would be Christians, learn Russian, and would not settle permanently west of the Ural Mountains. A communiqué from Beijing confirmed Stahl's offer.

The coup for Stahl, however, was the oil investment agreement between the EU, Russia and China. "Within five years," Stahl predicted, "All of Eurasia will be oil independent of the mid-East. Then let them see how much sand the world will want to buy from terrorist nations."

Barely coping with the repatriation of Europe's 13.1 million Muslins, the mid-Eastern nations now buckled under the prospect of the repatriation of Russia's 1.6 million. Even before the historic photographs of signing the Malta Accords, as they were called, were published, Muslins around the world demonstrated in the streets. Stahl, Franklin, King William, and Yeshenko were burned in effigy, their national flags dragged through the dirt by machine-gun mounted jeeps. In Detroit, over one thousand protestors were arrested and held for repatriation through E'tat de Guerre. In New York, another thousand were incarcerated at Ellis Island to begin their trip across the Atlantic. Franklin's approval ratings jumped to 80%. When London police rounded up fifteen hundred protestors, and notified their families to make preparation for repatriation, verses of *Onward Christian Soldiers* wafted out of every pub. Volunteer guards stood 24-hour duty around Buckingham Palace and Trafalgar Square, as people carried signs reading God Save The King.

199

It was an outpouring of relief and devotion Pope Edward could not ignore.

***

The loading was slow going. The bags were dead weight, stuffed full with random body parts and tissue. The men had to be careful that the bags didn't split open. The smell had dissipated somewhat in the tents as dead flesh was put in the bags. The men wanted no mistakes. A busted bag would release the stench of week-old rotten meat, and that meant cleaning up the puke of an entire platoon as well as carcasses. The unloading was quicker. The dump-truck backed up to the pit and dropped its payload, then headed back through Rome for another load. By three AM, tent one was disinfected and drying. Tent two was half empty and the men still had four hours till the curfew ended.

"With any luck, Sir," Jones told Georg, "We'll have enough room in tent two for two hundred fifty more bags."

"With that big dozer we won't have to worry about bags, soldier. We clear out some of the rubble, and we'll be able to load the dead directly into the truck."

"But the identification, Sir…"

"They waited too long to let us come in. Delay has consequences, Jones, water contamination especially. We have to get these corpses out of here."

"Yes, Sir. I understand."

There wasn't even a pretense of identifying the dead now. Loved ones who never returned were assumed to be in the mass graves outside Rome where Helmut erected an asymmetrical stone monument to the

Unknown Martyrs etched with the all of the names submitted to Milan. One by one the photographs on the fence disappeared as families came to realize the situation was hopeless. Eventually, even Madeline Churchill's photograph was removed. Helmut took it and put it with his other important papers.

***

On day sixty, Edward opened the door to St. Stephen's ready to greet his guards, but they were gone. He stepped into the glistening sun, slowly removing his face mask, and listened to the doves that had already returned to reconstruct their nests. "This troubles me, Nabu" he said to the man standing next to him.

"Why? It looks like the Germans have made miraculous progress. The air is breathable and the porta-potties are gone."

"Yes, it seems Herr Wolf has brought peace to Europe again, but at what cost? Can it really be the case that Stahl is right? That the only way to protect Europe is to rid the world of Islam?"

Both men had seen the morning news heralding the Malta Conference as a major breakthrough in the war on terror. The Big Four had reached an agreement that put Stephan Stahl in charge of the world's Muslin Problem. Just as the Mid-east countries were to be overwhelmed with repatriated Muslims, their economies that depended on selling energy to the Western nations, India and China were jeopardized with the agreement to develop Russian oil fields. It was possible that shortly millions of repatriated people would be starving to death with no *blitzretten* to assist them, and millions more would follow them into eternity in the next five years.

"Many people would have died without Stahl's help, Holiness. His paternalism is brutal, but without it I cringe to think what cholera would have done to the Eternal City," Nabu said.

"Is the key to civilization working toilets? My God, life cannot be that simple."

"Not simple, Holiness, tenuous."

"Why have libraries? Why have Universities?"

"Because cisterns are only the beginning —necessary but hardly sufficient."

"What do I do now, Nabu? When do I start to exert moral authority? Before or after Wolf rebuilds St. Peter's?"

"People understand, Edward. They know you aren't a worldly leader, but a spiritual one. Your job is helping them bear their grief and getting them ready for the next world. It's not up to you to give infallible answers to political problems or rebuild a basilica with your own hands. "

"The popes of antiquity made no excuses for their temporal power. They managed to build beautiful structures full of beautiful art. We in the twenty-first century can't even protect the structures, let alone rebuild them."

"They had a different sensibility, Holiness."

"That's my point. They would have helped Stahl, welcomed Wolf, and taken their own reprisals on Muslims, driven them out of Europe the way Spain expelled them and the Jews. They defended what they considered to be holy and would never have stood here, as I do now, jealous that I cannot wave my hand and do what this talented, relentless

202

boy has done. He bends his knee, kisses my ring, and then cleans the streets, feeds the hungry, buries the dead – all works of mercy – not for one or two, but for thousands while I watch television and drink tea."

"No good would have come from you trying to do what it took an army to do. Catholic peoples need you to live for Christ in desperate times."

"You are kind, Nabu."

"Realistic, Holiness."

Their tranquility was interrupted by the sound of shoes running on stone. A young boy ran towards them carrying a newspaper. Breathless, he bowed and said, "For you, Papa," and then ran back towards the perimeter gate across the square. Nabu handed Edward the paper shaking his head in disbelief. "Mussolini made the trains run on time. Wolf gets us fresh milk and the daily paper in the middle of catastrophe."

Edward opened the paper and read the headline. Frau Wolf was pregnant and making a visit to Rome to see her husband. A full-color photo of Helmut greeting her at the airport accompanied the good news. If there was evidence that Helmut had successfully secured Vatican City, this was it, Edward thought. He and Nabu could walk leisurely in St. Peter's Square now because German soldiers and German tanks patrolled the streets outside. German planes continued to bring in fresh supplies, medical equipment, and bullets, and Italian police and administrators continued to obey German orders.

"The world is waiting for your words, Holiness," Helmut told him as he sat in the vestibule of St. Stephen's. "Use your time to choose them carefully." Helmut provided a diagram of the speaker's dais that he'd erected in the square and reminded the Pontiff that the world's media would cover his first public address.

Edward would eulogize John and offer a message of hope to the relatives of the dead. He would offer hope and reconciliation to the Muslim world too, but would he condemn E'tat de Guerre? Would he denounce the regime that so nimbly brought order and relief to the devastated people of Rome?

"You must assume a tactful position, Holiness," Nabu counseled. "It wouldn't sit well with German Catholics if the Pope bit the hand that fed him, especially now. Wolf has found that portion of the Sistine Chapel that showed God giving life the Adam and has displayed it for veneration at the grave of the Unknown Martyrs in a temperature-controlled glass case."

The mere sight of the masterpiece calmed the crowds. Thousands filed past it. Thousands more gathered before it to say the evening rosary with black cassocked priests helping black uniformed soldiers dole out sandwiches, bottled water and juice for the children. Civilian clean-up crews, mostly young people, picked up trash, and assisted the elderly as the monument blossomed into a shrine complete with reported miracle cures of the sick and the dying.

The church had not been able to organize self-sacrifice on such a scale in the last hundred years, Edward admitted. He could not let Germany's assistance go unthanked no matter how dangerous he believed Stahl's regime to be.

As for Helmut, he won the gratitude of the Italian people, and when Teresa Jean knelt at his side to lead a decade of the rosary, she conquered their affections as well.

"Have you heard Wolf protected a Muslim family from the crowd last night, Holiness?" Nabu said as he and Edward stood at the gate and watched a crew of white uniformed medics administer tetanus shots to another batch of citizens. "He's sending them to E'tat de Guerre."

"Does Milan know?"

"There's been no formal protest, if that's what you mean," Nabu said. "It could be a PR stunt, I suppose."

"Nabu, I need to talk privately to Corigliano and Norman Wolf. How do I do that?"

"Not easily. But I'll see what I can do."

***

At Villa San Rafael the Cardinals had settled into a relaxed monastic life-style. Relieved of administrative duties, they spent their days doing light maintenance and gardening, and reading and contemplation in the evening. Umberto quickly immersed himself in diplomatic pursuits, mostly gathering information on the German occupation of Vatican City for the International Court. He soon arranged for Norman to visit the villa. Suspecting their phones were tapped, they made no mention of the Churchill affair after discussing the blood type test or the IC except to each other in private places. Their first opportunity to discuss the situations, then, was in the olive garden.

"Short of a civil war, there's no way to assassinate Stahl's Cabal," Umberto said using Pomeranz's moniker for the regime. "The IC is useless."

Norman didn't wince at the word as he had months earlier. Already in Berlin there was talk of making Stahl Kaiser, having all the prerogatives of a dictator, but with a kinder, gentler title, one that could be inherited by Helmut Wolf. "Well, we'd have to get every last one of them or there'd be a bloodbath. Oh, it's insanity. No one is strong enough to suppress the panic and the rioting that would follow a coup d'etat. Pomeranz knows that we have to have the people behind us."

Umberto broke off a branch and popped a ripe olive into his mouth. "That Olberman's a marketing genius. All those women drooling over Helmut, and now he's proved he's the world's stud too."

"It's Eisenbach," Norman said.

"Eisenbach wouldn't lay a hand on Teresa Wolf."

"No, you idiot. I mean Eisenbach's behind this marriage and family product Olberman's branding. I know it." Norman broke off a branch for himself and sat back against the tree. Halfway through his first olive, the two men suddenly looked at each other with the same wise eyes.

"He's the key," Umberto whispered. "I'll lay odds he knows where Churchill is."

"Sequestered in some unfathomable place until Helmut can safely visit her, no doubt," Norman said, continuing Umberto's line of thinking.

"Do you think Helmut knows where she is, Norman?"

Norman shrugged. "Hitler kept Eva Braun under wraps. Few German's knew the true nature of their affair."

"Then maybe there *is* a way to bring down the house that Stephan built. If we could prove that Eisenbach and Helmut conspired to secret a mistress from the saintly Teresa, Stahl would have them both shot."

"You're wrong about that, Umberto. Stahl would never sacrifice Germany for his daughter's pride. But the German people might see the tarnish on their golden boy and send him packing on the train to destruction. The question is, how do we prove it, assuming we're right about Eisenbach and Churchill?"

"Do we have to prove anything? One leak to the press…."

"The papers won't touch the story till after the baby comes. Even then, Olberman's got a lock on propaganda. But if the Holy Father told the press …"

"We can't involve the Holy See, Norman. Edward's a good man. Not politically savvy, but a good man. No character assassination allowed. I'll not make the mistake of confiding in him again, however."

***

Twenty miles away from Rome, Madeline Churchill hung freshly laundered sheets on the clothesline outside the back door of the Villa San Raphael kitchen. Like other young people from around the world, she had volunteered to help the Church recover from the terrorist attack. She knew how to cook for a hundred people and how to run a clean kitchen. She knew how to scrub and how to care for the elderly. In the chaos that followed the attack, her convent skills made her Captain Wolf's first choice to oversee the care and feeding of the Cardinals. After all, she was already at the Villa San Rafael – as someone else.

"What name do you want on her passport," Emil had asked Helmut as they planned Madeline's new life as his mistress.

"Helen Crabtree."

Emil had laughed. "Are you serious?"

"Half of a soap company. Evelyn and Crabtree. Not only will we hide her in plain sight, we'll give her a nanny's uniform and a name that sounds so British, no one will suspect her of anything."

"Helen" fell in love with the Villa the moment she drove through the back roads that connected the olive grove, orchard, and vineyards with the gardens that surrounded the main house. "You'll be comfortable, Signora Crabtree," the agent told her. "Many artists take these villa cottages for the summer. They're private, and," he said as an aside, "They produce income for the estate."

"I have no doubt I'll love the place, Sir."

"The kitchen is stocked. The phone won't be connected for another three or four weeks —if ever."

"I have a cell phone. It's no problem."

As they spoke, two locals unloaded her trunk, easel and canvases. She tipped them a five each, and they flirted with her shamelessly. She was pale and thin, but Helmut promised her, she'd be brown and healthy in no time. By that he means plump, she told herself, as she stared at her sunken breasts in the mirror. She turned out the lights and sat outside in a wicker rocking chair.

She and Helmut had spoken so briefly, just long enough for her to realize she would have to be content with stolen moments for the rest of her life. It was good enough, she tried to convince herself. She knew Helmut did love her. Emil had promised her a new life with ties to no one except Helmut, and she'd accepted the bargain. Sister Clare and Madeline Churchill were simply former incarnations.

"Do you know who owns this villa?" Helmut had asked her as they lay in each other's arms. "Cardinal Corigliano."

"Oh, shit, Helmut. The poor man would die if he knew he'd taken me from a convent to his own villa."

"He'll die if anyone *but* him knows. And it serves him right."

"He thinks he's doing the right thing."

"Sabotaging western culture is not doing the right thing. Fighting Stahl's efforts to rid the world of Islamofacism is not doing the right thing."

"Committing adultery is not doing the right thing."

"I'm not married yet."

"And when you are?"

"I'll think of you always. And I'll find a way to be with you if it takes every waking minute of my life and every dime I have." They made love again before Helmut rinsed off in cold water, pulled on his jogging shorts and his tennis shoes, and sprinted back to Teresa at the main house.

After the bombing, it seemed natural for a young British nanny-turned-art-student to help unload the Cardinals from the helicopter and ensure they were properly wined and dined. "You are truly an angle," Cardinal Chu said as she served them hot soup and told them they had fresh linen on their beds.

"The Italian government has instructed me to take good care of you, Your Eminence." Chu took her hand to shake it, she thought, but instead he kissed it and started to cry.

"I'm too old for this heartache," he said as Helen grabbed a napkin from the table and wiped his eyes. "We're all too old. How can we die in peace? It's all gone. Rome is aflame. You've heard the sirens."

"I've seen the white smoke too. We have a new Pope, and I swear to you, help is on the way," Helen assured him.

"You're here. Our angel," Chu said.

"Yes, you're here, Angel."

Helen looked up and saw a short young man with powerful shoulders and long, thick, black eye lashes that framed big black eyes. A small gold cross lay on his smooth brown skin. Under his arm, he carried a side of freshly slaughtered ribs wrapped in a blood-soaked towel. His other hand held a green wine bottle and a ball of provolone cheese. She put a finger to her lips to silence him. He broke into a naughty- boy grin and headed towards the kitchen. She followed him, watched him put the wine bottle on the table, and then open the freezer door. He put the meat on a hanger, closed the door and walked back to her.

"Umberto here?" he asked Chu.

"No. But he'll be here soon, I'm sure. Thank-you Helen, I'm going to bed now." Chu stood up on wobbly legs.

"Helen, hunh?" the man said when Chu had shuffled out of the room. "I'm Guiseppe…Joe to you. You're the artist chick who rented one of the cottages."

"I've been put in charge of housekeeping now. These Holy Men need care."

"Holy Men? OK. You're a believer."

"What do you do here, Joe? Besides being a smart mouth."

"I do the shit work for the unholy man who owns this place."

"Well, Joe, my orders came from Chief of Police Milan. Until I hear otherwise, I'll assume you work for me, until Umberto gets here. So take your muddy shoes and get out."

"Yes, Maam. Until Umberto gets here, I'll do anything you want me to, that is, if it's OK with your boyfriend."

210

"I don't have a boyfriend."

"Husband?"

"No."

"Good."

In many ways Joe was like Helmut, Helen thought. Arrogant, cruel, and harsh. Yet, when he was around her, he seemed as soft as lamb's wool. They soon worked out a work schedule, toured the Villa's vintage and olive presses, and spent many hours talking marketing strategies. They would turn Villa San Rafael around financially, they decided, making charts and graphs and doing internet research. For an art student, Helen did little painting. And their first kiss took place in Joe's beat up blue pick-up truck under the shade of an olive tree. It was dispassionate, almost an afterthought as Joe was getting out of the truck to talk to a pressman who had hunted him down to report the Germans were patrolling the streets of Rome, but it was comfortable.

Cardinal Chu had said Umberto was coming, so letting Joe into her cottage and into her bed seemed like a good strategy. Umberto had never really seen her, even at the convent. She had never looked him in the eye. Diverting one's gaze from others was one of the first things a postulant learned. And her veil covered most of her hair. She doubted he would recognize her, and he wouldn't suspect a British volunteer who was having an affair with the villa's lothario as being anyone but a naïve tourist. Would her accent give her away, she wondered? "If you don't sing it, Italians don't listen," Helmut had told her. "Corigliano never heard a word you said." What would Helmut think about her taking Joe into her bed so soon after he married Teresa, she wondered as well. She pushed her mental meanderings aside, just as the convent had trained her to do.

By the time Helmut's copter landed in Vatican Square, Helen was already in her second trimester. Humbly, she explained to Joe how her faithless boyfriend in England deserted her, and Joe did the honorable thing. He married Helen Crabtree. Now Helen Manetti, she was safe from discovery and safe from those who would threaten the life of Helmut's baby. But not entirely safe from Helmut.

"Who is this WOP?" Helmut demanded of Eisenbach when he delivered the news of Helen's pregnancy and marriage.

"A hired hand or Corigliano's bastard, depending on who you talk to and who you believe."

"Why? Why would she do such a thing? That's what I want to know," Helmut moaned. His agony was adolescent, but real.

"She's your mistress, not your wife, Helmut. She can't fold up and crawl into an envelope while you're with your family."

"I'll kill the son-of-a-bitch," Helmut vowed.

"And leave your child fatherless like you were? Maybe you're too young to have a mistress. The whole idea is to have parallel lives not intertwined ones. She's got to have a way to support the child. I can send her money, but who's going to help with the housework?"

"You think Stahl would care if I executed a looter?"

"Corigliano might mind, if Joe's his eldest male child."

"He has more then one?"

"To hear the Villa gossips, Corigliano has increased the population of San Raphael with a singular sense of purpose while saving souls and running political interference for the Vatican."

"I have to see her, Emil. Arrange it."

"It's done. I've given Corigliano a head's up that you'll go tomorrow to check on the Cardinals. The thought of losing Helen Manetti's organization skills terrifies him now that she and Joe have made San Rafael self-supporting. I hear they run a tight accounting ship. Ask to see the books and have Helen go over them with you."

Alone with Helen in Corigliano's office, Helmut melted into her arms and rubbed her bulging belly. "You have to leave him. I won't have my child grow up thinking this greaser is his father."

She pried herself away from him. "And be alone? I know what you must do politically. I'm no fool, Helmut."

"I know. How well I know," Helmut said. "What I don't know is what to do. What can I do, pretend this isn't my … our child? Pretend that beast isn't in your bed and in your body every night? For God's sake, Helen, at least demand I leave Teresa. Have a hissie fit. Scratch my eyes out. Be jealous."

"No, I won't. I have part of you and, until fate decides otherwise, Teresa has part of you."

"And what does Joe think of this? He knows this isn't his child."

"He's Corigliano's bastard so he knows what the word means. He doesn't care whose kid it is, it's his now. We're making a good life here, and Umberto's is becoming impressed with his first-born indiscretion. Joe isn't you, Helmut, but he loves me."

"Do you love him?"

"I love my life. I've learned I can serve God and have what I can, what I can never have with you. I don't want to be a mistress anymore than I wanted to be in a convent. Both require me to hide in shame."

213

"I was jealous of God and now I'm jealous of Joe." Helmut turned away from her. "I am a shameful man. Damn me. For all my bravado, I don't have the courage to walk away from being Stahl's son-in-law."

"Perhaps his successor?" Helen put her arms around him. Her breasts were as full as he remembered them, and her belly hardened under his hand. He sank his tongue into her mouth and he held her full buttocks in his palm. "No, Helmut," she said. "You have a duty that you can't escape as easily as I escaped mine. You are doing God's work. Of this I'm sure. You know where I am and where our baby will be."

"It may be years…"

"And we'll all be older."

Helmut told Corigliano that his English manager had the imprimatur of the German government. She'd been vetted and posed no threat to the elderly churchmen. "You know what I think," Umberto told Norman, "I think Wolf believed I was hiding Churchill somewhere at the Villa."

"Hiding her or her remains, if Eisenbach has anything to do with it."

"All this fuss about the books. It was chance to snoop, if you ask me. But if we could prove Madeline was dead and Eisenbach had something to do with it…"

Norman helped Corigliano to his feet. They had been summoned to a meeting with Edward and Nabu.

# CHAPTER XI

## Speak! The World is Waiting

The four men met in the ruins of St. Peter's Basilica, suspecting their office area was bugged. Edward was blunt. "Is Stahl instituting a repatriation program in Italy?"

Earlier that morning he and Nebu had watched the events in Vienna on the television. A Children's Army, led by Father Hahn under the auspices of the left-wing World Peace Organization, was taking center stage. Tormented by his participation in the Wolf's wedding, Hahn had dedicated himself to ridding the world of terrorism through a peace march on Jerusalem, resolved to offer himself up in martyrdom in atonement. Had the wedding been averted, Stephan Stahl would not have the roots of a devils' dynasty in Teresa's womb.

As word of his intention spread through the internet, thousands of equally dedicated pacifist youngsters were flocking to Vienna, there to board planes to the Holy Land. The streets swelled with visionaries, and vehement Junior Security League youths who taunted them with cries of "coward" and "queer". The confrontation was a media extravaganza. As the local police forces attempted to block the streets and contain both the march to the airport and the angered patriots, the two sides were only brought in closer physical proximity. Flame and dynamite were certain to meet. "God helps us, Nabu," Edward said. "Doesn't Hahn realize open opposition to the Stahl regime and the Repatriation Program only invites more government intervention?"

Both men knew the situation made Edward's afternoon address all the more crucial. Papal support for either side meant more German efforts backed by military force.

"I think Hahn's timing is impeccable. He absolutely knows the position this puts you in. He's trying to force your hand," Nabu said.

"His martyrdom is his business but taking thousands of children to the slaughter is insanity." The Junior Leaguers were throwing red paint, a symbol of the blood of the Unknown Martyrs, on the white robed pacifists. "The wounds of Rome are still bleeding, and Hahn throws salt into them. He's must be stopped. Stahl has to know the Church is not sanctioning this," Edward insisted.

"Hahn probably believes that Stahl won't take reprisals for the Vatican bombing if he puts those kids between Stahl and the Muslim world. He won't risk making them hostages…"

"They'll be hostages the minute they touch Muslim soil, Nabu, and they'll be treated like infidels. I need to talk with Stahl before Norman and Umberto arrive ..." It meant asking Helmut to arrange it, and Edward cringed at the thought. He wadded up the speech he'd been composing for the better parts of two days and threw it into the waste can. "Can you arrange a call, Captain Wolf?" Edward said as the Helmut strode into St. Stephen's.

Helmut glanced at the TV screen and punched in his direct line to Stahl. "Hall-o, Stephan. No, no, Teresa's fine. We're all fine but concerned about this Children's Army. His Holiness would like a word with you."

Edward took the phone from Helmut. "I'm very concerned. No, this is not sanctioned by anyone here in Rome. Yes, thank-you." He handed the phone back to Helmut. "He says it's under control."

"Then I'll leave you gentlemen to your thoughts."

Helmut left, and Nabu and Edward watched in amazement at what unfolded on the TV screen. The Eisenbach Brigade marched into the foray and the Junior Security Leaguers immediately formed squads and saluted. Told to return to their respective headquarters, they dispersed. Brigade leader Hans Holtzman took Father Hahn into custody and ordered his twenty-odd men to put the teenagers on the buses that were entering the area. One by one, with each pacifist requiring two men to carry him to the bus and up the stairs, the young people were placed aboard to be taken to hostels where their parents could pick them up. "We're told," an announcer said, "That Father Hahn will be charged with parading without permit, fined a hundred Euros, and sentenced to counseling." The incident ended without casualty.

"So that's it, Nabu. One man's crisis is another man's incident. How deftly these Germans restore order, defusing these zealots without firing a shot. And here I am fretting like an old woman. If I didn't know better, I'd think the whole scene was orchestrated as propaganda."

"Do you know better, Holiness?" Nabu turned off the television. "Is it possible Stahl bombed the Vatican to show the world the necessity of the Repatriation Program and disable the power of the Church to oppose it?"

It was a suggestion Edward could not ignore no matter how outrageous. Create a crisis to play the hero? It had been done before. But to do the unthinkable to justify the ultimate reprisal? "It *is* strange that no terrorist group has taken credit for the bombing. Al Jezeera remains silent on the subject, even after six months." Edward said.

"Perhaps the Muslim world is growing as fearful of Stahl as we are. If the result of Paris was the Repatriation Program, how will Stahl avenge the Vatican?"

That was Edward's next question to Norman and Umberto as they sat among marble fragments that had once been an altar.

Norman watched a worm inch its way into the grass. Such a vulnerable creature, he thought. God must see us that way too. "I am a diplomat in name only, Holiness. Castrato. Stahl doesn't share his plans with anyone except his inner circle. I deliver best wishes, not real communications, and I wouldn't even do that if it weren't for my nephew."

"You are my advisors, so advise me. Umberto, Nabu, what does God want me to say?" Edward pleaded.

Umberto looked at Edward. "God doesn't tell me things like that, Holiness. All I can say is that you are his voice on Earth. What you say matters to millions, and billions are listening. Speak the truth. We know what Stahl's plans are. Like Hitler in *Mein Kampf*, Stahl has told us a million times that he wants to rid Europe and the Americas of all Muslims. He doesn't care what happens to them, as long as they leave Christian shores. Someone bombed the Excelsior, but I don't believe it was terrorists. You know my heart, Holiness. You know I would be the first one to condemn the heathen if I believed they were responsible."

"What do you think, Nabu?"

"Umberto and Norman have told us they arranged for Madeline Churchill to be in the Excelsior, but she wasn't. They thought she and Helmut were killed in the blast, but they weren't. Someone wanted it to look like terrorists, because how would terrorists know of Helmut's planned rendezvous with Churchill? And the Vatican blast? It got Russia and China to work together. Who is capable of such orchestration?"

Norman and Umberto exchanged glances. "It's Eisenbach, Holiness," Norman said, sensing a solution to both the Churchill and the Stahl problem. "His fingerprints are all over both bombings. If we can take him down ..."

Edward held up his hand in protest. "I cannot be a party to murder."

"There is no other way, Holiness," Umberto said softly. "Eventually, Berlin must be stopped or else..."

"Or else, what?" Nabu said.

"Or else Stahl will accomplish what Hitler could not: world domination," Umberto answered.

"But maybe the world needs a global Charlemagne," Nabu countered.

Edward sighed as their tempers flared. "This is getting us nowhere, gentlemen. Norman, has Helmut told you anything about how long he plans to stay in Italy? I know his engineers have to stay for the reconstruction, but he's a consultant not an artisan."

"He and Teresa are very devout. I expect them to be in and out of Rome until the restoration is complete. Why?" Norman said.

"Well, as long as he's here, he's not building any more repatriation centers. Unless he does want to build one in Italy," Edward said.

"Umberto's right. Stahl has made his goals known – it's not the what but the how we have to worry about. It's possible Italy will be the site of a center. It's closer to Turkey than Paris is," Norman conceded.

"I have to withdraw and get my remarks together," Edward said. He had learned nothing. He walked away slowly, disappointed but understanding that it was neither information nor that advice he needed, but inspiration. He alone bore the burden of dispensing God's moral preferences to the faithful.

All too soon he was standing on the dais, looking out at the thousand of people crowded into the streets. Helmut had made an altar of the marble of St. Peter's Basilica. The locals claimed that the faces of Jesus and Mary could be seen in the fragments, and the Fatherland Security Force lifted the pieces with a rope and pulley, one on another, until the reflective pieces crowned a ton of stone. Before thousands of worshipers, Helmut and Teresa prayed for the people of Rome along with Pope Edward and the red-robed Cardinals who had been flown in from the villa. Everyone there was waiting for Pope Edward to speak to the world about the terrorism that wanted to destroy Christendom.

Suddenly the sound of rotor blades grew louder as a helicopter came into view and finally landed in the square. Edward turned, and followed the eyes of the crowd to see Stephan Stahl himself step out of the copter, Frieda at his side. The crowd exploded with cheers and chants – Viva Papa! Viva Stahl! People rushed towards the gates to get a brief look at the hero of Rome, greeting Stahl as the ancient Romans greeted a returning Caesar. Helmut and Teresa walked to greet them and embraced them warmly.

"Did you know about this, Norman?" Edward demanded, barely able to make himself heard over the roar of the crowd.

"I swear, I had no idea, Holiness," Norman said.

"Where is Eisenbach, I wonder," Corigliano said to Norman.

Stahl waved to the wall of noise that emanated from the crowd. Men threw their hats off to him and the women waved brightly colored scarves, the thousands congealing into one voice of ecstatic welcome.

The police were soon joined by German Fatherland Security Forces, and bullhorns and loudspeakers exhorted the grateful citizens to order. Soldiers with riot gear lined the perimeter of the fence, and Edward knew something had to be done to prevent chaos. "Children," he yelled into the microphone, "I stand before you today to declare the sainthood of those who rest in the grave of the Unknown Martyrs." A hush fell over the crowd. To many people, the instant canonization of their loved ones was enough to immobilize them. "Whatever their earthly sins, they died for the glory of God, trusting in him for their salvation in the face of evil. Yes, I said evil. Whoever tore down these stones was truly evil, but these stones only echo our resolve to raise them again in honor of God. Jesus Himself said, tear down this temple and in three days I will raise it again.

We cannot raise the temple in three days. We are not gods. But we have those here among us who promise to assist us in our efforts. We welcome our German brothers and sisters and thank them for their help in our time of trial. Without them, thousands more, perhaps millions would have died. God, in His mercy, enkindled the desire in the hearts of many people to come to help under their direction.

We are now recovering from shock, pain, and challenges to our faith and resolve. Our claim to the moral high ground of peace and charity is being threatened by those who do not hold peace and charity to be worthy of preserving.

If we could keep the enemy at bay long enough, he could perhaps learn by our example, and we could afford the luxury of complete pacifism. Unfortunately, we no longer have the protection of time and distance. Journeys that once took months, now take hours. Weapons that once killed a few, can now kill hundreds of thousands in less time than it takes to press a button. Modern technology has made it imperative that our response to the damage hate wreaks must be as swift as the weapons that destroy us. Yet, we know this is not possible forever. Eventually we will run out of resources and commitment. We will experience disaster fatigue.

What are we to do? Pray, of course. But while we pray, the enemy plots our destruction. Forgive, of course. But while we forgive, the enemy escalates his resentment against us. Hope, of course, that we can replace revenge and hatred with love and mercy. But recognize that we have a right to protect our lives *and* defend the innocent.

The pestilence of radicalism must be neutralized, whether it comes from Islamofacism or within countries in the grip of military and political dictatorship, by all reasonable means.

Thomas Merton, the saintly Trappist monk and former Marine wrestled with the same dilemma following World War II. Then, megadeath was a concept few could stomach to contemplate. What was the Christian response? That was the question Merton meditated upon. And his conclusion was that absolute pacifism was as immoral as absolute annihilation. Evil force must be resisted with righteous force, but only that amount of force necessary for self preservation.

There must be no retaliatory reprisals that escalate blood lust and perpetuate it. There must always be a willingness of heart to reconcile and forgive one's enemy when violence ceases. There must be no intentional infliction of suffering either during or after armed conflict. There must be no intentional destruction of infrastructure, water or food supplies that extend suffering and cause needless deaths. And always, the olive branch of peace and negotiation must accompany guns and soldiers.

To be Christian is not to be weak in the face of danger or threat to loved ones and innocents. To be Christian is to be brave, to defend the right, and to temper the might with mercy. God bless all of you, my children."

Edward blessed the crowd, a crowd stunned by the brevity of his words in reference to terrorism and what he expected from Christians around the world, and the not so thinly veiled references to the German government and what the Church expected from it in its fight against terrorism. Would Stahl speak to them as well?

Always mindful of the media, Stahl knew better than to upstage the Pope. He stood, and with Frieda at his side, knelt in front of the Pontiff for a papal blessing. Edward was caught a little off guard but raised his hand and made the sign of the cross over them. After them, Helmut and Teresa took their turn at kneeling at the feet of the Vicar of Christ. What the world saw was the solidarity of Berlin and Rome – the oneness of the sword and the cross with one mission: save the world from terrorism.

"We must talk, Chancellor," Edward said as they walked across the square to St. Stephen's. Norman escorted Frieda and Teresa to a make-shift reception tent, erected and maintained by the Italian government, where they could get cold drinks and protection from the Italian sun. Nabu, Corigliano and Helmut followed Stahl and Edward.

"It's why I came, Holiness. It's time we came to an understanding, even if we can't reach agreement."

"I think it would be better if we spoke privately."

"Alright."

"Gentlemen, why don't you wait inside while the Chancellor and I use the open-air office?"

Stahl and Edward went to the ruins. It seemed an appropriate place to talk about the dismantling of Europe and the reformation of the Holy Roman Empire. Stahl lit up a forbidden cigarette and offered one to Edward. "I haven't had one of these since I was seventeen —a hundred years ago," Edward said.

Stahl chuckled. "Isn't it funny how things remind us of our youth? For me, it's not cigarettes but the taste of Coke-a-cola."

"Ah … to be young again. I look at Helmut and I wonder if he's made those kinds of memories. He seems too serious. Does he ever laugh?"

"That's a funny question. Does it matter, considering the world is at his feet?" Stahl let out a cough. "I'm not used to these things anymore."

"Yes, it matters," Edward said. "He's the same age as many of the terrorist that plague us. If they had other things to do —make love for instance —they might not be so willing to throw away their lives in a war no one can win."

"The young seek meaning beyond their years rather than appreciate how wonderful irresponsibility and plain silliness really is. It's too bad but thank God they're willing to fight the wars. If old men like us had to do it… talk about silly."

"The whole damn thing is funny in a demonic sort of way. Absurd. People going around blowing up things and other people to have a world that is bleaker than any I can imagine. No pretty girls to admire on the beach. No dancing close. No western movies," Edward said.

"You're not anything like a Pope, Holiness. Too bawdy."

"You're not anything like a dictator. Too affable." Edward flicked his cigarette butt into the grass. "You forget I was married before I took Holy Orders, Chancellor. My wife was one of the funniest people I ever met. She thought everything had a hilarious side. Although I doubt she'd see any humor in deportations. God's not too thrilled about them either, I expect."

"It's hard to know what God thinks. We know so much about what he doesn't want and haven't a clue what he does want. War, for example. We know what war looks like, and we know He's against it. But peace? What does peace look like? I don't know, do you? Does he want it at any price?"

"I believe God expects us to do the best we can."

"And punish us eternally if we make the wrong choice? Read the mind of the ineffable. Do what cannot be done or suffer. I can't believe that God has set a trap for us, Holiness."

"That's where faith enters the picture. I trust God to show us the way."

"How? Through omens? Angels? The entrails of chickens? Democratic elections? Wouldn't it be easier, safer and kinder if the all merciful One just text messaged us?" Stahl said.

"I'll grant you life's not easy, but faith requires us to examine our actions. People know if they're doing wrong."

"Really? Pope Benedict condemned the Iraqi war while sixty million people applauded their liberation… especially the Iraqi women. Now, did Bush do right or wrong, Holiness?"

"Get thee behind me, Satan. You seek to trick me." Edward shifted with discomfort. He had asked himself the same questions Stahl was asking and had never found satisfying answers. "All I know is that innocents must not be killed."

"Even if they have explosives attached to them, like the mentally retarded homicide bombers?"

"Abortion, euthanasia, ethnic cleansing, human cloning – all of these subvert life and therefore violate the laws of nature."

"That hardly suffices as an answer to my question Holiness. It's rhetoric that addresses obvious deviations. What about the Iraqi war, Holiness? What about parting the Red Sea? Did Moses violate the laws of nature when he did that?"

"God parted the waters, not Moses."

"So, God can violate the laws of nature to save Jews, but man can't violate the laws of nature to save … say … crippled Muslims. Is God that capricious?"

"You ask me to read the mind of God." Edward wiped his brow with his handkerchief.

"No, explain it. You're his representative. Is it the will of God to let people be slaughtered until there's nothing left but the dead silence of peace?"

"You heard my speech. I said Christians have a right to defend themselves, but not the right to exterminate their enemies."

"Beat them, but don't vanquish them. Let them rise and fight another day? Is that the drill?"

"What's your point, Chancellor? I have admitted there is such a thing as a just war and defending one's life is a just cause. What more do you want? Permission to commit genocide through this repatriation scheme of yours?"

"No. I ask you to understand that God may be working through people who are willing to fight as much as through people who are willing to pray."

"Meaning?"

"I want you to name Helmut Wolf Defender of the Faith."

"Are you insane, Chancellor?"

"I want to make religious service part of world leadership. King William carries the honorific for the Anglican Church, why not have a Catholic counterpart?"

"You mean give the Church's imprimatur on the Repatriation Program. That is what you're after, isn't it? As we speak, thousands rot in refugee camps in countries that cannot possibly absorb so many. You might as well build the gas chambers and the ovens as send millions into desert countries that cannot possibly take care of them. Helmut Wolf is Heinrich Himmler lite. Absolutely not, Chancellor. Never."

"You may change your mind when you hear what I have to tell you. Such a title would give you some credibility after the inevitable. We believe you can be a uniting factor in what must be done."

Edward looked closely at Stahl. For the first time he noticed the glaze over his eyes. "You're on pain medication," he said as a half question.

"Anti-nausea medication for the chemotherapy."

"How long do you have?"

"The doctors tell me things are coming along fine. The chemo is working. My PSA count is down. It's foolishness. I'm exhausted."

"Do you want to make your confession?"

"Not yet. I know my penance would be – close E'tat de Guerre, and I can't do that now. Intelligence tells us that Iran's entire nuclear arsenal was moved to Mecca months before the Vatican strike. It looks like every Muslim country gets a turn to strike a blow to the West. King Saud now has a delivery system *and* the Iranian nuclear payload. All they need is training, and Israel and Rome are the targets. There's no way Germany can rescue Tel-Aviv *and* Rome —again. All Europe is at risk. The nuclear weapons will be moved back to Tehran after the Israeli attack."

Edward steadied his descent to one of the larger marble chunks, literally being swept off his feet at the news. "Oh, my God," he stammered hoarsely. He stared at Stahl and saw inevitability in his eyes. "You are going to war."

"Not exactly war. Tomorrow Helmut's off to RAF Cranwell in Lincolnshire with his squad of the Eisenbach Brigade They'll to learn to fly the B-3 Stealth. It's been improved since the 1990s. Virtually invisible. They won't even have to fly over their targets – with the computerized guidance system they can hit the target and destroy it before people are even aware they're under attack."

"Targets?"

"A pre-emptive strike. Helmut will hit Mecca. The Grand Mosque, the Kaaba. The other two crews will hit Tehran and Islamabad."

"Will they be nuclear bombs?"

"Tactical nukes. Low doses of radiation with the wallop of a MOAB. The B-3 can carry up to eighty, five-hundred pound bombs; sixteen nukes. I signed the order myself this morning."

"Jesus, Mary and Joseph," Edward said, and made the sign of the cross. "Do you realize millions will die? Millions. Mecca has almost three million people alone, and the dust cloud will travel thousands of miles. Yes, I remember Chernobyl. Thousands died from the aftereffects – cancers, sterility. It's unimaginable."

Stahl sat himself opposite the Pontiff. "The Muslims terrorists signed their death warrant when they bombed the Vatican with missiles but it's gone beyond quid pro quo. With the acquisition of both means and method, negotiation is impossible. Time has run out. Either we take out the Muslim terrorist centers and their nukes, or we're all dead."

"We don't know that terrorists bombed the Vatican, or the Excelsior. There's speculation it may have been a provocateur," Edward said, desperate to change the truth of what Stahl was telling him. "It might have been a mistake. An accident."

"No, Holiness. The Islamofacists have nuclear capability. The next strike will kill millions of Christians. I flew here today to tell you, President Buscolioni has agreed to let us use Brindisi's Popola Casale Airport as a staging area. B-3s have a range of six thousand miles. That means no refueling, so they just drop and exit. We're already building special hangars. Helmut should have his squad on line within six months."

"What about NATO's missile shield? Wasn't that supposed to protect Europe from missiles?"

Stahl just shook his head no and cast a wry smile towards the Pontiff. "The missile shield didn't protect you. It isn't worth a damn against an armada of planes or a missile fired from a submarine a hundred yards off shore, which we believe is where the Vatican missiles were fired from. If even one nuke gets through … and one will get through

229

eventually because we'll run out of interceptors eventually – no *blitzretten* will do any good."

Edward started to laugh. Stahl wondered if news of the strike had driven him over the edge. Edward saw the look of panic overtake him, and explained the irony. "Millions of people are going to perish within a matter of months and they don't know it. They sit in their homes and tents, they pray in their mosques and rejoice that another bastion of Christianity has been demolished, never dreaming that they're soon to be ashes because of it. And you know what is happening in that reception tent the Italian government loaned us? The man who is going to drop the first bomb is talking to three other men who don't have a clue about one insignificant woman they have all seemed to have misplaced. We're talking abut the immolation of millions while they wonder just where the hell Madeline Churchill is, thinking she holds the key to Helmut's rehabilitation as a human being. What fools we mortals be, and all in the name of God. Is He kind, or absurd?"

\*\*\*

Edward was right. While he and Stahl were contemplating the destruction of the Islamic world, Helmut, Corigliano, and Nabu were sipping lemonade in the tent. Norman joined them when he had Frieda and Teresa settled in at St. Stephen's with tea and cookies. He hadn't seen Helmut since the wedding. After a brief handshake, the two of them sat casually, as gentlemen do, discussing how Patricia looked forward to Helmut becoming a father.

Helmut made eye contact with his Uncle, and they both broke into quiet laughter. "If she's happy for me, Uncle," Helmut said, "It's because she believes a baby will get me out of uniform and into the foreign service. She hates children."

"She's softened, Helmut, "Norman assured him, "More like corduroy than armor plate."

Corigliano interrupted their small talk. "Did you know your father-in-law was making this surprise visit, *Captain Wolf*?" Nabu jabbed his elbow into Corigliano's side at the audacious question.

Helmut recoiled at his tone. "No, but I'm always glad to see him." What news of Madeline Churchill, *Cardinal Corigliano*?" Helmut shot back.

"Gentlemen, please. A little circumspection," Norman pleaded.

"We have serious issues to discuss, Norman. Why is Stahl here? Who better to hear it from than the horse's mouth?" Nabu thought he sounded conciliatory. "As for Churchill, Captain Wolf, I think it's time we add her name to the rest in the grave of the Unknown Martyrs."

"I agree," Corigliano continued. "How long should we wait before we tell her parents she's dead? Or do you have to run that by Eisenbach before you answer?"

"What's Eisenbach got to do with Churchill?" Helmut said. He looked for more ice in the bucket, but it was melted. He winced and poured some more warm lemonade from the pitcher. He hated warn lemonade.

Norman assumed his most diplomatic posture. "She didn't just disappear, Helmut. We know she was not at the Excelsior. She's either dead or alive, and somebody must know the answer to that question. If not one of us, who? Eisenbach has a vested interest in you and your marriage to Teresa Stahl."

"Assuming Churchill's dead," Umberto reminded them.

"What do you suggest? Helmut said, stifling his amusement..

"Investigate what Eisenbach was doing the night of the Excelsior bombing."

Georg walked into the tent and handed Helmut his cell phone. "Helen Manetti is on the phone, Sir. She wants to know when the Cardinals will be arriving at the villa."

"Signora Manetti? They're on their way. Yes, all went well…you heard His Holiness speak? He's a man of great perception. Bona sera." He handed the phone to Georg. "Tell Miss Teresa we'll be leaving for the hotel soon. She might want to get ready."

Norman watched Helmut carefully. There was something in the way he reached for the phone … was it anticipation or was he annoyed? Norman couldn't be sure. "I hear this Manetti is quite a find. I didn't get to meet her this morning…."

Corigliano sighed. "I never thought Giuseppe would find a woman who could tame him. Leave it to the English. She keeps him on a tight leash. No mistress in his future."

"She's English?" Norman said.

Helmut sensed more than idle curiosity in Norman's question and knew he had to subdue his interest. "Yes. She was Helen Crabtree, wasn't she, Your Imminence?"

"Amazing woman. Reminds me of Giuseppe's mother. Well, that's a story for another day. But yes, she rented the artist's cottage a few months before the attack. You know these English. Always wanting to paint sunlight. Helmut Ok-ayed her – checked her references, passport – before she was hired to look after the Cardinals."

"Really," Norman said. "I don't remember you running that by my office, Helmut."

"It was a military matter, not a diplomatic one. Hiring a housekeeper is a routine matter. Nannies often make good housekeepers."

"Yes, but who knew housekeepers can make good estate managers?" Corigliano said cheerfully. He seemed to be genuinely fond of his bastard's wife. "That may change once she has the bambino."

"Oh, that's right, you told me Giuseppe was going to be a father," Norman said. "Is Signora Manetti dark and short, or tall and blonde?"

Helmut caught his drift immediately. "Neither, from what I could see. Average height and she looks like an English girl," he said, knowing that as soon as Norman got a good look at the now plump Helen, he might recognize her as Madeline unless …. Madeline had a different look to her now. Gone was the sweet innocence of their college days. She was grownup. She had seen death and had all the more reason to protect life now that it was growing within her. She understood his mission now. Let Norman confront her, and he'll get the same no-nonsense attitude Helen gave him. "Aren't you going back to the villa tonight, Uncle? You'll certainly meet her."

Corigliano felt generous. "Why not bring the Ladies to the villa? It'll be more pleasant that staying at the hotel —if you can call it a hotel anymore with the rotten service it provides. You expect Stahl to return to Vienna tonight?"

"Obviously, his comings and goings are top secret these days. I have no idea what he and Frau Stahl will do, only that she needs the company of her mother now that the baby is on the way. But she loved the villa --- is there room with the Cardinals there?" Helmut said.

"You can have the artist's cottage now that Helen and Giuseppe have taken over the servants' quarters in the main house. It's a romantic place. Just ask Helen."

***

Stahl, Frieda, Teresa, and Helmut had little time for pleasantries. Stephan gave Helmut his orders to report to flight school, explaining that he and Frieda would fly to Vienna and expect Teresa there tomorrow night. Stahl told him of his conversation with the Pontiff. It had concluded with a promise from Edward that he would consider making Helmut Defender of the Faith, but on condition that the Christian Nationalists reconsider the pre-emptive strike. Stahl had agreed to explore alternatives but insisted Helmut and his squadron start flight training.

Teresa was heartbroken that Helmut might not be there for the birth of the baby. She and Helmut walked with her parents to the helicopter that would take them to the waiting plane, and then strolled around the villa's garden holding hands. "I wish we could make love," she said.

"The doctor says no. I'll be alright, Terri. The best things in life are those you have to wait for. Like this baby of ours."

"My father is happier than I've seen him in years even though he's worried sick about what may happen. I'm not a child, Helmut. Flight school can only mean one thing - a bombing mission."

"It's being sold as a defensive measure. Cross-training and all that, to maximize manpower. We're planning war games with out allies. Show of force. The Muslims think we're saber-rattling now that we've been to see the Pope. They think we're good Samaritans but lousy warriors."

Helmut saw a round form coming towards them and recognized Helen Manetti going about her business. She was pushing a cart full of stacked trays, dinners for those cardinals who chose not to eat in the hall with Corigliano and the "War Criminals". Thank God for the lengthening shadows, Helmut thought as Helen came closer. Perhaps Terri would not see the love and concern on his face for Signora Manetti. He was in emotional hell, but Norman would never believe he would chance the meeting of his wife and former lover, so it was a necessary torture.

"I don't believe you've met my wife, Signora Manetti. This is Teresa Wolf," Helmut said as the three came face to face.

"It's a pleasure," Helen said. Helmut listened carefully for some indication of pain as she spoke. All he heard was her melodious voice lilting on the soft breeze that cooled the garden at dusk. He hadn't expected to have another opportunity to see her before he left, and yet the gods had smiled, and he could say good-bye, in a way.

"We're leaving tomorrow," he said. "I'm off to flight school, and Frau Wolf returns to Vienna." He couldn't stop himself. He had to explain even if it was too much information to give a stranger. So what if Teresa thought it odd, how else was he to let Helen know he and Terri would not be together after tonight? Perhaps she couldn't have sex with Joe either. Perhaps the Doctor had told them to wait too.

"I wish you safe journey, Mr. and Mrs. Wolf. I'm leaving soon too."

"But … but … the business is doing so well. The villa is financially sound," Helmut stammered. "And the Cardinals …" He knew he sounded desperate.

"This is no place to have a baby. I'll spend my last three weeks in Milano. There are better doctors up north."

"Of course. Of course. Joe will stay with the Cardinals until… well, he'll be with you when it's time."

"I hope so. How long do you have, Frau Wolf?"

"Too long. Is it … is it what you expected? I mean, do you ever get over feeling you just want it to be over?"

"I haven't had that feeling, yet. Maybe I will, eventually. But, I'm fortunate. I'm not married to a soldier. I have to go now. Good-bye and be careful, Frau Wolf." Helmut let her pass and tried not to let his eyes linger on her full hips and she walked down the corridor.

"Good-bye Signora Manetti," Terri said. The pain he hadn't heard in Helen's voice, he now heard in Terri's. It was the sound of resignation, of knowing that she had lost something precious. She had lost the lie.

Lying next to Helmut in the big bed that filled the bedroom of the artist's cottage, Terri felt his hand wind its way over her belly and down between her legs. Would it really be so dangerous to let him have a little of her? His fingers found their way to lips and she let him get her wet with desire. "Helmut," she whispered, "If we're careful … if you do it slowly…" He was half asleep but gently pushed into her from the rear. She tried to sustain her passion, but the truth kept knocking at her mind's door. If Helen was Madeline, and she was almost ready to deliver, it meant Helmut had impregnated her before they were married. Why, then did Helmut marry her instead of Madeline when he was so obviously in love with her – so in love he would risk a scandal if Corigliano ever found out about Helen?

She remembered what Helmut had told her of Madeline, about her leaving the convent. Could it be that Helmut did love her, and Madeline was really just a troubled young woman he cared about? She smiled to herself. Given enough time a woman can find another lie when the old one is lost. Madeline didn't leave the convent and become pregnant, Teresa decided, she became pregnant and left the convent. Madeline's child wasn't Helmut's.

\*\*\*

Norman returned to Berlin and arranged to meet Fritz Pomeranz the following afternoon. Stahl's surprise visit and Helmut's subsequent departure for Cranwell made it excruciatingly obvious that the Christian Nationalists had eclipsed all other sources of political power in Germany. He learned of the war exercises with Britain, Russia and America with the rest of the public on a television newscast, and that Stahl returning to Berlin from Vienna from —of all people —Patricia.

"I figured that out when Frieda called about Teresa's baby shower."

"What about it?"

"She's not having one. Doesn't want one."

"She doesn't have any friends who take terrorist attacks and assassination attempts in stride."

"Oh, for heaven's sake, Norman. How's Helmut?"

"Top physical condition. Ready for flight school and the cameras."

"And Madeline Churchill?"

"I thought she might be holed up at Umberto's villa, masquerading as Helen Manetti, but … I mean she was no push-over, but Helen and Joe are a power couple like none I've seen. No idealism there. Run the villa like they own it. Umberto adores her."

"You believe Madeline's dead."

"I'm sure she died in the bombing. Even though Umberto would rather Eisenbach be at the bottom of a sinister plot. Did you listen to Edward's address?"

Patti was doodling on her crossword puzzle, drawing horns on the head of a bull. "The Pope's in the tank for Stahl. Maybe that's the right side of history, sad to say."

Norman sat beside her. "It's easy to be forgiving till you see the effects of one of those bombings up close and personal, Patti. Just when you think everything's been cleaned up, you stumble on a human foot, or see a blood-spattered car. It becomes your fight too. What did it for me was seeing the little coffins lined up outside the hospital tent waiting for the children medicine couldn't save. I thought about Baby Helmut being under all that rubble. His rescue *was* a miracle …"

Patti patted his hand. "We did the best we could."

"I watched them on stage. The Stahls, Helmut, and Terri – as the Pope spoke. I know its all propaganda, but Helmut does look different from the rest of them. Maybe he really does have a destiny and Emil and Stephan have seen it all along."

"What does Fritz say?"

"That the Center Socialists were too stupid to take action, and now it's too late. We're going to war. Period."

"I agree with him, Norman. The only way to stop the Christian Nationalists now, is to take out the Unholy Trinity. Helmut can't be spared." It seemed too much to contemplate, but Patti was only echoing Pomeranz who had called an emergency meeting as soon as Norman returned to Berlin.

"And leave a vacuum of leadership in Germany like we saw after the Berlin Wall fell? No. We'd have complete chaos. With no mechanism of rescue, the terrorists would seize the opportunity to hit us hard. We can't let party loyalty blind us to the fact that the Christian Nationalists are the only force strong enough to battle Islamofacism right now," Norman told the men seated at the table at Center Socialist Party headquarters what he had told Patti. "If we want power, we have to have an alternative structure already in place or we risk all-out civil war."

"We could take them out one at a time, but in a short time …," Tanzer suggested.

"Wait much longer and we'll be at war. Assassinations during a national emergency would have the same effect as taking out all three at the same time." Fritz was fiddling with a letter opener, turning it over an over, handle to point as he spoke. "What does Umberto say, Norman?"

"He says Pope Edward does little but pray and meditate since Stahl's surprise visit. He suspects Stahl told Edward the war games aren't games."

"No they aren't. Any fool can tell Stahl is preparing for an all-out assault on the Muslim world. The question is where and when? Do you suppose Edward knows the answers to those questions?"

"Does it matter? He can't reveal what Stahl told him. Even if he did, the information wouldn't do us any good, especially if the order was attack if any of the Unholy Trinity is attacked. There's something else we might want to consider."

"Which is?"

"What would we do differently if we had power right now? It wouldn't make the terrorist situation any better. Maybe it's wiser to let Stahl do our dirty work for us, and leave our party looking like the party of peace. I mean, we can never deliver peace as long as the Islamofacists are a *real* threat, so why not wait until Stahl dismembers them? We can always take the higher moral ground when the bloodshed has ended. You know, claim we would have done it without the killing even if it's a lie."

Fritz threw the letter opener up in the air and let it crash to the table. "You mean scream softly about the horrors and immorality of war until it's safe to scream loudly?"

"Precisely," Norman said. "Why should we be in such a hurry to confront problems no one has a good solution to? Now, if you gentlemen will excuse me, I have a conference call with Umberto pending … " He left, but not before tacking small recording device under his chair as he bent down to grab his briefcase. He excused this treachery as taking out an insurance policy for Patti should Tanzer persuade Fritz to pursue assassination despite the irrationality of the act. Did Stauffenburg feel the same way about the attempt on Hitler's life, he wondered. It seemed like a necessity at the time, but it failed miserably. Had anyone prepared for that eventuality?

Everything he had told them was the truth. Germany could not afford civil unrest when the Western world was depending on it to save Western Civilization, however messy and bloody the cost. He remembered the story Umberto had told him about the female archeologist from Iowa

240

who found a human eye impaled on the sharp corner of shard she'd cleaned in the debris. Her shriek numbed the senses of the other workers who stopped their labors and comforted her with a shot of whiskey.

The aftermath of the Vatican bombing was not like that of Paris. There was no Muslim community to quarantine and deport. There was only rebuilding, trying to piece together fragments of stone and canvas and marble and plaster. Everyday Edward and Nabu walked the square marveling at the dedication of artisans and engineers who worked with the quiet resignation of people who thought they would never live to see the restoration completed. There seemed too many slivers and chunks of man-made and human remains.

"It is immoral," Edward ended in an e-mail to Captain Wolf describing the eye incident. "We cannot continue to ask people like Scilla Moreno to do what cannot be done. We can only preserve what is intact. Stop the restoration of yesterday and begin to build tomorrow."

"No," Helmut shot back. "As long as we turn away from suffering, we will excuse those who inflict it. We must remind ourselves daily of the cost of forgetfulness. We owe it to the owner of that eye to keep seeing — always before us —so we do not lose our resolve. However, if Scilla Moreno wants to leave, we will not force her to stay."

Edward met with the woman and read her Helmut's remarks. She wept when he addressed her by name, stating that she understood his words. "His eyes have seen horrors that dwarf my revulsion," she said, and went back to work. Within a week, the workers were wearing t-shits that bore a fiery eye with the words "*Always Before Me*" emblazoned on the front. Edward wrote to Helmut about the shirts too. He was determined to reach across cultures and generation to establish communication with the future German leader. It was his only hope, he knew, of persuading Helmut to disobey his "holy" orders from Stahl. Did Helmut know the real reason he was at flight school? He couldn't ask, bound as he was by the seal of the confessional, but the question haunted him.

Norman's misgivings were ebbing away. His surveillance paid off. The tape of the conversation that ensued when he left the conference room identified Pomeranz and Tanzer as the masterminds of the Excelsior bombing and exonerated both him and Eisenbach. It also revealed an embryonic assassination plot that targeted Helmut as the first of three planned murders. His demise, Pomeranz and Tanzer agreed, would leave the leadership in tact for the duration of the war on terror, but force Stahl to look for another successor. It was a distraction the two men could use to their benefit.

Stahl was impressed. "How did you come to suspect them?" he wanted to know.

"I admit I had a hand in getting Churchill to Rome to see Helmut. As his Uncle, the goal for me was seeing that he married the right woman. Both Patricia and I liked Madeline," he lied. "You understand. A lover's quarrel is not the best reason to marry someone else. But, of course, Helmut's heart was stolen by Teresa, and now that I know her, I know why. What motives Pomeranz had, I think, are revealed on the tape. He wants to break the power hold Helmut has on the public. He's too popular. He threatens the entire political system of Germany should he have a change of heart … or loyalty."

"I just thank God the children were at the villa," Stahl said.

"What now, Stephan? Will you have Pomeranz and Tanzer arrested?"

Stephan popped the CD out of the player and slipped it back into its case. "They have to be neutralized. I hate the word purge, but I realize that having state power always carries a risk of internal enemies. At least I have the evidence to convict them in a court, thanks to you."

"I consider it my duty to you and Madeline's family. The bomb that killed her wasn't a terrorist bomb, but we still brought her to her place of death. It's a decision I regret. Yet, it was Helmut they were after."

"Is it possible these traitors can lead us to others?"

"Anything's possible Stephan. But I don't like the idea of these guys on the loose. God knows how far they've gotten with the assassination plot."

"Arrest is a given, but a show-trial would be counterproductive. We can't let the world know the dissension over our policies has reached critical mass. Eisenbach said it would come to this. Every regime has to set the threshold where free speech transforms into sedition." He thought for a moment and then said, "Spandau."

"The prison's a shopping mall now, Stephan."

"Yes, we'll build another just for traitors. Who can take over the leadership of the Center Socialists? Not you, you're too valuable to me in Rome. You understand that."

"I have political affiliations, but no pretensions. Halderman can step in. He's innocuous without Fritz telling him what to think."

"What does Edward expect of me? You know him. Is he really blind to what we have to do?" Stephan said, diverting the conversation to Rome.

"No. He's wrestling with the fact that there's no such thing as a kindly war. By definition, war means kindness and understanding have

243

dissolved into might makes right. Nobody wants to admit that the twenty-first century is one war away from barbarism. It's easy to send two criminals to prison, but where do we send millions?"

"Hitler faced the same problem. Only Jews, Gypsies, and homosexuals weren't violent enemies. The Jihadists are monsters," Stephan said.

"He tried to expel them as we're expelling the Muslims. Perhaps a Final Solution is the only solution, after all."

Stephan withdrew his cell phone from his pocket. He had it set on vibrate to remind him to take his pills so Frieda wouldn't have to. She was, joyfully, occupied with Teresa's pregnancy. He opened his desk drawer and perused the array of medicine vials, color coded by time —red for every four hours, blue for every six hours —and numbered for how many. He checked the text message and chose a blue/2 vial. Norman poured him a glass of water and handed it to him.  "The cancer's been damn inconvenient," Stephan said before swallowing two white tablets. "But instructive. Think about any wound. Inside or outside, once your immunity's been compromised, your security defenses if you will, the battle is to separate lethal bacteria and viruses from the benign and useful. What happens when you start to die? Science steps in and kills them all. There's no time to test each microscopic organism to see if its bad or harmless." He drank the glass empty. "Edward isn't familiar with that pharmaceutical concept in spite of a bout with the common disease: terrorism."

"He's Old Boomer. Give peace a chance," Norman suggested.

"Not possible without the warriors. An older world concept. Have you heard America is beginning a Hispanic repatriation program?

Congress passed legislation last night. Twenty-three nays in the House, four in the Senate."

"Let me guess, the dissents were all of Hispanic descent."

Stephan chuckled. "I don't know that all were, but some will be packing their bags if Franklin doesn't veto."

"Will he?"

"Franklin told me no when I talked to him this morning. He says a veto would cost him re-election and would be over-ridden anyway. His chances have improved one hundred percent since the Muslim Repatriation Program went into effect. Wall Street liked the stability it promises and there's been a huge rally in the market. He thinks he can reverse some of the socialist policies that have plagued the economy for the past fifteen years. It's about time America stopped giving away its wealth. And it's damn sure time for Franklin to grow a backbone and stop the Reconquistas."

"Edward will have apoplexy if America starts to rid herself of the Spanish disease. It will be the Bush Effect. He'll blame it on you, Stephan."

"I don't care. America is a useless ally if she can't get her house in order. Speaking of which, call Pomeranz and Tanzer and tell them I want a meeting. I won't tell them you're the one who ratted them out. You'll have to take some heat too, but don't take it seriously. It'll be cover for you."

"Where will you send them?"

"Downstairs. Forever."

# CHAPTER XII

## And Baby Makes Three

"Umberto tells me there's a new baby at San Rafael. The Cardinals are cheered by him. He's eight pounds of demanding humanity who runs Joe and Helen ragged. They have named him Gerald, of all things. Gerry, they call him. I have reminded Umberto that Helen is British, so he should expect odd things from her. Like increasing the sales by six percent with a new label for Sangia Christi wine. It bears the insignia of the Fatherland Security Forces —the blazing heart," Norman e-mailed Patricia.

Helmut looked at the picture of Gerry Eisenbach sent, and was so overcome with joy and terror and jealousy, he almost caught the next plane to Italy to claim him and Madeline. He kissed the picture and held it to his cheek, imagining himself at Madeline's side as she nursed their son who smelled of powder and baby shampoo. To be fair, he thought, Joe could have Teresa and her child in the swap of the century, then put silliness aside and returned to duty.

"Congratulations," was all Georg said, and only once Helmut felt his hand on his back in a friendly pat as he slid Gerry's picture into his wallet behind his driver's license.

Three months later, Terri delivered a seven-pound, eight-ounce son she named Stephan Helmut Wolf. He was baptized in a quiet Catholic ceremony at Holy Word Lutheran Church, with Norman and Patricia Wolf as Godparents. Norman held the infant as Patricia didn't want to chance getting anything babyish on her grey wool dress. Helmut watched the ceremony on a DVD Eisenbach sent him and placed Stephan's picture in his wallet behind his driver's license. It was difficult to tell the babies apart. They both looked like their father.

As testimony to willed ignorance, the people of San Rafael congratulated Joe on the birth of his son who, according to them, was a lighter colored version of him. "He's got your eyes, only they're blue, and your hair only it's blonde," they gushed whenever he would walk the baby through the narrow streets where the elders sat outside and talked of the old days. When Gerry first said, "da-da" Joe handed out another round of cigars.

"He'll be a great businessman like his father," everyone predicted, and Umberto agreed. He started a college savings account for the baby, and asked Norman to recommend a good college he could start schmoozing to assure admission for "the butcher's boy".

"Butcher's boy my ass," Edward remarked to Nabu. The first time he saw Gerry's picture, he knew he was Helmut's child and concluded Helen Manetti was Madeline Churchill, chalking up Umberto's and Norman's denial as wishful thinking. "I'd like to meet this female entrepreneur," he told Umberto when the Cardinal handed him a tightly taped shoe box, adding that "We could use some marketing expertise to bolster our coffers."

A private audience with the Pope was the last thing Helen would have predicted her first night at Villa San Rafael. Yet, here she was sitting across from him in the visitor's tent, amazed at a Pope with a British accent.

"Ceremonies, awards, monument dedications —all these keep the Vatican story alive and PR is absolutely necessary to success," she told

Edward. "Tourism was the Vatican's bread and butter, and can be again with a star performer and beautiful scenery."

"You suggest I market the restoration?"

"Absolutely. I'd also bring in all the vocalists and musicians I could find to make the place both a holy and an entertaining place again. The Square can again host choirs and symphonies and all kinds of secular performances without sacrificing sanctity or the work of the artisans, Holiness."

Edward knew instantly why Helmut loved Madeline. She was alive with energy and ideas, and voluptuous in a way that Teresa was not. She was scrappy and direct. She was the woman Helmut should have married – the one that would have kept him in line. How did she ever think she could lock herself away in a convent? More importantly, was there still a way for her to curb his excessive sense of mission even though they were married to different people? He caught himself wondering if all sins were really sins in the big scheme of things. Masturbation turned into fornication and then into adultery, but were any of them abnormal?

Madeline was the kind of woman Helmut needed to have an affair with. It would humanize him. Hell, it would make him happy and there was much to be said for a young man having a little happiness in his life. Edward made a mental note that, in a pinch, Madeline could be counted on to provide Helmut with some common sense.

He toyed with the idea of asking her why she had disappeared from her family's lives. Perhaps she would admit she was holding out for some miracle whereby she and Helmut could have a life together. Their only hope was anonymity. Improbable if not impossible.

While the world rejoiced at the birth of Helmut's son by Terri, 250,000 men, women, and children died of cholera at the Cyprus repatriation camp at Kyrenia. The International Court issued an injunction ordering E'tat de Guerre to halt all repatriation transports —it had ceased using the word deportations —and Stahl left the decision of whether to issue a moratorium on transports in Helmut's hands.

All of Ireland, the Norse Countries, and Latvia, Estonia, Lithuania, as well as Germany, France, Austria, Poland and the Netherlands had been declared officially Islamic-free, the Court observed. There was no need to proceed with such volume with disease becoming an issue in the repatriation centers. UN Ambassador Muller issued a statement that, though Islamic-free, the countries could not be considered terrorist-free given the Vatican attack. Germany would not honor the injunction, as it had withdrawn from the International Court. Captain Wolf, however, agreed to issue a moratorium on the transports for ninety days and agreed to send in teams of engineers to assess the water and sewage disposal problems of the camps. Primarily, these teams were advisory. If any actual repairs or alterations were done, Turkey had to pay for them.

Pope Edward called Helmut immediately after the International Court's announcement of the moratorium and the reason behind it. The megadeaths were just beginning, Edward warned. More were predicted if the social disruption and relocation continued. He begged Helmut to extend the moratorium indefinitely.

But the stability the Repatriation Program had wrought had ignited consumer confidence, Helmut explained to the Pontiff. Europe's economy had rebounded. Any sign of revanchism now would derail the recovery. Edward asked him to consider an alternative, if one could be found in the ninety days, and Helmut agreed. Edward sent for Umberto and Norman. "Think of something," he commanded. Reluctantly, Umberto left San Rafael and hunkered down with Norman at a meeting room in the now-restored Excelsior Hotel.

"We both know Edward is asking the impossible," Norman said. "Islamic nations have too many people, too much sand and oil, and not enough water, food, and medicine." He took off his glasses and rubbed his eyes with his knuckles. "It's what everyone's known all along. Without Western resources, Islam is doomed. It's what Stahl understood when he started the Repatriation Program. That choking sound you hear is the Islamic world coming to grips with its own inadequacies."

"A Holocaust not of Stahl's making, or so he tells himself." Umberto had spread a map out on the fifteen-foot table, and secured the corners with ashtrays. "Where the hell do we put them all? All of North America is off limits, and South America can't even feed its own bulging birthrate."

"How about Greenland?" Norman snipped.

"You're half-way there. It has to be somewhere isolated, but big enough to allow for a nomadic life, if that's what they want. But the land has to be able to produce food." Umberto was thinking out loud.

"Think Australia would take them in, Umberto?"

The Cardinal rolled his eyes. "We have to be serious about this. Siberia? They'd freeze their veils off. South Africa? Drop them off at the Cape of good Hope and hope for the best."

"And let the blacks slaughter them? Death by disease or death by machete. What a choice."

Umberto sighed. "Can the Turks contain the cholera?"

"In Kyrenia? Maybe. In Ankara? No. Too big an urban population. As we speak, another thousand people are dying. If we deliberate long enough, the problem will disappear."

"I swear, you sound more and more like your infamous nephew every day, Norman." Umberto threw up his hands.

"Cholera has to be treated quickly with clean water and salts and where're they gonn'a get clean water when it was dirty water that made them sick in the first place?"

"I surrender to the will of God. I certainly can't come up with a solution." Umberto sat down in a green leather chair with a plop. "If they die, they die."

"Unacceptable, Gentlemen," was Edward's conclusion when they told him it was hopeless. As the words left his lips, a bullet went screaming by his ear and grazed his shoulder sending a river of blood down his white cassock. Norman grabbed his left arm as he went down to the floor, while Umberto came crawling around the corner of the desk.

"Get underneath, Holiness" he whispered desperately. The three of them crouched between the desk and the bookcase in back of it. They could hear shouting and shooting, and suddenly the door of St. Stephen's was being kicked in. It was Omaha Jones, whose mission, it seemed, was protecting Edward's life. "Get a doctor, I see blood," he yelled as he ran to the desk.

Seeing the three men contorted like jumbled puzzle pieces made him smile. "Help me, Jones, I'm stuck," Edward said trying to wriggle out of the crawl space between the desk drawers. Jones, Umberto, and Norman dragged him out by his feet. Within seconds a doctor appeared and was eying the scratch and the burn the bullet had made in his flesh.

"Who was it?' Edward said.

"The son of one of the artisans Captain Wolf brought from E'tat de Guerre to help with the restoration. God help them when Wolf finds out."

"Oh, God. Don't tell him, Jones," Edward pleaded. "Please, I'm alright."

Norman was shaking. He knew what an attempt on the Pontiff's life meant. The media would make it a *cause celebre*, pressuring Stahl to take retaliatory action. The hope of getting Helmut to extend the moratorium was the real victim of the attack. "They never learn. They never learn," he mumbled.

"I'm sorry, You Holiness, but I have to report this as a terrorist incident." Jones motioned the other soldiers out of the room.

"Why not report it as a crime? Why punish other people for what one misguided young man did? Can't you handle it another way?" Edward sat down. "Where is the young man now?"

"Dead."

"Perhaps if I talk to Wolf. Can you get him on the phone for me, Omaha?"

"I can try, but he may be flyin' high in a friendly sky."

The assassination attempt struck Edward to his bones. It was the provocation Stahl needed to order the strike on Mecca. A new wave of hatred would sweep the Western World, and news of more cholera deaths would only be met with sighs of relief, just that many fewer radicals to deal with. "I want no revenge, Helmut," he said as their private conversation began around midnight. "I won't be the excuse for spilling innocent blood. You must restrain the response to this unfortunate incident."

"We cannot let any act of terrorism go unpunished, Holiness. Even an unsuccessful one. To do so would embolden the enemy."

Edward decided it was time to play a trump. "I know where Churchill is, Helmut. And I know Gerry is your child. If you don't want that information made public, quell your anger."

Helmut collected his thoughts. "So, you bargain three innocent lives for a million. Is that the plan?"

"That's the plan."

Helmut suppressed a laugh. "It's not a very good plan. What do you think the world will say about a child conceived before my marriage to Teresa? I'll tell you. The world will rejoice – an heir and a spare only the spare is older. I can see the headlines now. Pontiff becomes *paparazzi* —mercy for Muslims but none for ex-nun. Miracle Baby becomes super stud. You'll only aggrandize my reputation and sully your own. Which of us can least afford a scandal? My money is on you."

Edward huffed in frustration. "That was clumsy of me. But can't you see the position I'm in? You'll get another reason to carry out your mission. Just wait a few more days and these stupid jihadists will hand it to you boxed, wrapped and tied with a bow."

There it was. The naked truth that knew no hiding now. Yes, Muslims were stupid, kept that way for centuries by a religion that saw every change as a challenge to the faith of power rather than a challenge to the power of faith. Didn't they see Americans still praying though prayer was stripped from their schools? Didn't they see all of Europe return to the churches when Paris fell? Didn't they see the resolve of Europe and Russia to rebuild every shrine? Yes, didn't they see Helmut Wolf ready to do battle against them to save Christendom?

"Stupidity can be lethal, Holiness. Think of all the women who died in childbirth because doctors were too stupid to wash their hands. Remember the educational fiasco when teachers switched from phonics to sight reading. What about the Serb who shot Prince Ferdinand? I could go on, but you get my point."

Edward grasped at the last straw. "Helmut, treat this incident as a crime and I will confer on you the title of Defender of the Faith as Stahl requested. To the Muslim world it will serve as a warning, and to Christians it will recognize what they already believe."

Helmut transferred the call to his headset. Edward had capitulated in the name of a faceless terrorist who would have blown his brains out, given half the chance. "I'll tell Stephan of your decision. He'll be pleased."

"Alright," came the dry reply.

"How's the restoration coming along, by the way," Helmut said, trying to lighten Edward's load.

"Slow. Painful. Rewarding."

Helmut couldn't help thinking all life could be summed up in those three words. Slow childhood. Painful adulthood. Rewarding old age. If one made it that far. Surviving was reward enough for people who had nothing either to live or die for. He could hear his future in the Pope's words and wasn't impressed. "The greatest architectural wonders of the world took generations to erect. Are we less disciplined and patient than they?" was all he said to Edward in response.

"Tell Stephan to call me, Helmut." Edward put down the phone and sent for Nabu. Rome was to have another media event in less than a year. The whole world would watch the accused war criminal become the champion of Christianity. But maybe, it would be enough to persuade the brash young man that he needed to temper his mission with compassion, if not for Muslims, then for his own sons.

Helmut took three days off and flew to Rome for what was supposed to be a local ceremony. But, coming on the heels of an attempt on the Pope's life, the event exploded into a royal coronation. Pictures of heads of state, monarchs and aristocrats glutted the tabloids and U-Tube. Once again, Helmut was put on public display with the looming figures of the other members of the Unholy Trinity and the Christian Nationalist regime. To an outdoor stage, draped in purple and white and clouded by incense smoke, Helmut walked like a Wagnerian hero, the crowd holding its breath in awed silence as the golden-haired god approached the Holy Father with measured, humble steps.

"I call upon you, Helmut Wolf," Edward said as he crowned the kneeling Helmut with an olive branch wreath in front of TV cameras and video recorders, "To defend, not just the existence of the faith, but the principles of that faith, including patience, mercy, hope, love of neighbor and of stranger alike, remembering that the greatest of all warriors was the Good Samaritan who battled indifference and cruelty with alms and assistance without consideration of cost and convenience."

From the tops of the newly constructed colonnade that arced the square, snipers watched for signs of danger. People jostled each other to get a glimpse of their protector proclaimed by Rome and of his beautiful wife and child.

"Thanks be to God," Helmut said.

"Go, and serve the Lord," Edward directed him and the thousands of faithful that crowded the now-open St. Peter's Square. Gone were the fences that separated the bombed area from the streets of the holy City. They would go up again over night so the restoration could continue, but for today, the throng ohhed and ahhed in amazement at what they saw. The Vatican was being rebuilt. The beauty of the new material mixed with the old evoked cultural memories, memories of centuries of incremental contributions by countless geniuses now resurrected quickly by modern machinery.

Helmut's first act as Defender of the Faith was to send an emergency response team to Cyprus that included an engineering crew and equipment, and two hundred public health workers. Within sixty days, Kyrenia had a refurbished reservoir and water treatment facility, and a rationing system that included instructions in sanitation as people received their Dukoral shots. Cook it, peel it, boil it or don't swallow it, read the ten-foot posters plastered throughout the refugee center. People who had cursed the infidel and burned German flags were now touching their heads to the ground before white-uniformed, bare headed nurses who rehydrated their dying children inside squalid huts. When one female worker was murdered by a man who accused her of trying to seduce him, Helmut immediately aborted assistance to Ankara. The city mustered enough local talent to begin a water treatment facility in its refugee center, but another hundred thousand people died of the disease before it was completed.

Pope Edward wept in sheer frustration as the television newscaster delivered her report.

*Katrina Miller, a twenty-two-year-old nursing student from Quebec, was stabbed to death by a Muslim man as a crowd of men on their way to Mosque services looked on. Though her cries for help could be heard over the call to prayer, her fellow volunteers were not able to penetrate the ring of onlookers soon enough to save her life. They did, however, protect her body from mutilation. Her attacker has not been identified.*

Helmut lifted the moratorium, and the repatriations resumed with eleven hundred Muslims being flown to the ten largest reception centers in the Mid-East. Ankara got three hundred.

With Helmut graduating from flight school in six weeks, Edward knew time was running out. Helmut had given him ninety days to come up with an alternative, but he could not afford to honor the timeline. Politically, the Miller murder was a valid reason for an all-out assault, and Edward had no logical or philosophical weapons to prevent it.

Nabu heard his sobs and came to his side at the altar steps. "I am a blind man, Nabu," he said. "I caused the death of that young woman as surely as if I'd plunged the knife into her heart myself. What is the definition of insanity? Continuing to do the same thing and expecting a different result. I continue to urge love and forgiveness and the result is always the death of someone who heeds my words. I can't continue making martyrs of Christians and excusing the evil that kills them. I just can't do it. It is a sin against justice."

"If only one of the men had tried to stop it. If only one had identified the killer. Lot said, if I can find one righteous man in Sodom and Gomorrah, will you spare the cities, Lord? But there wasn't one to be found. Katrina Miller. One life, but how many destroyed because of it? Her parents and aunts and uncles and brothers and sisters. Her friends, her boyfriend, her future children. It is too much to bear without a response," Nabu said.

"Jesus said put away your swords …"

"He knew the inevitable had to be done to redeem us, so it was useless to fight, but it isn't useless to fight to protect the Katrinas of the world. It wasn't useless to kill Nazis or the Japanese who subjugated and tortured their captives."

"Do you think the Repatriation Program is morally right, Nabu?" Edward said pensively.

"I do now. I think Stahl and Helmut and Eisenbach are doing the best they can. We sit in judgment, but we offer no alternative other than the self-annihilation of Christendom. God cannot want that."

"What do you think about a war? Does He want that?"

Nabu hesitated. "Oh, I see. Helmut being in flight school isn't a prelude to German ally maneuvers. Who's got the nuke? Iran? The Saudis? Whoever has it must be stopped."

"I don't know who has it," Edward said, truthfully. "I doubt even Norman knows. Nabu, send Helmut an e-mail and ask him to see me on his way to Brindisi."

# CHAPTER XIII
## All Things Come to Him Who Waits

Edward knew this would be his final conversation before the war with the solemn young man who was hated by half the world and idolized by the other. Helmut and his squadron were going to commit genocide in less than a hundred hours, and the weight of that mission bore down on Edward like boulders. Yet, he saw resignation, not zeal, in Helmut's eyes when the two met in St. Stephen's church. Edward wanted Helmut to know there was peace to be had in the darkness of the sanctuary; that there was the hope of life and the desire of love left for him to experience. He would find it too, Edward believed, if he would only see the future in the eyes of his sons. Perhaps a war was inevitable, even necessary. But there were ways of fighting wars that minimized collateral damage – to spare the sons of other families.

And, suddenly, nothing else seemed important. Agonizing over angels dancing on pin-heads seemed a waste of time in view of the tsunami to come. In desperation, he would urge a man to sin.

"You asked to see me, Holiness," Helmut said. Centuries of burning candles and floating incense gave the church interior an exquisite, ancient aura that he and Madeline loved so much about old buildings. They reminded him of her every time he opened their wooden doors and heard his footfalls on their stone floors. To some they stood for eternity. To him they stood for the permanence of his passion for her.

As if Edward could read his mind, he sat back in the pew and said, "I spoke with Madeline. Oh, yes. There's no question Helen is Madeline, and there's no question in my mind why you love her. What a fire. But a controlled burn. If I was you, I'd forget my misguided directives and make the only decision that counts – run away with Madeline and Gerry. Take them and run into oblivion, Helmut. She knows how to disappear. Live in a small house in the woods or a tee-pee in Wyoming. Grow old and fat and eat cookies for breakfast."

Helmut did nothing but stare at the altar. Edward followed his eyes to the cross and immediately knew escape was not an option for the young anymore. Their eyes had seen too much of the world – a world he had only heard about.

"If only it was that easy to say goodbye to duty." In Helmut's words, Edward heard the sad, heavy voice of truth. "Once you see the enormity of suffering, as I did in Paris, there is no running away from taking a stand. What happens, Holiness, if every man runs away when it's time to fight? Who will protect the women and the children? A long time ago, people understood that peace was valuable because it was so rare. Now, we feel entitled to it. Our anger is that of the child who is frustrated when he learns there is a price to be paid for everything, especially peace."

Edward thought it was as though he and Helmut were calling to each other across a great canyon of conflicting convictions. Was it possible to make a man a boy again? At least part of him.

"Did you know that Corigliano went to see Madeline's parents? He told them she was dead – an Unknown Martyr. They gave him a memento to give to you, to thank you for taking on the cross of saving civilization. They made him promise not to open it and then wrapped it with packing tape." Edward handed the still-unopened box to Helmut. "I hope that whatever was important to her is equally important to you." Helmut took it from him eagerly.

"Thank-you, Holiness."

"But you know it belongs to her, not to you."

As he promised Edward he would do, Helmut took the box to Madeline. They met in the villa's arbor to open it together, they decided. Joe was with Gerry, walking through San Rafael and visiting with the townspeople he knew so well. Teresa was with Stephan and Frieda, watching them play with their grandson in a garden corpulent with Spring flowers. For this brief time, they were alone with their memories of future promises, and Helmut savored the minutes.

Inside the box were Helmut's love letters, and one of the white gloves he wore at his graduation from Boswell. There were movie ticket stubs from the Cineplex in San Diego where they saw *Gone With the Wind*, and a piece of wood from the Petrified Forest. There was a key to Madeline's apartment in Boston, and a picture of them at the Grand Canyon, at Yellowstone, standing in the Pacific Ocean, and one of Helmut in his dress uniform. And there was a small white envelope that had one word scrawled on the outside: Lisa.

Which one of them would open it, Helmut wondered, or would it remain the one closed chapter in their lives? Madeline stared at it for a few minutes before she carefully unsealed it with a fingernail and removed the picture of a newborn baby girl. "Do you ever wonder who adopted her, Helmut?"

"I'm sure she is loved," Helmut said, fearing Madeline's tears. "We were too young and stupid to realize what we were giving away."

"We did what we thought was right at the time, I guess, but it wasn't right for us after all." Madeline returned the photo to the envelope and the envelope to the box. Their stroll down memory lane always ended with stumbling over Lisa. It was after her birth that their relationship fell apart. The secrecy, the distance, the lies they had to tell – all bricks of an insuperable wall between them. A wall that became a convent wall.

"Damn it! Why didn't I just do my duty and marry you like I wanted to?" Helmut turned away from her, remembering his warning to Brandt the night he shot the looters. If only someone had been there to warn him the night Madeline told him she was pregnant. "Can't we undo this, Maddie?"

"I don't see how, Helmut. We're not young and stupid anymore. We can't leave Gerry and Stephan behind like we did Lisa."

"In eighteen years we can. When they're grown, and it doesn't matter anymore."

"In eighteen years, Joe and I will have other children. You and Teresa will too."

I'm not having anymore children with Teresa, Maddie. Stahl has what he wants. Everybody has what he wants except me."

"What do you want? And don't say me because you wouldn't have married Teresa if that was true. How many times did you tell me to wait just a little longer? How many things became more important to you than me? I can't wait forever for you to choose me, Helmut."

She was speaking the truth, much as he hated to hear it. He married Teresa for one reason only, to be Stahl's successor.  To be his successor, he had to be the son Stahl wanted —committed, courageous, and cruel.

"You're falling in love with Joe," he said. The simplicity of the words took them both by surprise.

"He's as ambitious as you are, but his arena is San Rafael. Yours is history. He'll be content. You'll be remembered. The love I have for Joe is not the love I have for you, Helmut. I've learned that to survive in this world, I have to do what you do, put people into compartments. There's no security in ambiguity."

"Just don't love Joe so much that he takes my place, Maddie. I *will* find a way to undo this," Helmut said. "And when I do find a way, be ready. To hesitate is to die." He left her in the arbor. The certainty of her prediction he carried with him well into the night as he traveled to Brindisi by train. It was odd to go by rail in the days of private jets, but Emil convinced him at the last minute that the best way to foil plots is to do the unexpected. Georg agreed, and Helmut obeyed the head of his security detail without question.

Eisenbach traveled with him in a private compartment, both men ruminating over the text messages they received from Stephan about Pomeranz and Tanzer and the assassination plot. Grotesque as it was, it was still easier to confront than the magnitude of what the Eisenbach Brigade was about to do.

"Norman was smart to jump ship. It's hard to imagine what would happen to Germany if anything happened to Stephan," Emil said. Helmut saw the concern in his eyes and thought how fortunate Stephan Stahl was to have a man like him at his side.

"I think my Uncle was determined to solve the Excelsior bombing too, because of Madeline." Helmut added.

"As if that was a mystery. The only difficulty was proving Pomeranz's guilt. Stahl's been waiting for Norman to wise up."

Emil's frankness made him uneasy. He chalked it up to the stress of the mission. "I'm not privy to the inner workings of party politics. I get my orders and I do my duty," Helmut said, hoping to close the subject. One look as Emil, leaning back in the seat and so deep in thought, made him realize there was more to the story. He could see the gears of Emil's mind meshing as they turned the information over and over, grinding facts into narrative. "What is it, Emil? What's troubling you?"

"What would you have done with Pomeranz and Tanzer, if you were in charge?"

"Where are Pomeranz and Tanzer now? In a jail. They ought to thank God they didn't have to answer to me. The Russians taught me how to deal with murderers and would-be assassins." Helmut said.

"Yes. Now Stahl's enemies have other opportunities to hurt him. Why would he allow that? It's beyond comprehension."

Helmut asked himself the same question silently, but to Emil, he said, "What would happen if something did happen to Stephan?"

Emil answered swiftly. "You'd take his place. None of us —me included —have the wherewithal to lead the nation through such a crisis. Olberman, Frict, and Beuhler would be at your side. Stephan has groomed you carefully, but you've got the instinct, and they know it." Emil reached up and shut off the light above his seat, taking his mind into the darkness where he knew plotters resided. "Stahl knows it too."

Helmut mentally followed him but halted at each twist and corner. His Uncle could navigate the maze of politics so much better than he.

Norman had instinct too, Helmut thought. Perhaps it was a genetic trait. If Norman sold out the Center Socialists, it was because he knew their time in power was limited. The world would be so grateful to Stahl for getting rid of the Muslim threat, he would be master of Europe. Would the Americas be next?

Helmut felt a rush of optimism remove the sadness he'd borne since his visit with Madeline. Emil had made his position in the hierarchy definitive. There would be no opposition from the Christian Nationalist Party faithful if he had to assume the role of Dictator of Europe as well as Defender of the Faith.

Helmut shut off his overhead light too. Like pimp and whore, they sat in silence, each weighing their positions relative to the mark. Stahl must know the rest his cabinet would suspect something was amiss if he refused to destroy the men who plotted against him. On the other hand, he and Emil were always a comfortable distance from Stephan. The others were in the thickest part of the forest.

"Stahl's made a fatal blunder, Helmut," Emil said. "He's tipped his hand whether he knows it or not. We're about to kill millions who threaten civilization as we know it … why spare two German politicos?"

"Momentary weakness? Longtime associations? Pity for their families? Stahl's job is to handle the politics of our cause. He probably sees his mercy as a rational political move," Helmut offered.

"Bullshit. He's keeping them on ice for a reason. He knows he can trot them out at any minute and blame them for anything at this point."

"Fall guys. But for what?"

"He beat the cancer and he has a successor, one that won't threaten him for decades. Caesar doesn't need us anymore, Helmut."

"Why make Pope Edward name me Defender of the Faith? So he can make me a martyr?" The thought of Stephan turning on him made him nauseous.

"No. He has Edward name you Defender of the Faith so that when the world decries the destruction of millions of people, Pomeranz and Tanzer will testify you plotted with them and Catholic Church to overthrow his merciful regime."

Helmut felt an unfamiliar sensation in his belly. Fear. Emil's words were searing his brain. It did deem odd that the entire Repatriation Program was put in the hands of a young low-level officer. Treaties were negotiated about it, world organizations discussed it, and leaders alternately praised and condemned it, but it was he who made the decisions about the details. The Pope did not beg Stahl to end the program, but him. When the world pointed a finger at Germany's solution, and screamed "Holocaust!" they referred to him, not Stahl.

"Stahl's last enemy is the Church," Emil continued. "He can't be master of Europe unless the Vatican comes on board or is destroyed. The surprise visit? He had to study his enemy. Why didn't we see it? He had to find out how politically astute Edward was, or if he was a man of real faith."

Helmut swallowed his revulsion and fell back on his military training. No matter what the situation, he would not give in to panic. "Do the Iranians have a nuclear bomb and a missile to deliver it?"

"Intel says yes."

"If we strike the big three —Arabia, Iran, and Pakistan —doesn't that make us heroes?"

"It makes us war criminals if Stahl can say he didn't order the strikes. Who's to say otherwise? Edward is bound by the seal of the confessional, if he knows. Remember the Night of the Long Knives? Hitler's former pal Rhome, head of the SA, and his forces wiped out. Hitler chose Himmler's SS black uniformed thugs over brown. The Eisenbach Brigade is going to be purged. You're the misguided renegade bomber, and I'll be the blamed for the assassination plot."

"Then what?"

"Genocide. It's what Stahl has wanted all along. You're the one who insisted on clean dormitories and health care for the repatriates at E'tat de Guerre. At some point, humanitarianism becomes too expensive."

"Are you sure? Absolutely sure?"

"What is your son's name?"

"Gerry," Helmut answered without thinking.

"And what of Stephan Wolf? Why don't you claim him?"

"Father Hahn was right. He's the demon spawn of Hades. Stahl's successor he grooms with me out of the way." The anger in his veins spilled into his words. "I'm willing to kill millions of people for you," Helmut said coldly. "All I ask in return is that you kill three for me – the Stahls."

"What are your orders, Helmut?"

"What about our loyalty oaths?"

"Don't be a fool, Helmut. Stahl wants us dead. Shall we let him use Pomeranz and Tanzer, or shall we use them to save ourselves?"

Helmut opened the door of the compartment and motioned Georg to come in. "Who is the best man we have on the maintenance crews of the B-3s?"

"An American named Lincoln Bradley, knows them inside and out."

"Have him check the flight programs of the computer system on each plane. I need the data by the time we reach Brindisi."

"I'll get him on it. What's he looking for?"

"Sabotage. Anything that suggests the pilots are not in control of those planes after they take off. Anything that suggests a change in the targets or scuttle procedures including the ejection protocols. I want him to check every bolt and every piece of equipment – everything that's there, or should be but isn't."

"Yes, Sir…."

"What is it, Georg?"

"Something I read in your mail caught my eye. It's your graduation card from the Provenkos." Georg got Helmut's suitcase from the shelf and opened it. Inside was a leather pouch with the word "mailbag" on it —a gift from Teresa to Helmut. He shuffled through the envelopes and handed Helmut one with a satiny finish. Vasily signed this, but Natya chose it, Helmut remembered thinking when he saw it. It wasn't something a gruff giant like Vasily would send. The card was just as feminine as the envelope with the word "Congratulations" embossed on the front. Helmut took it and read aloud:

*To the standard bearer of the Goddess of Justice —remember that war games are dangerous when both sides have patriots. Warm regards —Vasily and Natya.*

"Damn it!" Emil swore. "One or all of the targets have interceptors. Is that proof enough for you?"

268

"Get hold of Bradley and get him started. We need to know how this sabotage is supposed to go down," Helmut said calmly.

"Yes Sir."

"Emil, how did our enemies get these weapons? Traitors in NATO? Traitors among our allies?"

"None or all of the above. The Provenko's obviously know our enemies have them and if they're warning you, they know about the strike. The big question is who are our real enemies —will the interceptors deploy before you drop your payload or after?"

Helmut tore Vasily's card into pieces and tossed them out the window. He wanted nothing incriminating the Provenkos in his luggage. "Didn't the Russians have heavy duty oil contracts with Iran during the late 1900s and early 2000s?"

"And a non-aggression pact of sorts too," Emil said. "They were piqued about America's failure to underwrite drilling in Siberia – how stupid to keep giving the Saudis money while Russians starved. Yet, here the Russians are having war games with America in the Pacific while Germany cavorts with Britain in the Mediterranean Sea. Alliances change with circumstance."

"Ahhh, allies – friends who can change with the wind."

"All nations leave their options open, Helmut."

Helmut was weighing the consequences of aborting the strike. It was too late to contact Vasily for clarification without raising suspicion, yet to abort on a hunch was politically costly. Stahl would be put on notice he'd been found out. "If the planes check out, we'll abort mid-air for two of the targets. They'll take-off but return to Brindisi. Mecca is the go. That's the jewel on the crown anyway."

"If you're leading a coup, you can't fly that plane, Helmut. It's either go to Berlin or go to Mecca. You can't do both."

Helmut smiled one of his engaging, enigmatic smiles as he remembered the technological tipping point. "Not a problem, Emil."

\*\*\*

*How many passengers thought about death as they boarded those four planes on 9/11, Helmut wondered. Did any of them have a fleeting sense of foreboding as they checked their luggage or made a last trip to the bathroom? Perhaps one tipped a cabby big that morning, or another decided on ivory roses for a centerpiece. All the mundane things they did, they did for the last time. Did it those banal acts matter when they saw the building loom before them? And what about the tourists in Red Square, the Parisians, and the devout Catholics from around the world visiting St. Peter's? Did they have any inkling that their devotion would cost them their lives? No, Helmut told himself. No one ever expects tragedy will claim them.*

"You Bradley?"

"Yes, Captain Wolf," the black man said. Who would believe, he thought, that the man dedicated to eradicating terrorism from the world would be enlisting his help. Just being in his presence infused him with pride and commitment. Whatever Captain Wolf needed, Bradley vowed, he'd make sure he got it.

"Where you from?"

"Macon, Georgia,"

"You ever play video games?"

"Yeah. Once in a while."

"Well, Mr. Bradley, what we need to do is make this war game a video game."

"Tell me what you want these planes to do, and I'll program them to do it. Except the dishes, of course." Bradley displayed two gold front teeth when he smiled.

*This was the morning that began like any other for two million people who would be dead by noon. They got up from their beds, and because their religion demanded it, they prostrated themselves in submission to Allah, a god they would be meeting soon if the Qu'ran was accurate. They would walk into the center of Mecca for their Hajj, joining their fellow believers who were probably strangers to them. Just like the strangers who boarded those Pan Am planes, and the strangers in Moscow, Berlin, Paris, Tokyo, and Rome, they never imagined they were fated to die together.*

"We take off at 0700, cruising at 50,000 ft at 600 MPH. Fifteen minutes into the flight, two of the planes will turn back, but you won't report it. I'll bail out of my plane. A sea plane will pick me up, and bring me back to Brindisi, where a small jet will to take me to Berlin. Clear so far?"

"Yes, Sir." Bradley showed Helmut how to program the GPS "smart" guidance system, commenting, "You want a seven hundred million dollar aircraft to behave like a drone."

"You got it. Don't worry about return. We'll let it run out of gas somewhere over the Arabian Sea ... or be destroyed." Helmut programmed the system to fly to 25 degree 0' 0" North latitude, 45

271

degrees 0' 0" East longitude —three hours and fifteen minutes out of Brindisi —and to fire two missiles from one hundred miles at the target. As it passed over the target, it would drop all twelve 2000 pounders at two second intervals.

"What next, Capt'n Wolf?" Bradley asked Helmut.

"I'm going to drink a beer with my squadron." He and the five pilots who graduated with him, went to a pizzeria. They ate heartily and drank the local wine. They listened to the local tenor sing arias from *La Traviata* and the *Barber of Seville*. They laughed when they were invited to join in the singing, following the white bouncing ball across a six-foot screen that displayed the words. They drank a toast to Eisenbach, and Helmut reminded them to obey his orders without question. Their lives depended on it, he told them. To hesitate was lethal.

To Georg, the next morning, Helmut said, "Today the ghosts fly this plane and avenge themselves," as he shook his hand. "When the plane drops to twenty-thousand feet, I'll eject," he explained. "It will go back to fifty-thousand feet in exactly one minute and continue its flight. Get it on film. We'll tell the news people the plane veered off course and I couldn't get control, but the mission was completed."

Eisenbach pulled Helmut out of the crystal Mediterranean near the Greek Island of Gavdos as planned. "If the plane is shot down before the bombing, it's the Saudis who have the interceptors. After, the bombing, we know it's Stahl's work," Helmut said as the seaplane took off for Brindisi. "All we have to do is wait two and half hours, and we'll know." By the time the B-3 was firing its missiles, Helmut and Eisenbach were entering Berlin.

*The Muslims were better off than the 9/11 passengers. They were required to pray five times a day, so they were spiritually ready to die when the bombs began to fall. The first two missiles were a direct hit on Masjid al-Haram – the Center of Mecca – where over two hundred thousand pilgrims walked in a slow circle around the Kaaba. They instantly evaporated into molecules. Another hundred thousand more were blown apart. Five hundred thousand more died shortly of wounds inflicted by flying debris and body parts. The third, fourth, and fifth bombs hit the Grand Mosque, and the perimeter of the city, setting off gas and electrical fires. Seven more bombs leveled the cityscape to rubble. Thousands of people died of asphyxiation, unattended wounds, shock, hunger, and thirst as the Saudi government scrambled to amass resources to assist them, then abandoned them to disease and looters. The world watched the film footage in both horror and relief. Seventy-two hours after the strike, two million, three hundred thousand Muslims were dead, and the Mid-east was put on notice: their cities were not safe because the patience of the West had reached its end.*

A British destroyer off the coast of Yemen plucked the B-3 from the sky as it left the Arabian Peninsula and radioed the base at Brindisi the rogue aircraft had been intercepted. Eisenbach called Olberman from the Chancellery. "Go," he said. Olberman called Frict and Beuhler who took Pomeranz and Tanzer to the Stahl residence. There, Stephan, Frieda, and Teresa were herded into the velvet draped meeting room and executed. Pomeranz and Tanzer understood their part in the coup and waited for the inevitable. Frict and Beuhler would announce that a meeting among the opposing party members was a ruse for the assassins to gain entrance to the Stahl residence. Frict and Beuhler could do nothing but execute them on the spot. "Sic semper tyranis!" Pomeranz shouted before Frict fired six bullets into his body.

Olberman called Eisenbach. "Done," he said, and immediately issued a press release about the assassinations and a subsequent government announcement from Helmut Wolf.

From the Chancellery balcony, with Eisenbach holding baby Stephan in his arms behind him, Helmut spoke directly to the German people. The ringleaders had been executed, but the other members of the Center Socialist Party would be investigated. The "Loyal Opposition" was not longer loyal and would have to be suppressed. Outraged Germans agreed, beating party members and burning Center Socialist party flags in the streets. Helmut called for reason and restraint but didn't order the Eisenbach Brigade to quell the rioting. He described the rioting as "An outpouring of grief that mirrors my own," to the crowd and the world media, adding, "My heart is devastated and if it were not for the love from and for the German people, I would be tempted to succumb to grief's retreat."

Patricia and Norman flew to his side, standing, for the first time, shoulder to shoulder with Emil and Francesca Eisenbach. Old scars made family loyalty stronger now that Stephan Stahl was dead and the country needed Helmut to guide it. Stahl had given him plenty of opportunities to manage crises and he had proven equal to the task.

"In the name of Katrina Miller, I put Islam on notice this day. If there is another terrorist attack, if another Christian is killed, Tehran will be destroyed. Then Baghdad, Islamabad, Jakarta, Istanbul, Mogadishu – wherever there is a mosque there will be bloodshed in the millions. We have shown the Islamic world it exists at our pleasure. Our weapons cannot be stopped. And, if it takes the annihilation of every Muslim in the world to make Christians and Jews and Buddhists and Hindis and Taoists safe to worship in peace, then so be it," said Helmut from the pulpit of Holy Word Church in Vienna.

Thousands of people had gathered outside the humble church that had become synonymous with Stahl milestones, and now three matching ebony caskets lay in from of the altar as Helmut delivered the eulogy that was more fire and fervor against terrorism than memorializing the lives of his family. The assassins, Helmut told them, were pro-Muslim factions within the government. "What these senseless murders show is that no family is immune from the treacherous tentacles of terrorism. Not even my own. Here lies my dear wife; my heroic father-in-law, and my sainted mother-in-law, who were as dear to me as the parents that were taken from me in the Brandenburg Massacre. No wonder I weep with the families of the victims of this world-wide pestilence. But today, I say to terrorists around the globe, your reign of terror is over. Amen."

"Amen," echoed the congregation inside and the congregation sprawling over the adjacent lawns, roads, and driveways. The caskets were carried by the Eisenbach Brigade down the center aisle, through the vestibule to the small church cemetery, and lowered into the ground on Easter Sunday.

"History has come full circle," James Turtletaub said in a televised interview. His picture of Eisenbach holding the son of the Miracle Baby —a miracle made possible by the quick-thinking Frict who gunned down Tanzer on his way up the stairs to kill the child —made the front page of every newspaper and magazine in the world.

\*\*\*

275

Pope Edward sent his condolences to Helmut, and his gratitude for sparing Tehran and Islamabad in the Good Friday attack. But he pleaded with Helmut, would he urge the Western nations to send humanitarian relief to Mecca?

"Infidels are not allowed on the holy soil of Mecca, Holiness," Helmut reminded him.

"How about infidel medicines, food, water, and bandages?" Edward replied.

"That we can manage."

Donations to the Red Crescent poured in by the millions of dollars. Much of it was sent back. "We don't need money," King Saud said. "We need doctors and nurses, experts who can advise us how to organize the rescue. Will you send personnel?"

Helmut replied, "No. I can't guarantee their safety and I will not order anyone to risk his life again for a Muslim cause. However, I won't and can't stop volunteers from helping the survivors if they assume the risk."

"In view of the humanitarian catastrophe in Mecca, will you reinstitute the moratorium on repatriation transports?" Edward begged.

Helmut replied, "No. The sooner the Muslim virus of Islamofascism is eradicated from Christian lands, the better. Mecca lost 2.3 million people. That means there is room for that many new arrivals on Arabia's shores."

As planned, Reinhardt and Lt. Rudolph took command of the Repatriation Program. In addition to E'tat de Guerre, a transport center was built in Tbilisi and administered by ally Vasily Provenko.

"The refugee problem is overwhelming, Helmut," Edward said. "They need a respite."

Helmut replied. "What they need is to get busy and solve their overwhelming problem. We're solving ours – and without their donations, I might add. When was the last time a Mid-east nation donated anything to the West?"

"And we thought Stahl was the worst thing since Hitler. At least he had middle-aged fatigue to slow him down. This youngster combines the worst of fanatic zeal with the stubbornness of youth. Truly, the world is doomed," Nabu said when he read the latest communication from Helmut to Edward. "At least we have the consolation of knowing he'll never be free to walk the streets without bodyguards."

Edward gave him a doleful glance. "Helmut Wolf was never free to walk the streets unguarded, Nabu. That's the trouble. He has never known freedom – or love for that matter. The media condemned him to a life of celebrity and we blame him for the result. If he walks away from his duty now, Europe is left leaderless. Do we really want that?"

"I suppose not. Look at what Umberto is going through with the loss of Helen. He has to rely on Joe ..."

"What about Helen?" Edward motioned Nabu to come to his desk. "What about Helen?"

"I didn't want to trouble you. One death seems so trivial compared to millions. She was killed in an auto accident just two days ago." Nabu pulled up San Rafael's newspaper's web-site and showed the report to Edward. The picture of the automobile was grisly, a mass of tangled metal and charred upholstery. Burned beyond recognition, the story read, but miraculously the baby thrown from the car received only slight head trauma. He couldn't say da-da anymore, but it wasn't permanent. He would recognize Joe again eventually, the doctor said.

What the doctor didn't say was that the baby the police retrieved from the gully wasn't Gerry, and the female found in the car wasn't Helen even though she was buried under that name. "Babies' eyes can begin to darken after six months, so that they're now hazel blue is no cause for concern," the San Rafaelians told the grieving father. "And blonde hair turns reddish brown sometimes - he looks more and more like you everyday – just be thankful Gerry is alive and healthy."

Joe meant what he said. It didn't matter whose baby it was, he was the father now. The Cardinals still fawned over the "bambino" and prayed for Helen, and the Villa San Rafael was still solvent a year after "Helen's" death.

In Berlin, another miracle had been wrought. Madeline Churchill walked out of the shadows and into the hearts of the German people. Unable to recall where she'd been or what caused her disappearance, she was nonetheless ready to care for Stephan Helmut Wolf as though he were her own child and tend to her husband's needs as a dedicated Christian Nationalist wife. Six weeks after she and Helmut married, Madeline was pregnant with twin daughters.

Those who knew the lie about Gerry and Madeline Churchill —Umberto, Norman, Patricia, and Edward— knew the lie kept Joe and little Stephan alive and kept silent. Perhaps Madeline had, at last, found her true vocation: keeping Helmut satisfied. The "good engineer" had toppled the governments of Germany and Arabia in less than four hours, and would level entire cities, if necessary, to keep the Western World from barbarism. Who were they to begrudge a measure of happiness to a man who had the courage to face an uncertain eternity of a soldier's soul? Whether he was a hero or a war criminal, millions of people slept safely in their beds because of him, and millions cursed his name in the hellholes of the repatriation camps. His enemies trembled before him, and those he protected revered him.

*The role of the Prince is to maximize his power to insure the continuity and safety of his kingdom. He must be ready to use force swiftly and surely. Whatever strengthens the Prince is good; that which weakens him is bad. So wrote Machiavelli. Collective security seems rational, but in the end, every Prince must insure his own security through his own strength. That is his duty – a duty he must keep always before him.*

Emil and Francesca Eisenbach, like good parents, stood by their Miracle Baby. "You and I are accidents of fate, my boy," Emil once told him. "You were supposed to die in the rubble, and I was supposed to let you. We defied time and space."

Now, they defied Mohamed.

# CHAPTER IVX
## Epilogue: Heil Helmut

*December 7, 2041, a day that will live in infamy, saw the destruction of Pearl Harbor by a missile that was fired from a hijacked Russian submarine. President Franklin condemned the attack and called for a reprisal on Tehran. "This rogue nation has been the perpetrator of unspeakable horror upon the world since the 1973 and we fear, with our Christian and Jewish brethren, that Israel is the next target. Iran must be brought to justice."*

Helmut and his cabinet ministers listened to the broadcast inside the bunker at the Berlin Chancellery. America was on alert, awaiting a second strike from Iran. A plane was readied for Norman to go to Rome, ordered by Helmut when German intelligence reported a large explosion somewhere in the Pacific. They both knew the significance of the date – one hundred years to the day after the Japanese made their fatal passes at the American naval installation.

Helmut handed each man a copy of the communiqué from Pakistani President Kalil Hamid inviting the German government to send inspectors to count his nuclear missiles. The number hadn't changed, he assured Helmut, since the last count. It had been four years since Helmut took on the mantle of European leadership. The destruction of Mecca had sent the mother of all shock waves through the Muslim world even as the Western world breathed a sigh of relief. Maybe now Muslims would understand how it felt to have their shrines desecrated by other than imaginary slights. Maybe millions of rotting corpses would get them to accept the fact that the world was not going to give into Allah-ism, that Islam could not break the will of Christians and Jews. Pakistan, Algeria, Jordan, and Turkey had all opened their doors to German inspectors. Weapons were catalogued, counted, and crated off to secure sites where they were inventoried every six months as a condition of economic development aid. There was hope, Helmut told Edward.

Yet, there were those in the West that still believed the way to peace was through diplomacy, not force. The International Court indicted Helmut for war crimes and crimes against humanity in absentia the day after the Mecca attack, but the charges were moot when he became Europe's Holy Roman Emperor. The United Nations cautiously issued a censure over the bombing, terrified it would be disbanded or disappear from desertion. Its criticisms were weak, but steady. Helmut ignored them.

"Tell his Holiness, I have no other choice. Tehran is next. I can't spare it twice," Helmut instructed Norman. "It's been a threat for seventy years."

Norman said nothing, just shook his head in silent agreement before leaving the stone-walled office.

"It never seems to end," Buehler said. "Are you going to give the Iranis any warning?"

"No."

Eisenbach smiled approvingly. This was why the cabinet chose Helmut to replace Stahl. He was decisive. There was a stark honesty that shone through Helmut's quick responses and the people of Europe rewarded him with loyalty. Helmut would not just punish evildoers, he would protect Europe from attack in the same way the Bush Doctrine was supposed to protect America. Forty years after 9/11, and the Americans still recoiled from its central premise: get the enemy before he gets you. Helmut believed it was idiocy to abandon a successful strategy.

Confidently, Europeans waited as the minutes ticked by, sitting in pubs and cafes and restaurants in the early morning hours, sipping lattes and tea, waiting for word of the reprisal strike they knew was on the way. They had become as complacent about the bombings of Muslim cities as they had about the Repatriation Program.

"Hamid has promised Pakistan's complete and unfettered cooperation and has given it unconditionally. Listen to this," Helmut read, "We deplore and denounce terrorism and invite the German Fatherland Security Forces to use our bases and their own here to root out the scourge."

"He knows Islamabad's next unless he can squash these brutes. You think he'll invade Afghanistan now?" Eisenbach said.

"He's offered to set up a grid to explore and de-Talibanize every cave in the mountains separating their respective countries," Olberman said. "It's a tremendous undertaking, but it can be done."

"Let's hope so, Gentlemen," Helmut said. "Hamid's a McDonald repatriate, so he knows what he has to do. Where are we on the aid to Pearl?"

"Russia's got two transport ships on the way. Medical supplies and personnel mostly." It was Frict, who was on his laptop exchanging e-mails with Moscow. "Japan is sending in food supplies and water purification systems. These new ones they make are portable and cheap…"

"Any word who's taking responsibility for this, Emil?" Helmut said.

"Like all of the attacks now, no one is taking responsibility for anything in the Muslim world. They're scared to death of reprisals."

"Beuhler, talk to Hamid. He may be able to tell us something."

"Right. I'm on it."

"Are you waiting to get Edward's input, Helmut?" Eisenbach said.

"No. It's just a courtesy. I want to give Norman a chance to do his job. He needs to give Edward some warning so the Vatican can handle the blow-back from the press."

And Norman did his job the moment he arrived at the Vatican.

"My God, Norman, between Mecca and Tehran Helmut will have killed more people in six hours than the Nazis did in six years," Edward said as they walked in the newly replanted Vatican Gardens.

"Eventually, the other nations will do as Pakistan has done —police themselves. Until then, the re-education and de-terrorization will continue, Holiness. Europe and Asia have had no more attacks. That means over a billion people have been spared tragedy. Maybe Pearl Harbor will be the last act of insanity."

"After Tehran, which city will be next?"

"Jakarta."

"Not Islamabad?"

"President Hamid has wisely come over to our side. He's even promised protection for Christian minorities."

"Will there be any help for Tehran?"

"No, Holiness. The other nations are so crippled with repatriates, they can't offer anything."

"Is there no way to relieve the suffering?"

"For Pearl or for Tehran?"

The question was like a mirror and Edward didn't like his reflection. He hadn't asked about Pearl. "I pray for the Hawaiians too," he said quickly.

"America has sent aid from the mainland, but Washington is hesitant to send assistance since the Island Secession. The Conservatives will give him grief over it. The price for independence comes high —the Hawaiians didn't know how high, it seems. Small nations are like teen-agers. They want to do whatever they want and be able to run back to Uncle Sam if there's trouble, but American taxpayers aren't in the mood to be generous."

"Does Helmut know who's responsible for the attack?"

"No, the sub was scuttled with all hands aboard. More suicide jihadists. No one has claimed responsibility."

"Such an incredible loss of life. Mother of God. Things are better in Europe. I admit it. But, I cannot condone the price of peace for some at the cost of the suffering of the many. What ever happened to the goal of peace on earth?"

"It's still there, standing next to the reality that peace is a two-way street. There will always be those who exploit our desire for peace," Norman said sadly.

"How is Helmut holding up under the pressure? He's such a young man."

"There's nothing a man can't bear with a good woman at his side, Holiness."

"Ahhh, the enigmatic Madeline Churchill. How naïve we were to think of her as a delicate flower when we knew Helen Crabtree was a businesswoman with nerves of steel."

Norman looked away. It wasn't prudent to mention Frau Wolf 's other identity, not even in private. If it was discovered that Joe's "Gerry" was the rightful heir to Stahl's German regime, it would be a threat to Helmut he would not tolerate.

"Do you know that in earlier times it was believed by many that women were incapable of serious crimes because they lacked the wits and the aggression to commit them?" Edward continued. "We want so hard to believe that women are the guardians of peace and gentleness that we often force them to do what they don't want to do, and then burn them at the stake when they revolt."

"Madeline is no Eva Braun, believe me, Holiness. She's as politically ruthless as Helmut and extremely fertile. It seems she and Helmut are as committed to rebuilding the Wolf blood line as Umberto is to perpetuating the Corigliano's."

"No Lebensborn program in the works, I hope."

"Not quite. But he offers child-care options for women that let them have their cake and eat it too."

"And the old, the sick, and the disabled?"

"Eldercare is available everywhere, but with so many people working he's able to keep taxes low. It's quite remarkable really. Helmut once told me he would never replace competition with altruism. He would make them parallel tracks. So far, he's been able to pull it off."

285

"And when he can't?"

"Then the world will change again."

***

"Turkey and Jordan have reported. Our inspectors are invited to come at your pleasure, Helmut," Beuhler said.

"And Algeria?"

"We haven't heard from them yet."

"Get the inspectors into Pakistan, Turkey and Jordan within four hours. Contact the Algerian government and tell them we'll be there too."

Frict looked up from his laptop. "Just got an e-mail from the Algerian government. They finished their count and want us there pronto. President al-Dari thinks there's been a security breach."

"They don't have nukes or long-range missiles, what's missing?" Helmut said, as he waited for Georg to answer his call.

"Twenty RPGs and some plastic explosives. He wants us to protect him and his ministers. He fears a coup."

"It could be a lead, Helmut. The bastards scuttled that sub with something they could easily get aboard," Beuhler observed. "Al-Dari's afraid we're going to bomb the Great Mosque in Algiers."

"Send al-Dari an e-mail, Frict. Tell him we're sending help. Georg? What do you know about terrorists in Algeria?"

"It's the home of the Barbary pirates —or the Ottoman corsairs or the Marine Jihad, depending on preference. Muslim pirates operated from North Africa from the time of the Crusades till the nineteenth cventury. Nasty beggars. Eventually, much of the coastlines of Spain, Portugal and

286

France were abandoned until the nineteenth century because of their assaults on commercial vessels and incursions inland. It was captured by the French, with the usual accusations of planned extermination of the Algerians. The country won independence in 1958, became oil-income dependent and was ruined economically by the oil glut of the 1980's. So, if you're asking me could the Pearl attack have originated in Algeria, the answer is most definitely yes, given what's there and given its history."

"Get a division and get in there quick. Al-Dari's an ally I don't want to lose."

"What about Tehran?" Eisenbach said.

"Algeria has the know-how to get the sub alright, so they steered the boat. But Tehran supplied the firing skill, no doubt learned from the North Koreans. We'll take it out. America's still too weak to act."

\*\*\*

"Why strike Pearl Harbor, Norman? Helmut must know."

"It's oil, Holiness."

"Hawaii doesn't have any oil."

"Right, but it has a substitute."

"Pineapple juice?"

"A refinery that can stretch a gallon of Russian crude to thirty gallons. Helmut has assembled a team of German, Russian, and American chemical engineers in Honolulu to develop synthetic oil by 2045. A sort of Manhattan Energy Project."

Edward thought for a moment, remembering his conversation with Stahl about the development of the Russian oil reserves. "The Mid-east will have nothing of value the West wants or needs. Synthetic oil will destroy every Muslim OPEC nation as well as Mexico, Columbia, and Venezuela —all nations that are propagating like rabbits. Billions will starve."

"Yes, Holiness, billions will die from another kind of black death."

"Then it's not about religion anymore."

"No. Helmut won that war with the bombing of Mecca. Now it's an economic war the Muslims will lose also. There was a time when Africa and the Mid-east could have insured their survival, but that time has passed. Perhaps those who died in Mecca were more fortunate than those who will die from starvation. A few will live, but the ancient world threw away its opportunity to flourish and save its culture, as many traditional cultures do, when they fight the inevitable instead of adapting."

Edward surveyed his words. He remembered telling Helmut to stop the restoration project, convinced it was hopeless. Yet now, from the Vatican gardens, he could see the dome of St. Peter's reflecting the Italian sun once again. Every one of the Cardinals who survived the Vatican Attack lived to see the Basilica rise from the ashes while German guards patrolled the streets with machine guns and night-vision goggles. There was no looting of Vatican treasure, and Vatican Square was once again filled with visitors and pilgrims. Helmut kept his promise to return the Holy City to Christians.

"I don't know what to think about Helmut, Norman. Where do I put him in my catalogue of historical men?"

"You can't fault a man for not being able to save everyone and everything, Holiness. Two billion plus should be enough for one man in one lifetime."

Edward nodded in agreement. "I have unreasonable expectations of him. If he can save two billion, why not seven? Why not everyone? Perhaps because I am convinced his life does have a purpose..."

"Just not your purpose and the way you want to have it fulfilled?"

"Everyone he saves is white."

"African-Americans aren't white. The Chinese and the Japanese aren't white. Indians on the Asian Sub-continent aren't white, Holiness."

"But they are ... nationally, ideologically..."

"They are modern people, Holiness. That is the difference. And they are Christians and Jews, and Shinto, the Hindi, and Buddhists —all able to tolerate religious differences. For some reason, Muslims cannot. Too close to their politics, I suppose."

"Corigliano and Nabu say the same things."

"Listen to them and spare your emotions."

"One of them should have been pope, not me, Norman. They are modern men whereas I'm still praying for miracles and believing they will happen."

"They have happened, Holiness, but your heart aches for those in pain. Your sympathy has blinded you to the good there is still left in the world. Already four Muslim nations have signed peace treaties and anti-terrorist agreements with Berlin. Already economic development projects are underway. Helmut is adamant that nations who cooperate in stamping out terrorism within their borders will get recognition and help in their fight."

"And annihilation for those who resist. So, you've become a Christian Nationalist Party member, and Patricia too, I imagine."

"We have learned there is nothing to be gained by protesting from the grave. So far, the regime has resisted the temptation to interfere in the private sector... or with the churches."

As they spoke, the B-3s flew above them. In another hour and a half, three million Iranis were obliterated, and another two million waited to die in the aftermath.

***

Helmut and Madeline stood on the balcony of the Chancellery as they always did on holidays, displaying their children as evidence of continuity, and waving to the throngs of people who cheered and chanted the name of Wolf. In summer, Helmut and his family flew to their Wolfslair mountain retreat in Bavaria where the children rode their ponies and played in the wild-flower fields as well-armed soldiers looked on. All of Europe celebrated its freedom in union with their English, Asian, and Russian brothers and sisters. People shopped and went to the cinema, ate at outdoor cafes, and drank in beer gardens while in places like Chad, and Somalia, and Indonesia people lay dying in homes, huts, and hospitals for want of medical care and sanitation amidst murderous violence.

"Their leaders have decreed that no non-Muslim may put his foot on holy ground," Helmut explained to Edward again and again. "So be it."

"What good is medicine without people to administer it properly? What good are bandages and cartons of food without people to deliver them to those in need?" Edward implored him to "do something". "Intervene! Violate national sovereignty, if you must, but don't leave innocent people to their corrupt leaders. You have the power to punish, but not prevent? Well then, punish the Imams and the Mullahs, but save the innocent, Helmut."

"I cannot, Holiness. The balance of power in the world depends on the stability of the nation states, and that stability depends on the concepts of borders, sovereignty, and leadership remaining in tact. I will not challenge the lessons of history. Nations must save themselves first. If I intervene, there will always be those who foment a resistance that threatens the West. Self-determination means determining that your nation will be destroyed as well as determining that life is more precious than your ideology, and each nation must make that choice. Now, the terrorists know they take millions with them to their Islamic paradise. Theirs is an informed decision."

It was an exchange Pope Edward and Helmut would have every day new information on the "Mid-east crisis" was released from Cairo. Edward died still begging for help for those who refused help. It was reported that his last words were, "Oh the price of freedom…such a price…"

Helmut died still providing the greatest good for the greatest number with Madeline Churchill at his side. Madeline died never seeing Lisa or "Gerry" again, but with her other six children at her bedside.

Was Helmut happy? Was he ever remorseful or plagued by doubt or guilt? These are questions Germany left to historians to debate in later centuries because they were irrelevant questions for the time. Helmut's cabinet ministers never asked or answered those questions for their world,

291

and their world didn't care. It was enough that damns and bridges and reservoirs and skyscrapers and monuments and hospitals and grammar schools and universities and graveyards and sports arenas and churches and shrines and temples and neighborhoods and parks and theaters and opera houses all over the Western world remained untouched by Islamic perfidy.

In homes across four continents, people venerated Turtletaub's picture of Eisenbach holding the Miracle Baby in his arms on Easter Sunday the way they venerated pictures of the Nativity, for this was the day that their deliverance from terrorism began.

# NAMES AND IDENTIFICATIONS

Helmut Wolf: the "Miracle baby" saved from the Brandenburg Massacre
Norman Wolf: Helmut's Uncle and German Ambassador to the Vatican
Patricia Wolf: Helmut's Aunt and Norman's wife
Madeline Churchill: Helmut's love also known as Sister Clare and Helen
Crabtree/Manetti

Emil Eisenbach: the man who rescued Helmut; Minister of Fatherland
Security; creator of the Eisenbach Brigade
Francesca Eisenbach: Emil's wife

Stephan Stahl: Chancellor of Germany
Frieda Stahl: Stephan's wife
Teresa Jean Stahl: daughter of Stephan and Frieda, Helmut's wife

Inspector Picot: French Chief of Police
Abu Al Muhammad: French terrorist, mastermind of the Paris attack,
"Mighty Mo"
Sgt. Georg Reinhardt: Helmut's Aide de Camp and Security Chief
Lt. Vincent Rudolph: tank commander and 2nd in command of E'tat de
Guerre

**Christian Nationalist Party Members:**

Leopold Stassner: Bundestag member and Stahl's mentor
Herman Beuhler: Stahls' secretary
William Olberman: Minister of Propaganda
Gerhardt Frict: Minister if Intelligence
Bruno Muller: Stahl's UN Secretary

**Center Socialist Party Members:**

Fritz Pomeranz
Karl Halderman
Alexander Tanzer

**World Leaders:**

President Franklin: America
King William: Great Britain
Prime Minister Alastair Howe: Great Britain
President Buscolioni: Italy
President Kalil Hamid: Pakistan
President Al-Dari: Algeria
President Yeshenko: Russia
President Matisse: France

**Representatives:**

Vasily Provenko: Russian Representative for German Affairs
Natya Provenskaya: Vasily's wife
Abnel Sadr Ibrihimi: Egyptian Representative for German Affairs

**Church Officials:**

Umberto Cardinal Corigliano: Norman's friend and Papal Legate to Berlin
Pope John XXIV: Pope killed in Vatican bombing
Edward Cardinal Hugh: elected after John's death as Pope Edward I
Philipe Cardinal Nabu: Cardinal from Sudan, Edward's secretary, bombing survivor, Secretary to Bishop Meyer during the Brandenburg Massacre
Anthony Cardinal "Tony" O'Malley: Umberto's friend and bombing survivor
Xioa Cardinal Chu: Cardinal from China and bombing survivor
Father Willem Hahn: Pastor of St. Mary's Catholic Church and leader of the Children's Crusade
Rev. Kohl: Pastor of Holy Word Lutheran Church
Bishop Meyer: Bishop of Berlin during the Brandenburg Massacre
Mother Ignatius: Director of the Carmelite convent

**Miscellaneous Names:**

Charles Turtletaub: photographer who snapped the picture of Helmut's rescue
Paul Brandt: Helmut's friend
Selah Chaobli: terrorist who ransacked the Lourvre Museum

Sister Agnes: Madeline's charge
Nicholas and Lena Grothe: Paris terrorist victims
Anne Carpenter: Paris terrorist victim
Federico Milan: Chief of Police, Italy
Scilla Moreno: volunteer worker who found the eye of a victim
Katrina Miller: murder victim in Cyprus
Stephan Helmut Wolf: Helmut's son by Teresa Jean Stahl
Gerald "Gerry" Manetti: Helmut's son by Madeline
Giuseppe (Joe) Manetti: Umberto's bastard son and "Helen's" husband
Lincoln Bradley: aircraft expert from Macon, Georgia

# Other Titles

Kill the Beautiful Bastards
Paint the Town Dead
Wanted Ones: Published Stories Vol. 1-7
Tales from the German Mind
Raphael: Guardian of the Arts
Retrolands
Murder, Mayhem … Tea Anyone?
Coward No More
The Ninth Circle
everything glass: poems for the sane

Writing Beyond the Self: How to Write Creative Non-fiction that Gets Published (Vine Leaves Press, 2018)